THE FRENCH HOUSE SHARE

GILLIAN HARVEY

Boldwood

First published in Great Britain in 2026 by Boldwood Books Ltd.

Copyright © Gillian Harvey, 2026

Cover Design by Alice Moore Design

Cover Images: Shutterstock

Every effort has been made to obtain the necessary permissions with reference to copyright material, both illustrative and quoted. We apologise for any omissions in this respect and will be pleased to make the appropriate acknowledgements in any future edition.

A CIP catalogue record for this book is available from the British Library.

Paperback ISBN 978-1-83656-147-7

Large Print ISBN 978-1-83656-146-0

Hardback ISBN 978-1-83656-145-3

Trade Paperback ISBN 978-1-80656-194-0

Ebook ISBN 978-1-83656-148-4

Kindle ISBN 978-1-83656-149-1

Audio CD ISBN 978-1-83656-140-8

MP3 CD ISBN 978-1-83656-141-5

Digital audio download ISBN 978-1-83656-142-2

This book is printed on certified sustainable paper. Boldwood Books is dedicated to putting sustainability at the heart of our business. For more information please visit https://www.boldwoodbooks.com/about-us/sustainability/

Boldwood Books Ltd, 23 Bowerdean Street, London, SW6 3TN

www.boldwoodbooks.com

for Lily

PROLOGUE

'Do you want to do the honours?' Pete held up the ridiculously enormous key that had been handed to them by the agent an hour earlier.

Bella took it from him, feeling its cool weight in her hand. This was the moment. The moment she could finally put her past behind her and step into the future.

She inserted it into the lock on the oak-panelled door and for a moment struggled to find purchase. Then, with a final look at Pete, she smiled and turned it.

Inside, the house smelled musty, like the stately homes Bella's parents had used to drag her around as a kid – the scent of age and neglect. But the smooth stone of the walls, the polished wood of the staircase that stretched before them, the original tiles scattered in a haphazard pattern underfoot promised a beauty that would be easy to unlock with a little fresh air and elbow grease.

She looked around again and caught Pete's eye. She could see that he was feeling it too: a sense of awe that somehow, they owned this house – or at least owned the mortgage on it. That this would be their forever home. That in a few months' time they would be welcoming the first guests through the door.

'Thank you,' she said suddenly.

'Thank me? What for?'

'For believing in me. For coming with me. For buying into this dream.'

'You are far too romantic for your own good,' he joked, gathering her to him. 'I just wanted to quit my job and sip wine in the sunshine.'

'After the renovations are complete?'

'Yes,' he kissed her. 'Obviously after the renovations are complete. Just give me – what – ten, fifteen years!'

They laughed, their mouths still almost touching. Because the truth of it was that they had those years – ten, fifteen, maybe even fifty or more. They were young and had a bright future ahead. And having this business, living this life, meant she could walk away from the mess she'd made – her dead-end job, her failed exams, the disappointment she felt on behalf of a mother she no longer had.

Moving to France meant she could shed her former life like a snake might wriggle out of its skin, leaving it entirely behind and simply stepping away. No more of Kitty's meddling or her father's half-hearted visits. No more seeing the places she used to go to with Mum and feeling that pain over and over. A new start in every sense of the word.

'Come on,' she said, pulling away from Pete and moving towards the darkened windows. 'Let's get these shutters open; let some light in!'

1

NOW

'I'm back!' she called, closing the door against the February afternoon and almost instantly feeling her whole body relax. The house was warm; the wood burner had been lit early that morning and Pete had clearly been feeding it all day. She turned the key in the lock behind her and the bolt slid into place, leaving the darkening garden firmly outside.

The welcome sound of the kettle whistling on their stove met her ears and she grinned. Pete knew her only too well – the instant she got in, she was always gasping for a cup of tea. She smiled as she unwound her cream wool scarf and hung it over the dark wood of their coat stand, unbuttoned her black winter coat and hung it up beside his.

They'd argued this morning again – this time about the *habitation* bill that he'd forgotten to pay. But that seemed a lifetime ago – and there was something reassuring about being here, being home, being with him. Shutting the door against the winter weather and knowing that while there were still leaks to fix, gardens to maintain, the website to update and more tiny snagging jobs than she could bear to think about, they still had this: their home, the life they were building together, their adventure.

It had been harder than they'd imagined living in rural France; the business less lucrative, the move less a happy ending than a new beginning. They were managing though: she was working hard to prepare the garden for spring; Pete was spending most of the time fixing small leaks on the roof. But soon it would be done, the season would start, and things would feel possible again. Each year in France had been a learning curve, but they were growing and beginning to stream-line the business. Things were good. They would be good.

'Hi,' she said, walking up to him as he poured tea from her favourite teapot into two large mugs.

He nodded. 'Hi,' he said, adding an extra slug of milk to his own mug, along with a heaped spoon of sugar, making it look more like gone-off milk than proper, honest tea.

He passed her a mug of her usual – stronger – brew.

'Thanks.'

She pulled out a chair and sank onto it, plonking her elbows on the heavy farmhouse table that they still hadn't got around to sanding down. Pete pulled out a chair opposite.

She sipped her drink, feeling the warmth of it flood her senses and begin to thaw her cold body, and they fell into silence.

Pete added a log to the wood burner and she watched the flames encased behind iron and glass flicker and throw out a weak halo of light.

Usually, by now, they'd be discussing their day; talking about tomorrow. Arguing about who would do what. One of them might mention their lack of bookings, suggest they join another site. But tonight, every time she opened her mouth, something stopped her from making a sound.

She could sense something in him. Something different.

'Are you OK?' she said at last, setting her mug down.

He did the same, before sitting up straight for the first time that evening and fixing his steady brown gaze on her.

Later she'd wonder if this was when she'd known. When she'd had that horrible lurch of dread that comes when you sense something is wrong. Perhaps. Still, even that anticipatory feeling hadn't prepared her for what was to come.

Then he cleared his throat. 'So, I mentioned that I wanted to talk to you about something...'

'Uh huh.' She nodded.

'I love you, Bella, you know that.'

She swallowed, suddenly feeling nervous. It wasn't the kind of 'I love you' that happened in isolation. This was the kind of 'I love you' that happened before a revelation. 'Of course,' she managed to say.

'But I just can't do it any more.'

'Can't...?'

'This isn't working, is it. We can't—We work so hard and it's so difficult. I haven't—I'm not happy, Bella. I haven't been for a while. I think we have to stop.' His eyes searched her face looking for something. 'Or *I* do at least.'

'Stop?'

'Stop pretending this is ever going to work.'

'The B & B?' She looked around at the carefully carved work surfaces, the cupboards they'd painstakingly renovated. Outside, now in darkness, was their acre of land, their newly dug allotment. The grass they'd spend days on end cutting once spring arrived. Everything she'd dreamed of.

Admittedly, dreams weren't reality, and the life they had was more fraught, less idyllic than she'd imagined. But just because something is complicated doesn't mean you love it any less.

'Well, yes... and...'

'But this is... I mean, it's everything we've always wanted!'

'Bella, listen.' He reached out and covered her hand with his. 'I know you had plans. They're great plans in many ways. But... I've given it eight years of my life. I've just—I can't. I want out.'

Something sank inside her: 'Out of France altogether?'

His gaze shifted to the table, a finger moved to trace one of the splits in the worn wood. 'Out of all of it. Out of us.'

'Out of *us*?' She could hear a waver in her voice, an almost childlike quiver.

There was a pause; she could feel the hammer of her own heart against her chest.

At last, he spoke: 'I love you. You know that. And I thought this was what I wanted. But...' He made brief eye contact then looked around the room, holding out his arms as if illustrating his point. 'It was never my dream, not really. You know that. And I miss England. I miss who I was in England.'

'But you were...'

'What? Just an apprentice living in a bedsit? Maybe. But I had prospects. Friends... Don't get me wrong, I wanted to come. It was... *has* been amazing. But I'm only thirty-four, I just can't see myself spending the rest of my life here.'

Bella worked hard to steady her breathing. 'I can't go back. You know I can't.'

He shook his head. 'I'm not asking you to.'

'But I can't stay here without you either! How would I cope?'

'You'll be fine. Come on, Bella. You're stronger than you think.' He reached and tried to take her hand again but she snatched it away.

Her breathing was erratic now, sweat beading on her forehead. Recognising the signs, Pete came around the table, sat next to her. Held her. 'Come on,' he said. 'Breathe. In. Out. In. Out. That's it. Shh. It's OK.'

She nestled into him and for a moment let herself believe that the last few minutes had been in her imagination. Because he couldn't be leaving, could he?

'Please stay,' she said. 'I know it's been a struggle. But please, give it another chance.'

He shook his head. 'I've tried; believe me. But France was always *your* thing. And it's been fun. I just don't belong here.'

'You can't leave me,' she said then, her voice stronger, more insistent. 'We'll try something else! We can do anything we want! You can't throw away a marriage because a business has... well, not *failed* exactly, but...'

'We don't want the same things. And lately we just argue all the time.'

'But that's normal! Marriages are like that. That's why you work on them!'

He was silent for a moment. 'It's just too much. It's too hard.'

'So, what? You want a separation? A break?'

'I'm sorry, Bella. I know this seems out of the blue. But for me... I've been thinking about this for a while.'

'How long?' Had he been thinking about it last summer, on their eighth wedding anniversary? Last week when they'd snuggled on the sofa in front of a romantic movie? Had he been thinking about it last night when he'd moved over to her side of the bed and begun kissing her ear?

'Does it matter?'

'How long?'

'Just a few... well, months.'

'A few months!' Her voice was loud in the empty kitchen; the shrillness of it shocked them both.

'I'm sorry,' he said.

His words hung in the air. Their eyes met. And she felt her heart rate accelerate, her fingers tingle. She took in the face as familiar as her own: his short, sandy brown hair, the sun-kissed tone of his skin; the brown eyes that seem to look right into her. This was the person who'd been at her side for over a decade, who'd come with her on this adventure. She'd watched him grow into himself, mature – and knew every new line and wrinkle. Her life was anchored to his.

She saw how nothing they had built could survive his leaving – she couldn't afford to run the B & B alone; wouldn't be able to buy him out. She'd have to sell. Move.

'Please, Pete. You can't just—'

'Look, I know you like it here. But it can't be just about you.'

'Me?'

'Your happiness.'

'You're happy too?'

'I'm not!' He stood up abruptly. 'And maybe you'd notice that, if you weren't so wrapped up in yourself all the time!'

'Wrapped up in myself? All I do is work!'

'Work and order me about.'

'What?'

'*Oh Pete, the roof is leaking again. Pete, can you change Room 2's bedding? Pete, make me a cup of tea,*' he said, his voice becoming a sneer.

'But... I mean, that's your job. Our job.'

'I thought I'd come here and be... free. But it's worse. Because here we don't have any money, and this is meant to be our business, but somehow you seem to think you're my boss.'

She tried to steady her voice, now fizzing with held-back anger. 'I take charge because *someone* has to, Pete. If I didn't tell you the roof was leaking, you'd probably not even notice!'

'Seriously?'

'And if anything, I'm working twice as hard as you most of the time.' The last thing she wanted to do was argue, but suddenly it was as if she'd opened a floodgate, and the anger she'd suppressed over the last few years was escaping in a torrent.

'Oh, here it comes,' he said, rolling his eyes.

'Yes. Here it bloody comes! You say you're in this business with me, but most of the time you just complain, or go out to "price materials" and spend most of the day elsewhere. You haven't kept up with your French, you haven't made any friends here. If I'm honest, you've stopped feeling like a husband. It's like... it feels like I'm your mother!'

He looked at her, his face thunderous. 'And that's what I mean. It's over, Bella. You don't respect me. And I'm not happy.'

'What about me?'

'You said it yourself, *Mum*, you're old enough to sort out your own life. Apparently.'

'Look,' she said, swallowing her anger for a moment, reaching for him. 'I'm sorry. I know it's been hard. But could we try again? Try to... I don't know, recapture what we had? Think about what this would mean, Pete. We'd have to sell, move on. Where would I go?'

'What about Kitty? Maybe go back to her place for a while. God knows she'd be pleased to have you.'

'You know I can't do that!'

'Still not sure I understand why. You love Kitty, right?'

'I know, but she's so overbearing. Judgemental. And...' She waved her hands, unable to express the way Kitty made her feel. Inadequate. Small.

He made an awkward face, gave her no answers. She realised that, even now, the Pete she'd known was gone. The one who'd sit down and work out problems with her, however insignificant. She was stuck.

'At least think about it for a bit. Give it some time?' she suggested.

He at least had the humility to blush at this, to look away. 'I've booked a plane. Tomorrow. I'll go to my mum's for a bit. We'll have to pack up. Sell the place.'

'Hang on... You're going tomorrow?'

'I should have said something earlier, it's just...'

'You're getting on a plane tomorrow and leaving me?' She stood up, sending her chair rocking backwards noisily. 'Leaving me to do everything? Sell the house? Wind up the business?'

'I'm doing it for you! I thought you'd want me out of the way once you—'

'No, Pete. You can't do this. You can't just disappear because you've changed your mind!'

'I think it's for the best. We can't stay here together. Not now.'

'For the best? The best for you, you mean! Pete, you're expecting me to deal with this news, deal with the bureaucracy of selling the house, the business. Pack it all up, and what? Send you a cheque with no hard feelings?'

'Oh, come on, Bella.'

Bella wasn't given to temper tantrums or outbursts. She was more likely to deal with something with passive-aggressive silence than a huge explosion. But the man she loved – and yes, she'd known they were in a rocky patch, but that was marriage, wasn't it? – had dumped her in the most callous and selfish way.

She'd never thrown anything in anger before. But she suddenly felt the teapot in her hand, still weighed down with half a pot of cold, stewed tea and couldn't resist the urge to fling it with all her might. The pot sailed almost gracefully through the air, before plunging onto the terracotta tiles and smashing spectacularly, sending dark liquid and sodden leaves across the floor.

They both stood for a moment looking at what she'd done. Then Pete simply walked from the room.

When the door closed, she sank onto a chair, all the vibrating, jitter-inducing energy and shock dissipating for a moment. She lay her forehead on the table's hard, smooth surface, smelling the familiar aroma of the wood and polish, and wrapped her arms around her face. She tried to breathe, to focus on what had happened, make sense of it.

But there was no sense to make. Pete – her husband, her best friend, her business partner – was leaving. Everything she'd imagined for her future was falling away. And she had no idea what she was going to do next.

2

2006, FRANCE

'This is boring,' her best friend Sarah whispered.

Bella nodded in agreement.

The teacher – a stern-looking woman with a shock of short, blonde hair – turned to look at them and they returned their eyes to their clipboards and the checklist they were expected to complete during the tour of the ninth century church.

She hadn't wanted to admit to Sarah that she was fascinated by the rudimentary stained glass in the windows, that she longed to light a candle and make a wish, or say a prayer, she supposed. Bella didn't believe in God, not really. But she could feel the history in this building, the collective prayers and hopes and dreams of the people who had gathered there for the past thousand years and more, as if they'd seeped into the stone walls, the mottled wooden pews, the flagstones underfoot.

Later though, as they sat with their French counterparts in a restaurant and ate *steak haché* and *frites*, chattering loudly in a mixture of French and English, even Sarah had a smile on her face. 'It's been a good week,' she admitted to Bella later. 'Sucks that we have to go home.'

'Yeah.' Bella hadn't actually wanted to go on the French trip. It had been Sarah who'd convinced her. But she was glad she had. It was her first time abroad – family finances didn't stretch to foreign holidays. Here, everything felt the same, yet ever so slightly different. It meant that she could be different too.

She felt as if she'd lived more in this past week than in the preceding sixteen years. They'd visited Limoges and taken a harrowing trip to the ruined village of Oradour-sur-Glane and learned of its tragic history. They'd gone to see a play they'd only half understood and eaten in a variety of restaurants. They'd attended lessons at a French school and learned to kayak on the river. She'd fallen in and out of love with a boy named Isaac with whom she'd shared a secret kiss on the first night.

Back home, life was limited. She was the baby of the family, and nobody seemed to notice that she was actually sixteen and technically an adult. Curfews and homework and talk about A level choices, eating her greens. And Kitty, unbearably older – working her first job and actually living with a boyfriend – had left her far behind.

Here, people actually saw her. This week, she'd experimented with her hair, tried different looks, spoken a language she only half knew and stayed up late giggling with friends. This was what she wanted in life – to be her own person, independent of all the things that held her back.

Home was boring. Life was dull and predictable. 'Wish we didn't have to leave,' she said.

3

NOW

'No, wait. I'm a quick learner. I can—'

'I'm sorry, Madame Baker, but there are other candidates with more experience.'

'So you're not even going to give me an interview?'

There was a long pause, followed by a breath that bordered on a sigh. 'I am sorry, Madame. There may be more opportunities in the autumn.'

'But it's only March. I need a job now!'

'I am sorry.' The line went dead and Bella found herself letting out a roar of frustration. A part-time cashier opening, at her local supermarket. The kind of thing she'd thought of as a last resort when she'd started the search two weeks ago; and now she'd just practically begged for an interview.

Her hand dropped to her side, the phone almost slipping from her grasp. She was utterly exhausted, dejected, tired of crying, and had put on at least two kilos in chocolate weight alone since Pete had left three weeks earlier.

The knock on the door made her jump. As she went to answer it, she glanced in the hall mirror and saw herself for the first time that day. Hair wild and escaping from her ponytail. Eyes red-rimmed and dark-circled. She thought back to her innocent entrance to the house that fateful evening; her warm scarf, neat coat. Her hair, light make-up, her smile. At that moment in time, she'd thought they were simply having a bit of bad luck. Bookings were down, the plumbing had needed a fix and they'd heard that social charges were increasing this tax year. Yes, they'd been arguing – who doesn't?

But life had pulled the rug out from under her.

There was another knock. Then, 'Bella?' came a voice.

It was enough, even in this situation, to make her smile. 'Juliette?'

'*Oui*, open the door. It is warm this evening but it is not *that* warm.'

'Sorry. Sorry.' She wiped her hand roughly across her face and pulled back the latch, opening the door on the half-light of early evening.

Juliette, her blonde hair neatly bobbed around her face, wearing a jacket, jeans and walking boots, was there, holding a foil-covered dish in one hand and a lead in the other.

'Oh, and Jolie!' Bella exclaimed, dropping into a crouch and wrapping her arms around the golden lab. 'It's lovely to see you.'

'Me, or the dog?' Juliette enquired drily as she followed Bella into the hallway. She looked at Bella quizzically as she handed her the dish – slightly warm – and unhooked the lead from Jolie's collar before removing her coat. Somehow, she maintained eye contact throughout.

'Both of you, of course.' Bella leant forward and lightly kissed her friend on each cheek. 'And thanks for this.' She lifted the dish slightly. 'You didn't need to.'

'Didn't I?' Juliette said as they made their way into the kitchen. 'Have you even been eating in here? Or just snacking?'

'Both?'

'Eating meals?'

Bella shrugged. 'It's hard, cooking for one.'

'Pah! That is a pathetic excuse. I am cooking for one most of the time if you don't count Jolie. And I manage just fine.'

Even in her miserable state, Bella felt the edges of her mouth turn up. Juliette's forthright manner was a breath of fresh air in her current confused state. It had been Juliette who'd convinced her to apply for a job, to give herself a financial stopgap. Time to think. She'd felt quite buoyed up about it last time they'd spoken. That was before she'd realised just how unemployable she was.

'Yes, but you like being single.'

Juliette shrugged. 'Sometimes. Anyway, this is not a visit to talk about me. We need to talk about you.'

Bella had met Juliette a couple of months after moving to France. She worked with the *maire* as a secretary, as well as running the local social club. When Juliette's grandparents had come to visit, they'd stayed at Bella's B & B, somehow cementing their friendship.

'Do we have to?' Bella moaned, sitting down on the sofa.

'Yes. We do. Because I can see that you are not well.' Juliette peered at Bella's face. 'You have been crying, *non*?'

Bella shrugged. 'Is it that obvious?'

'Yes, Bella, and Pete is not worth your tears. You know this! He left you in a terrible situation.'

'He doesn't love me any more.'

Juliette shrugged as if this were an insignificant detail. 'Perhaps, but he still has responsibilities. A business. He left that all with you. You should be angry, not sad.'

Bella nodded. 'I know.' It was hard though, when she felt Pete's absence in every corner of the house. 'Anyway,' she waved vaguely at her face. 'These tears aren't about him. Not this time.'

'Oh?'

Bella explained how she'd spent the afternoon enquiring about local work, but since she had no experience in doing anything here bar running a B & B, she'd been pipped to the post by other candidates. 'It's not that I'm not good enough,' she said. 'It's just that they're better.'

'I doubt it,' Juliette said, loyally.

'Well, I even applied for that job at EcoMarché. You know the one I said I wouldn't touch with a barge pole? And guess what. Not even an interview!'

'Perhaps that is a blessing?' Juliette detested the cheap supermarket in their local town, preferring to visit the butcher's and buy the rest of her food from the market.

Bella shook her head, unable to join in with their usual humour. 'I'm in serious trouble. Financially, I mean. The agent, Nathalie, is pretty sure those last viewers are going to make an offer. But even if they do, it'll be at least three months before I see any of the equity.'

'Well then you need to strategise,' Juliette said. 'Cast your net a little wider.'

'Wider?'

'Yes! You are not tied to Peyrat. Or Aubusson. Why not try Paris? I have a friend there, and she says the hospitality industry is crying out for staff.'

'Paris! I won't be able to afford to live there.'

'If you have a job, you might?' Juliette raised an eyebrow. 'And there are lots of attractive men in Paris.'

'Forget it. I'm off men for good.'

Juliette nodded, all mock seriousness. 'Of course. How could I forget.'

'I just don't think... I mean, going to Paris. It's a lot. I'm not sure I could...'

Juliette shuffled closer and put her arm around Bella's shoulders. '*Mon coeur*, you are looking at it the wrong way! Maybe it's what you need. To get away. Have an adventure. Forget about the house and the village for a while. Why not?'

'I love you, Juliette, you know that. I love your... faith in me. But I've just failed at one business. I have no idea what I'm doing. And everyone but you can see that. I have no qualifications, no experience that seems relevant to employers. I can't see myself getting a job at all.'

'You want to borrow money? I have a little saved, you can have it if you need?'

Bella shook her head. 'No. I mean, I need money. But I won't. I can't. You know that.'

'Then why not give Paris a try?' Juliette gave Bella's knee a squeeze. 'Look, if it were me, I'd just apply for every job I found and take whatever I can get. Cleaning, housekeeping, office work. Just to buy you some time. And in Paris, the wages will be better, even for those kinds of work.'

Bella nodded. 'I know. I'm going to have to. Or it'll be destination Kitty's.'

'Would that really be so terrible?'

'Yes, actually. Anyway, you're right. I just have to take whatever I can get. Even if it's just a stopgap. Even if it's – I don't know – scrubbing Macron's underwear or something.'

Juliette pulled her in for a hug. Jolie, sensing the emotional moment, came and lay her warm head on their hands, looking up at them imploringly. 'See, even Jolie wants to help you,' Juliette said.

Bella felt her eyes fill with tears. 'Oh Jolie,' she said, pulling her hand away and rubbing the dog's head. 'I know you'd employ me in a heartbeat.'

Juliette laughed. 'Yes, she'd have you walking her and cooking special meals. Unfortunately, she can only pay you in love.'

'If only the bank would accept that.'

'*Oui*, indeed.'

Later, when her friend had left, Bella lifted the foil lid from the dish she'd been given to discover a rich *pot-au-feu*, a casserole made with well-marinated chunks of beef and vegetables in a rich gravy. She heated a little in the microwave and tried to eat, but it was difficult.

Juliette had been right. She hadn't been eating properly. Just picking at this and that. Working through the batches of cupcakes she'd baked to get her mind off things. Feeling sick of them and sick with herself.

Something in her body reacted to the sensation of proper food, and she closed her eyes as she chewed and swallowed her first decent meal in an age.

'Enough,' she said to herself. Enough of the wallowing. She would get a job if it killed her. She opened a bottle of wine – something she'd ordinarily never let herself do when alone for fear she'd finish the whole bottle – and poured herself a generous glass. Then, roughly clearing off the kitchen table, stacking dishes and mugs in the corner to deal with later, she opened her laptop and began to search.

She didn't want to leave her lovely home. Only that was going to have to happen whether she liked it or not. So maybe moving away from Peyrat for a time would be a blessing. How would it feel to rent a home in the village and see someone else living her life in the house she'd thought she'd be in forever?

The tears threatened but she forced herself to regain control. It would feel awful. Awful.

Juliette was right, she should cast her net farther afield. Find a job to fill the months between sale and completion, give herself something to think about and money in her pocket. Keep the bank happy by paying her share of the mortgage. Then reconvene, decide what to do next.

She opened yet another application form and began to fill in her details, sipping from her wine as she did so. Every job she'd applied for so far in the local area had criticised her lack of experience. She'd run a business for eight years, but clearly that wasn't impressive enough. She hadn't worked in an office, she'd never worked in a larger organisation. Her face, her skills, just didn't seem to fit the mould. Her meagre qualifications from the UK weren't even recognised here.

She thought of Kitty's offer. Her sister had suggested she move back to the UK even if it was just for a bit. But staying at her sister's and observing her perfect life – married bliss, a toddler, a successful career to go back to when she was ready – would be too much.

She wouldn't be happy there, living in Kitty's shadow, feeling every ounce of her inadequacy. France was the place where her happiness lived, and she had to stay.

What would Kitty do if she were in this situation? she thought, opening up yet another questionnaire.

She didn't need to ask. Kitty had always been the confident one. She'd aced her exams, got into a top university, landed a coveted graduate scheme. She'd met the love of her life, got married, conceived easily and now had a perfect little boy. Her CV would impress anyone.

She thought of Juliette. Of her forthright manner, her strength. If Juliette were in this situation, she would sell herself.

She had the confidence to overcome the sort of reticence that Bella had when talking about her skills.

If she wanted to get anywhere, she'd have to forget all about who she was, her limitations, and try to become the kind of person she wished she could be.

4

2006, ENGLAND

Mum wasn't home when Bella got back from school, although she'd left a note on the table.

At supermarket. Back soon.

Bella checked the cupboards and managed to find one slightly crushed packet of salt and vinegar crisps. Hopefully Mum would bring some more snacks back with her.

This was the sort of moment where a mobile phone would come in really handy, she thought to herself. Everyone else seemed to have one and she was the only kid in the world whose parents thought she was too young. She was doing her A levels now, for God's sake!

Of course, *they* all had them. Mum, Dad, Kitty. It was only she who was left out of the loop, having to borrow Mum's phone to send a text, or use the landline in the hallway where everyone could hear her.

They'd argued about it ever since the French trip. 'Mobile

phones are expensive!' her dad had said. 'We've just spent two hundred quid sending you on holiday.'

'But that was for school!' she'd whined.

She'd keep at them. They'd have to give in eventually. If not, she'd have to save up for one, she supposed. Only at the rate she earned working in the bakery one Saturday a fortnight, it would probably take until she was a thousand years old.

The key scratched in the lock and she flung down her crisps, scattering a few but ignoring them, and went into the hallway to help Mum carry in the shopping, hoping to root through to see what she'd actually bought.

The dark feeling came seconds later when she stood in front of the unopened door. A kind of heaviness; a dread. Like in a horror movie when the idiot girl goes down to the deserted basement even when she knows there's a murderer on the loose.

So as the door swung open to reveal not her mother's face but Kitty's – or a version of Kitty's, a swollen, red-eyed, pale-skinned version whose eyes didn't quite make contact with hers – she already knew something was very wrong.

'Kitty,' she said. 'Where's Mum?'

5

NOW

The cocoa formed a thin film of chocolate over the batter and she watched as it folded in, turning the cream-coloured mixture the colour of toffee. Bella added a little more until the mixture was sufficiently rich.

Her phone flashed up the name 'Kitty'. She swiped at the screen to accept the call, leaving a trace of chocolate, and put it to her ear, cradling it between her shoulder and her head. 'Hi.'

'Hi.' There was a pause. 'So, how are things?'

'OK,' she lied, scraping batter into yet another set of cupcake cases.

'Seriously?'

'What do you want me to say?' She could hear the sharpness in her tone and grimaced. Whatever this was, it wasn't her sister's fault.

There was another pause.

'Sorry.'

It was very unlike Bella's sister to be so hesitant. Since Pete had left three weeks ago now, she'd phoned almost every day. She'd counselled Bella through fits of tears or anger, helped her start to get the house organised for the imminent sale. Even emailed an agent who had come to value the place. She deserved better than that.

Only, when Bella was baking, all the other stuff seemed to fall away. Her sister ringing now was like someone piercing the bubble of a dream and letting reality in.

'We've accepted that offer.'

'That's really good!'

'Is it?' Bella looked sadly around the kitchen; she wasn't sure how she felt about it now, without Pete there any more. The house was large, empty, fairly remote. It felt odd to be here solo. But she wasn't in a hurry to leave either.

'It is. Come on, Bella, you can't afford it on your own. You said that yourself.'

'I know. But... what am I meant to do? This is my business too. I won't have a job or anything once it goes.'

'Come home.' Kitty's voice took on an older sister authority. 'Just get on a plane and come home.'

'*This* is my home.'

'It *was* your home. It's not now, Bella. We'll look after you here. You can find a job. Start again.'

Bella shook her head vehemently; the tears that hadn't been far from her eyes over the last three weeks began to threaten again. 'No,' she said, her voice sounding slightly strangled now. 'I can't, Kitty. I don't want to give up on France, even if I do have to give up this house. And I haven't got time to start again.'

Yet another pause. 'I do try to understand, I do,' her sister said. 'And I know France is beautiful. But I honestly can't understand why you hate visiting the UK so much. It's not that bad, you know!'

'I know that!'

'So let go of France for a bit. Come back, see me. Get to know your nephew a bit more.'

Now it was Bella's turn to be silent. Then, 'I can't,' she said, her voice small, reluctant.

'But what will you do?'

'I don't know. I've applied for – I don't know – a thousand jobs? One of them has to come up, surely.'

'But you can get a job here, there's loads of temping work around at the moment and...'

'I can't do it, Kitty. At least not yet. Because if I do, then Pete's taken everything. Don't you see that? He took my marriage, and my home. But I've had this dream of living in France for as long as I can remember. He can't take that part of me too.'

'He won't. You'll still be you.'

'Look, maybe I *will* go back to England one day. But if I do, I want it to be on *my* terms.' She sniffed loudly.

Kitty was silent. 'OK,' she finally said.

'OK?'

'I understand. But if that is the case, then you have to stop making cupcakes and start actually being practical.'

Bella looked around the kitchen – at the mixing bowls piled by the sink, the plates of pink-iced cupcakes, chocolate swirls. 'What makes you think I'm baking?'

'Bella?'

'What?'

'Bella...?'

She sighed. 'OK, yes. I'm baking.'

'And?'

'And I'll stop once this batch is finished. I'll get back online and find something if it kills me.'

'Atta girl.'

6

2006, ENGLAND

Her tights itched. Mum would never have bought cheap tights from the local shop. But Dad didn't know anything about tights. These were thinner than her usual ones too; already they had a small ladder on the right ankle.

She didn't understand why everyone had to wear black, either. Kitty and her, obviously. And Dad of course. But there were people there at Mum's funeral whom she'd never met. Some of them were crying. It didn't seem right that these people were here to mourn her mum when she'd belonged to Bella and Kitty and their father and no one else. Not really.

And why had Dad decided to have the ceremony in a church? Mum hated churches – said they gave her the creeps. She'd hate to know that she was in a coffin in front of the pews (although a part of Bella still didn't believe that Mum was in that thing in front of the altar). Mum had liked outdoors and sunlight and happy places.

But Mum was dead.

The word 'dead' seemed to flit across her mind every few minutes. It was such an odd word. Such a flat, final word. It didn't seem to fit the lively, loving mum who lived in her memory. She thought again of the last time she'd seen her, her back to Bella as she rinsed out her coffee cup at the kitchen sink.

'Bye, then,' Bella had said, bag over her shoulder, annoyed that she had to go to school.

'See you, love!' Mum had called.

And she'd left.

Bella had relived this moment hundreds of times since – when Kitty had given her the news about Mum's accident; when Dad had come home, ashen-faced, and told her the same story all over again; that night when she'd been lying in bed and it'd felt like the house was holding its breath; and in the morning when she woke up feeling normal, and it had hit her thirty seconds later – a blow enormous enough to take her breath away.

She'd thought back to that final exchange and hated herself. Why hadn't she turned and given her mum a hug? Slipped her arms around her and leant into her and sniffed her lily of the valley perfume and just said something like 'I love you'. It would have taken a second. Maybe if she'd said that, things would be different. Somehow it felt as if Mum hadn't died because of the van that had ploughed into her car at a round-about, but because Bella hadn't loved her enough, hadn't made it impossible for her to leave.

A woman turned and looked at Bella, her face creasing in sympathy, and Bella looked sharply away. All people did now was look at her, or ask her how she was. Even Kitty, with her sad face, her worried questions.

Of course she wasn't OK. Nothing would ever be OK again.

After the service, they all crowded back to their three-bed

detached house and ate sausage rolls and little sandwiches. They drank tea and coffee and orange juice.

As soon as she was able to, Bella escaped to the garden, away from the gaping mouths filled with half-chewed bread, the inane chatter, the ordinariness of it all. The funeral had been awful, but the sandwiches were worse. They reminded her of packed lunches and picnics and boring 'this will do' teas. Of everyday things that had come before and would come again. She couldn't understand how easily people could put food in their mouths and chew and talk about what a lovely woman her mother had been.

She couldn't understand why people wanted sandwiches.

She'd had one forced into her hand by Kitty, and as she stood behind the huge oak tree in their garden, she shredded half of it into crumbs and threw it, piece by piece, to a blackbird that was hopping at a safe distance, regarding her with its side-facing eye, its head on a tilt.

The bird table was empty. Mum had always been the one to cover it in titbits for the birds, to hang disgusting fat balls from its special hook. Bella walked over and crumbled the rest of her unwanted sandwich onto its surface.

As she turned away, she noticed a feather at the base of the structure. Bending, she picked it up, remembering times when she'd done so as a child; how exciting it was to find one. And she thought of Mum. And she tucked the feather into her pocket before making her way back into the house.

7

NOW

As the train jolted, Bella's forehead banged lightly against the window. She sat up with a start, realising she'd fallen asleep. The man opposite was looking at her with undisguised amusement. She glared back, feeling her head throb, and he looked back down at his phone screen as if nothing had happened.

Checking her watch, she saw that there was now only an hour to go until she reached Versailles. She felt the familiar spike of anxiety that she'd kept experiencing ever since she'd made the arrangements.

The call about the job had come unexpectedly. The woman's voice on the phone had been clipped; efficient. 'Is that Madame Baker? It's Claudine from Hôtel Benjamin.'

'Yes. Speaking.'

'I'm calling about your job application.'

'Oh. Yes. Great.'

'I appreciate this is short notice, but the person we'd offered the job to has had to pull out. And you mentioned on your application form that you don't have to give notice on your current position, is this correct?'

'Yes. I mean, there isn't really... no, there's no notice period.' It wasn't technically a lie after all.

The woman had asked her a few further questions; and Bella had expected to perhaps be offered an interview. Which meant she'd been stunned at what had happened next.

'So, this is a temporary position, with the possibility of permanence after six months.'

'OK.'

'And if you are still interested, we'd like to offer it to you.'

'Yes! Of course. Yes, please. I mean, I'd be delighted.'

'Wonderful.' The woman had given her a start date and details and simply hung up.

In all honesty, it had sounded like it might be a scam. But Bella had looked up the hotel website again and found Claudine on it. The CEO.

Then an email had come, confirming her appointment, and she'd begun to feel more than a little excited.

'So what exactly is the job?' Juliette had asked, as they'd walked the length of the small village a few days ago. Jolie was bouncing on her lead, anticipating a longer walk and not realising they were only going as far as the café.

'I'm not completely sure,' she'd admitted. 'I applied for so many. Something in the admin department, I think.'

'You don't know?' Juliette's eyes had widened.

'Not exactly.'

'And you didn't think to ask?'

She'd looked at her friend. 'How could I? I wanted to sound interested in it!'

Juliette had thrown back her head and laughed. 'Oh, I'm sorry,' she'd said afterwards, grinning at Bella. 'But I love it! You have accepted a job, but you could be cleaning the toilet, or perhaps running the whole enterprise! You don't know! It is funny, *non*?'

Bella had smiled, although her own good humour was skating on a deep sea of anxiety. 'Ha. Yeah.'

'You will be fine, you know,' Juliette had said, perhaps sensing Bella's mood. She'd linked her arm through her friend's. 'You are more than capable.'

'Of the toilet job?'

'Of *any* job. Although I still don't fully understand why you would take a job in Paris over spending time with your sister. No rent, no job. It sounds wonderful!'

Bella had sighed. 'It's complicated.'

'*Oui*, I can see this.'

'I mean, she's only four years older than me. But after Mum... well, she became almost like a surrogate mother. Even now she has this kind of pull over me. And I'm afraid that I'll give in. Things have been so, so hard. I hate being alone and she's offering me an out...'

'But surely this is kind of her?'

'It's just... if I go back, I feel that—I'm not sure I'll ever have the courage to return.'

'*Ah bon?*'

Bella had nodded vehemently. 'Yes. And it terrifies me. Because coming to France – living here – was something I always dreamed of. And I'm afraid that if I leave... France is the place I'm happiest. It's where my life is now.' It would be complicated too, she'd realised; right now she had the *carte de séjour* afforded to expats who'd come over pre-Brexit. Things would be more difficult if she had to forfeit that. 'I know the job situation isn't ideal, but like you said, I just need a way to... survive, I suppose. To keep going while the house sells. Give me some breathing... thinking space.'

Over coffee, she'd told her friend about the house share she'd secured in Versailles, the cheapest she could find. 'I'll be living with students, commuting to Paris,' she'd said. 'But it might be fun?' She hadn't told Juliette that, in order to secure her room, she'd allowed the agent to assume she was a student herself. Juliette would only worry, would offer her money she didn't want to take. This way she could afford to live close to the capital without falling into more debt.

'Well, this is wonderful news,' Juliette had said firmly. 'A whole new adventure.'

Bella had tried to smile. 'I just... I've never even been to Versailles. I've never met these people. Haven't even seen the hotel. It's... I'm dreading it, if I'm honest.'

'Pah! You will have a blast. It's exciting.' Juliette had fingered the four-leaf-clover pendant she wore.

'Maybe I should take your pendant, for luck.'

'Ha! Then what would *I* do?' Juliette was superstitious about the necklace, given to her by an aunt when she'd taken her baccalaureate exams at seventeen. 'No, you do not need luck. You have everything you need.'

'I guess you're right.'

Still, it felt strange to have accepted a job without being sure exactly what she'd be expected to do. She'd scoured the hotel's website, but they were advertising vacancies in several departments, so there was no clue there.

She'd considered writing an email asking exactly what the job might entail, but she'd been too afraid to do anything that might jeopardise this opportunity: it was her only chance to stay in France, stand on her own two feet, and she had to see it through, no matter what came of it.

The email had addressed her as Isabella – her full, given name and the one she'd used on the application as it sounded so much more serious. She'd always hated it, but if Mum were still alive, she'd probably be delighted. She'd always insisted on calling Bella by her full name, especially when she was in trouble. Bella remembered the way Mum would call her down for tea as a child: 'Isabella! It's getting cold!' Then, as was often the case when she thought about her mother, she felt the welling of threatening tears. As the train continued its way towards Versailles, she forced her mind to focus on something else.

* * *

The street where the house was situated looked better than it had on Google Earth. A couple of shops that had been derelict and covered in scaffolding in the online images were now shiny, new, and open for business. There was a restaurant, and something that looked like a laundrette. As she walked on, the buildings became residential, with rows of bells outside, bikes leaning against railings, curtains in the windows. And then she was there: No.12.

She paused, looking up at the building that would soon become her home. It was a pretty terraced house, probably nineteenth century – three storeys with two windows apiece – each with an ornate, black balconet. The powder-blue shutters on the first and second floors were thrown open, revealing wooden windows in cross-hatched white. The front door – *her* front door – was curved and split in two, and painted a deep blue.

Hesitantly, she climbed the two front steps, lifted her hand and knocked.

'*Oui?*'

The woman – or girl, really – who opened the door was dressed in a loose-fitted shirt, covered in flecks of paint. Her fingers were stained red at the tips and even her hair – auburn and pulled back into a messy ponytail – sported little dots of accidental colour. The afternoon sunlight rested on her face revealing smooth, porcelain skin, naturally arched eyebrows, a rosebud mouth. She was young – no more than twenty. Bella thought of her own skin, already starting to form fine lines around her eyes, and wished she'd never lied about being a student.

'I'm sorry, I'm interrupting,' she said. She should have just used the key; the agent had said she'd be free to come and go as she pleased. But it would have felt odd just letting herself into someone else's home for the first time without any sort of introduction. They'd probably have called the police.

True, at five foot four, with her neat, shoulder-length hair, fitted jeans and wheeled suitcase, she probably didn't look like a hardened criminal. And the young woman didn't look the type to rugby-tackle an intruder to the ground. But you can never be too careful – and the last thing Bella wanted was to get off to a bad start. She'd had enough bad starts – and come to think of it, bad middles and endings – to last her a lifetime.

The young woman looked at her, tilting her head quizzically. 'Can I help you?' she asked in heavily accented English.

She was clearly trying to be helpful with her language choice, but it made Bella aware that despite her continually improving French, her accent must have given her away. 'Sorry,' she said automatically. She wondered whether she'd ever behaved quite so Britishly in her life. She'd said five words so far and two of them had been 'sorry's. 'I'm Bella. I'm—I've rented the spare room.'

'Odette,' the girl said in response.

On autopilot, Bella held out her hand for a shake. Both of them looked down at her clean hands, her neat, manicured nails. The girl shook her head. 'Do not be offended, Madame,' she said, 'but I do not want to get paint on you.'

'Sorry.' Bella cringed at her own word now and noticed a flicker of amusement in Odette's expression. Odette was speaking in her second language and she'd still managed to use a wider vocabulary than Bella in this small exchange.

In all honesty, she was a little put out by the 'madame' part. Surely, at thirty-four, she was still 'mademoiselle'? She knew that some younger French women found the term archaic and sexist, but 'madame' sounded to her like a woman of at least twice her age – someone who ran a café and wore her grey hair in a bun, chain-smoked and sported scarlet lipstick.

She was not there yet. Quite.

'*Entrez.*' Odette turned away, leaving the door open behind her.

Tentatively, Bella stepped into the hallway which was laid in parquet, something showcased in the photos she'd viewed before committing. What the photos hadn't revealed was that the wooden floor was worn and uneven; it squeaked under her weight. But then this was student accommodation.

In the past she'd have spent ages researching before choosing somewhere to live. Or to work, for that matter. But a combination of misery and late nights meant she'd put down a deposit on this place sight unseen.

In fact, her whole life right now was sight unseen.

The hallway also sported an old-fashioned coat stand in one corner, with several mismatched garments hanging from it: a powder-blue jacket, a heavy wool coat, two hoodies and what looked like a pair of running shorts. A pile of post sat on a small table next to it, together with a couple of sets of keys and – for no apparent reason – one shoe.

There was also a painting on the wall; a large, wooden-framed seascape in oils – beautiful, confident strokes of blue and green to make up whirling waves, the abstract form of a ship being tossed on a playful ocean. The contrast between the fine art and its lacklustre surroundings made it seem almost comically incongruous – a neglected animal with a diamond collar or a battered car sporting expensive alloys.

'Thanks,' she said, although she knew Odette, like her, would just be renting a room. It wasn't as if she'd offered Bella her hospitality. Still, after three 'sorry's in a row, at least it was a new, slightly less apologetic word.

'Didn't they give you a key?'

'Oh. Yes, they did. I just—it felt too weird to just walk in.' Bella smiled but it felt forced; unnatural. Recently, she'd felt more conscious of herself, her actions, her appearance than she had in a decade – as if she'd travelled back in time to her late teens.

She'd been with Pete for over a decade, married for eight. They'd come to France together to run the B & B and pretty much spent every day in each other's company. For better or for worse. Latterly, obviously, for worse.

Now that she was an individual again she felt strangely vulnerable, exposed, with no Pete buffer to fall back on.

Inside, Odette gestured at the stairs. 'The spare room is on the right at the top.' She smiled, but almost instantly turned back towards another door, propped open with a pile of books. 'This is mine,' she said, looking over her shoulder before stepping through and pulling the door to, so just her face was exposed in the gap.

'Right.' Bella continued to smile. What was actually wrong with her? Had she literally frozen to the spot?

Odette looked amused. 'You will be OK to find your room?'

'Yes! Yes, of course.'

'Well, I will get back to my painting. But come ask if you need anything. Knock first, please.' Then, still smiling, Odette turned and disappeared like a cat slinking out of sight. The door clicked firmly into place.

'Well, that went well,' Bella muttered to herself before pulling her wheeled suitcase to the edge of the stairs, then adjusting it so she could carry it upwards.

As she made her way to the second floor, she could feel any hope she'd had of finding a friendly welcome, of fitting in, drain away.

8

NOW

'*Bon Dieu!*' The cry was loud and echoed around the en suite.

With a gasp, Bella stood back against the wall, feeling for some sort of weapon and seizing the only viable instrument in sight – a toilet brush that had seen better days.

She'd found her room easily. It was quite sparse – just a chest of drawers and a bed with a bedside table, but it would do. Then she'd noticed a door in the corner. Perhaps a closet. She'd pushed open the door and gasped; it was an en suite! They hadn't thought of mentioning this in the property details. Things were looking up! She'd found herself grinning, but her face had fallen when she'd realised she was not alone. Because there appeared to be a naked man, half-covered in soapsuds, standing in the shower, clutching at the plastic curtain and trying in vain to cover his modesty.

'What are you doing in my bathroom?' she managed.

'Madame,' he said, drawing himself up – although it was hard for him to demonstrate the authority or gravitas he was clearly trying to show when half-wrapped in a plastic shower curtain which left very little to the imagination. 'My question is: what are you doing in *mine*?'

'Yours?'

'Yes, of course! Do you think I would break into somebody's bathroom and have a shower?'

It did, on reflection, seem rather odd. Bella lowered the toilet brush to her side. 'But I've—This is *my* room! I've—I literally signed the contract two days ago!'

'I have lived here for several years.'

'But this is—'

'Is it possible,' the man said in a voice that sounded as if he were only just holding onto his temper, 'that perhaps you are mistaken?'

'But—'

The bedroom she'd passed through had been uninhabited. Immaculate. She'd lain on the bed for a moment, revelling in the fresh cotton sheets someone had clearly put on for her benefit. It hadn't looked like a room that someone was actually living in. It was too tidy, too empty.

But she *had* wondered about the dressing gown on the back of the door.

And the shoes just tucked under the bed.

She'd just assumed they'd been left behind by the previous occupant. Not the present one.

Oh, God. She had just walked into someone else's room, into their en suite, and then accused them of trespassing. First impressions just didn't get any worse than this. 'I'm so—I'm— Oh, God.' She turned on her heel and made for the door.

'Madame!' he cried after her. 'The brush!'

'Oh, sorry,' she said, noticing the toilet brush still clutched in her hand. She turned swiftly to return it and in doing so, flicked some dirty droplets into the air. They sailed almost gracefully in slow motion across the room before delicately sprinkling themselves across the wall and onto the man's bare chest.

'*Bon Dieu!*' he cried again. '*Merde!*'

'I'm—' But she couldn't bear to look at the mess she'd created of him, his bathroom and her life. Instead, dropping the brush, she ran back into the corridor where she noticed the door to a smaller room, slightly ajar. It was almost comically obvious, yet somehow, she'd missed it before.

She flung herself onto the smaller, harder, sheetless mattress of her actual room and let out a scream of exasperation into its muffling surface. What the hell was wrong with her? And why exactly was this now her life?

It was at moments like these – although thankfully this exact situation hadn't occurred before – that she missed Pete most of all. He'd been her husband, sure. But in the years they'd lived together in France, he'd also become her best friend; her family. She could have rung him, told him about this and he would have found a way to make her laugh at it, helped her to move on.

She couldn't talk to Kitty, who would probably just share her horror. And she didn't feel able to speak to Juliette about it – this sort of thing would never happen to someone like her.

Mum had been gone for years, Dad was now also a dad to two little boys and lived in Clapham; he'd melted away after Mum died and had been swallowed up by a new life.

She didn't have anyone. Or anything.

All she had was squirming shame, and an almost overwhelming desire to run out of the house, get back on the train and disappear into the haven of Peyrat and the house she'd loved for almost a decade.

* * *

The tentative knock on the door made her jump. 'Come in,' she said after a pause, hoping to heavens that, if it was the half-naked French guy, he'd at least pulled more than an off-white shower curtain over his manhood.

When she saw that in fact it was Odette, she gave a sigh of relief. '*Bonjour*,' she said. 'Hi.'

'Hi.' Odette stepped in, looking around at the rather shabby room with its faded wallpaper, heavy vintage wardrobe and overlarge carved bedframe. 'You found the right room now?'

'Yes.' Bella probably would have blushed if she hadn't already been fully coloured from her earlier embarrassment. 'Did you hear what I—what happened?'

Odette gave a little smile and sat next to her on the bed, slipping an arm around her back. 'It's OK,' she said. 'Do not be embarrassed. Henri told me.'

The arm around her back was a surprise; Odette seemed a different person to the one who'd answered the door less than an hour ago. The unexpected touch caused a prick of tears which Bella quickly swallowed away.

'Henri?' she said, nodding in the vague direction of the other room.

'*Oui*. That was Henri, our other housemate. He told me what happened, but don't worry. He thinks it's funny, now he knows you are not a burglar. Or an assassin.'

'He thought I might be an assassin?'

Odette rolled her eyes. 'You will have to excuse Henri. He is training to be a professor of literature. He has too much of an imagination. Too many stories.'

Bella laughed. 'Oh – well, I hope you put him right.'

'Yes. He is reassured you are quite harmless!' Odette's tone was teasing and Bella felt something tight within her uncoil, relax.

'Well, good. I'm so embarrassed just walking in like that.'

They smiled at each other for a moment, then Odette stood, stretching her arms above her head and yawning. 'I wanted to ask you to join us for some wine, if you drink? We often have *apéros* together at seven.'

'Oh. Yes, please.' In actual fact, the thought of seeing Henri again so soon made Bella feel a little light-headed, but better to get it over and done with. Be a grown-up about it.

And while she'd rather not have been confronted by Henri's – albeit rather attractive – naked body, if it turned out that this was what it took to thaw the ice, well, she'd learn to cope.

All was not lost after all.

9

2008, ENGLAND

'Remember...' Kitty reached over and grabbed Bella's wrist and waited until her sister turned and looked at her.

Bella made brief eye contact then looked away. Why did Kitty have to be so bloody intense all the time?

'Remember, whatever happens, whatever results you get, we're all proud of you. Me, Stu, Dad and Linda.'

'Oh yeah, I bet Linda's *really* proud,' Bella said, deadpan.

'You should give her a chance, you know,' Kitty said softly.

Bella looked at her again, incredulous. 'Why? So I can have a brand-new mum and forget all about my actual one?'

'Don't be silly. She's a nice woman. She's kind. And you know, she's trying.'

'It must be very difficult for her.'

Kitty let go of her wrist and sighed. 'I know. I get it. It's hard for all of us. But Dad seems happy. And you know, Mum's been gone nearly two years now.'

'Oh, so we should just forget about her; is that what you're saying?'

'Look, let's not talk about this now,' Kitty said, a bright artificial tone returning to her voice. 'I just wanted to say good luck. And you know, don't worry. We'll get you sorted.'

Bella grunted and exited the car.

At the school, pupils were already streaming in and out; some with groups of friends; some with family; others, alone. There were whoops and screeches from some; others simply melted away into their future, clutching the paper that would go some way to dictate it.

She already knew – and Kitty already suspected – that the news wouldn't be good. She hadn't worked hard, had been unable to somehow. I mean, what were A levels anyway? Something some professor had invented a hundred years ago. A piece of paper. Everything seemed so pointless. University had once been a goal, but she was almost certainly not going to get the place she'd applied for.

It was weird, but she didn't really care. If Mum's death had taught her anything, it was that your future comes and hits you full in the face whether you like it or not. You could try to shape it with qualifications and dreams, but at the end of the day, if fate had other ideas, your plans meant nothing at all.

10

NOW

Half an hour later, Bella ventured downstairs, changed into a simple white summer dress. The idea of *apéros* sounded quite sophisticated – the tiny nibbles and drinks served before an evening meal had been something she and Pete had sometimes offered guests. But they'd rarely had the chance to have any themselves.

In fact the more she thought about it, the more she realised how many of the dreams they'd had had fallen by the wayside – there had been no trips to Paris, no weekend jaunts to the Riviera. They hadn't visited the lakes in the Loire or gone on a wine tasting tour. They'd stayed, for the most part, in Peyrat and although their world seemed expansive to those they'd left in England, in many ways it had shrunk.

Before arriving in Versailles, she'd been determined to keep herself to herself – to work the three months until her house finally sold, then disappear. Only when Odette had asked her to have a drink with them, it had seemed impossible to say no. Perhaps because of her embarrassment over Henri. Or perhaps just because, if she were honest, she'd never felt so alone.

As she reached the bottom of the stairs, for the first time in a couple of tumultuous months, she felt a lift – as if something were holding her upright. Hope.

It was kind of nice to be living in student accommodation; her own uni days existed only in her imagination. She'd wanted to go once, but after she'd failed her A levels and taken a job in a pharmacy, it hadn't seemed to matter. She hadn't cared back then, at a time when life had seemed to pass at a snail's pace, every moment drenched in grief. But she sometimes liked to imagine what it might have been like, living vicariously through Kitty's stories of wild nights out and exhausted days in lectures.

When she entered the kitchen, Odette had already opened a bottle of cherry wine, and placed it next to a bowl of tortilla chips and an open pot of dip. Two little glasses were set out on the table.

It wasn't quite the decadent spread Bella had pictured. But it was a start.

'*Voilà!*' Odette passed her a glass and she took a sip.

'Oof!' she gasped involuntarily after the thick, syrupy liquid burned down her throat. It took all the willpower she had not to spit the whole mouthful out.

'You do not like?'

'Oh no. It's lovely, just... strong.' 'Strong' was an understatement. In fact, it reminded her of the cough syrup her mother used to force down her when she had the flu, but with a shot of turpentine in it for good measure. 'Yummy.'

'It is good, yes?' Odette asked with a sideways glance, refilling her own drink.

'Yes. Lovely.' Bella grabbed a few tortilla chips, but it was going to take a lot more carbs to soak up something this strong. She hadn't got anything in the cupboards, no plans. Her stomach grumbled reproachfully. 'What do you usually do for dinner?' she asked. 'Is there somewhere local you like to go?'

Odette shrugged. 'Sometimes we eat, sometimes we forget.'

'Oh.' Her stomach grumbled again in protest.

There was a creak on the stairs and she turned, aghast, remembering suddenly that there was a third person in the house. Before she could prepare herself properly (if that was even possible), Henri strolled casually in, wearing a short-sleeved black shirt and jeans, with the casual air of one who hasn't had his genitals on display to an unexpected stranger.

'*Bonsoir*,' he said, giving her a nod and reaching out to accept a glass of wine from Odette.

He really *was* handsome. She hadn't noticed his face much before – her eyes had been drawn elsewhere. She'd noticed he was brown-haired and slim but hadn't got as far as studying his features. His eyes were kind, his expression amused, and she felt herself relax. He looked, she thought, a little like a hero from a period drama, a nineties Mr Darcy, or a modern Colin Bridgerton. She could just imagine him riding up on horseback, or arriving in a carriage, that dark, thick hair blowing in the breeze, his—

With a start she realised he was talking to her.

'...university?' he finished, eyeing her over the top of his glass.

'Well, no. I'm working, actually. Just a temporary thing,' she said, trying to keep things vague.

'Like a gap year from your degree or an internship?' Odette chipped in.

'Well...'

'It must be hard for you to be so far from family?'

'Yes, in some ways. But...' She shrugged in a way she hoped would indicate things were not straightforward when it came to her family situation. 'So you're both at uni?' she prompted, trying to shift the conversation away from herself.

Henri nodded. 'Well, *I* am. Odette lived here throughout her degree, but she graduated last year.'

Odette nudged Henri: 'She is probably only asking because you look so old!'

'I'm really not— I—'

'Henri is a *mature* student,' Odette confided.

'No!' Henri gave a mock scowl. 'I am not an old man who wants to study in his retirement,' he said. 'I am just someone who is keeping his options open.'

'This is his second degree,' Odette said. 'And he will soon start his Master's. But he is old – twenty-five!'

'Oh!' Bella found herself saying. 'Your second degree?'

Odette laughed. 'Henri is an eternal scholar. He plans never to enter the real world if possible.'

'I don't blame you,' Bella said. She opened her mouth to say that she'd kill just to have one chance to go to uni, live that life, but remembered just in time.

'And you. Your job. What are you going to do?' Odette asked her.

She flushed. 'I've got a job in a hotel. It's not really a proper job. I mean, it is a job, of course. But not a career. I'm basically making ends meet until...' She trailed off, unable to bring herself to mention her divorce, the house sale, the reason for her temporary cash flow situation.

'I understand,' Odette says. 'It is not what you want to do forever.'

Bella nodded. This, at least, was true.

'I am the same. I work in a bar, but painting is my passion.' She looked a little sad. 'Perhaps one day it will pay.'

Henri laughed – a rich, indulgent sound. 'Look at us!' he

said. 'Let's not be miserable. I think at our age it is normal to be a bit lost, *non*? We can make the most of this time. We are only in our twenties!'

Bella opened her mouth to say that she wasn't *his* age. But something stopped her.

Why not be in her twenties, at least for just one night? Her own twenties had been spent in a haze of depression, before she'd met Pete and they'd – as he put it – run away to France on a whim. Perhaps life was giving her a second chance. So instead, she raised her glass with them, then took a deep gulp of the cough-mixture wine.

'So, welcome to Versailles,' Odette said. 'To student life! *À la France!*'

'Ha. Yes,' Bella managed.

'And you're single?' Henri asked.

'Henri! I apologise for my friend, he is not subtle,' Odette said, giving Henri a small punch. 'Clearly, he wants to ask you on a date.'

'Not at all. I was wondering because I might be able to introduce her to my single friends.'

'What single friends do you mean? I don't think you have any, except perhaps Brad.'

'Oh, *bon Dieu, non*! Not Brad! He is too old for sex! I cannot think about it.' Henri laughed.

'Who's Brad?'

'Oh, the proprietor! Of course, you came through the agency, *n'est-ce pas*? Brad is an *américain*. He lives in Bordeaux but comes to Versailles sometimes for business. The house was his grandmother's.'

'He is grumpy, but then he is old. Perhaps even forty,' Henri added as if this explained everything. 'He cannot help it.'

'Forty?' Bella couldn't help her surprised interjection. 'But that's—' Was forty old to these people? She tried to think back to when she was in her early twenties. Life hadn't kicked in, or kicked her in the shins at that stage, and the idea of forty had been both terrifying and reassuringly distant.

'*Oui*, he could be our father.'

Bella took another long slug of wine and nodded. 'Hmm hmm.'

An hour later they were in the living room, a pizza box and two bottles open on the table between them. Everything had become pleasantly soft-focused and wibbly in the early evening light. She'd learned that Odette poured wine at a local bar most afternoons and that Henri was studying classical literature.

'It is completely useless in the modern world of course. But it doesn't matter,' Odette confided in her, 'he is rich, and his parents could pay for him to study his whole life if he wishes to.'

'Ah, but they have other plans for me,' Henri said darkly. 'They pay for me, so they feel they own me.'

Odette laughed. 'See? Too much literature. Henri, you are becoming quite dramatic!'

Bella was no longer feeling awful about her lies. Everything was mashed up in a state of blurry contentment. No need to tell people about ex-husbands, or B & Bs, mortgages or bank accounts with scarily small balances.

So they thought she was twenty-something, and on some sort of work experience or gap year? She leant back against the buttoned leather of the chesterfield. Perhaps this was one of those times when she was allowed to be a little loose with the truth, when she could be – for once – whomever she wanted to be without having to live up to anyone's expectations. She'd thought back to that final exchange and hated herself.

Nobody here could compare her to Kitty. Nobody knew that

she had just 200 euros left in her bank account and would have to make it stretch. Nobody knew that she'd accepted a job without fully knowing what it would entail.

So maybe it would be fun to be twenty again she thought, allowing her eyes to meet Henri's and feeling a shiver of something long forgotten. If only for a little while.

11

NOW

'Oh my God, you're alive!' Kitty's voice was carefully upbeat, but there was a definite edge to it.

Sitting on the bed as she tried to paint her toenails, the phone balanced between shoulder and ear, Bella grimaced and almost lost her grip. 'Sorry. Sorry,' she said, her tongue flicking at the side of her lips as she concentrated on applying yellow varnish to her big toenail. 'I meant to call but—'

'You texted to say you'd arrived in Versailles and were going to the house. Then nothing!'

'Yeah, things kind of—it's been eventful.'

'I know, but still... You can't go from calling me every day to ignoring my calls after going to live in a house of strangers.'

When she put it like this, Kitty had a point. 'Yeah, sorry.'

'It's OK. Well, it is now. Now I know you're not lying in the gutter somewhere.'

Bella had slipped after going out for drinks last night and had almost fallen face first in the gutter, but it probably wasn't a good time to tell her sister this. 'Not quite.'

'So,' Kitty settled into her usual tone. 'Tell me all about this new job. It starts tomorrow, doesn't it?'

'Yeah. I mean, it's no big deal. Just an admin job, really... probably.'

'Probably?'

'I mean, yes. It's an admin job. Like I said. I mean, I don't have to prepare or psych myself up or anything.'

'In Versailles?'

'Paris.'

'*Oh là là!*' her sister replied in a thick French accent. 'You must tell me more about this glamorous role!'

Bella laughed. 'Not sure it's that glamorous. But it's in this little boutique hotel which does look pretty cute.' She described the building, narrow but tall, like many of the buildings in Paris, attached on one side to a restaurant, on the other to an insurance office. Despite its apparent diminutive frontage, it had twenty rooms.

'And your job title?'

What was this? An interrogation? But Kitty had always been curious (she and Mum had used to laugh and make comments about curiosity killing the cat), and also had a rather scary sixth sense that detected when she was being lied to. 'It's... oh I don't know. PA or something.'

'Sounds good.' Kitty's voice was impressed. 'How did you land that?'

'I'm not completely useless, you know!'

'I know that. It's just you said about all the applications and the ghosting and... well, you haven't really got any admin experience have you, so...'

Bella felt a strange sensation in her chest. She reminded herself that her sister was just being supportive.

'Yeah. Anyway,' she said dismissively, determined to change the subject. 'What about you? Have you been up to anything?'

Kitty snorted. 'Oh well, we went to the park yesterday so that's something!'

'And how's Ty?'

'Adorable. Annoying.'

Bella smiled, thinking of her two-year-old nephew. 'Hopefully more one than the other?'

'Yes, but I'm not saying which. Anyway, my life is nothing new. I want to know about this house share. What are the others like? Are you getting on?'

Memory footage from the last forty-eight hours scrolled through Bella's mind as she inspected it for suitable titbits. Naked Henri? No. Getting unfathomably drunk on three glasses of cherry wine, then finding out it was more of a liqueur, something to be enjoyed sparingly? Best not. The fact that she was off out again tonight despite the fact she was starting a new job tomorrow? Probably best to keep that to herself. That and the fact her friends thought she was a twenty-something student on a degree break rather than a thirty-something woman with dodgy finances.

'It's good. They seem... nice,' she said at last.

'And Pete hasn't been in touch?'

'No.'

'Good.'

The fizz she had been feeling in anticipation of the night out dampened at the mention of his name. 'Good?'

'Sorry. I liked Pete, obviously. But after he left you like that? It was so heartless. It made me question everything about him.'

'Well, I loved him. And whether you liked him or not, I miss him.'

'I know, I'm sorry.'

When she'd got married in her twenties, people had commented it was young. Plus, emigrating to France and opening a business? Nobody had said much out loud once the move had been finalised, but she'd always suspected people had wondered – how long it would last.

She wondered how long it would take her sister to say, 'I told you so.'

'So. Are you all ready?' her sister continued.

'What for?' She had, in the past, wondered if Kitty might be psychic. But how could she possibly know Bella was preparing for a night out?

She'd selected a yellow dress she'd bought years ago and never worn, and Odette had helped her to style her hair with more of a tousle, using mousse and tongs. She'd even promised to help her run a little colour through its brown length to give it a bit of a pop. She'd lent her a dark red lipstick and when Bella had put it on earlier, she'd looked in the mirror and gasped.

In place of the rather sensible, neat, and passably pretty Bella she'd become accustomed to seeing was a new woman – someone who looked vibrant and fun and bright and confident. It was as if she'd stepped into a magical clothing store and bought a whole new persona. Eat your heart out, Mr Ben.

'Ready? What do you mean?'

'For work! Got everything ironed? Have you bought your ticket? Thought about lunch? It's probably better to take something just in case... I—'

'Oh yeah, I'll be fine.' Bella straightened up and held her leg out, looking at her toenails in the still bright daylight. They glimmered.

'Good. And you're not going to spend the evening fretting?'

'I'll try not to.' She smiled, thinking about the theatre, the musical she was being dragged to at Théâtre Darius Milhaud. It was a performance of an original play penned by one of the students and although she'd never really been one for musicals or theatre – or, latterly, even going out after 7 p.m. – she had really been looking forward to it. Henri had said he'd bring a couple of people he knew from the uni, and one of Odette's friends had managed to secure them tickets at half price.

She managed to deflect further questions by asking Kitty about her husband, Stu, and his new job. It worked... just.

After they'd said their goodbyes, she set her phone down on the cotton duvet, stood and opened one of the doors of her rather ancient wardrobe, taking in her appearance in the mirror on the back. Her newly styled hair was falling softly around her face. The dress hugged her waist and fell gently to her knees, just enough to reveal her lightly tanned legs without being too short.

But what struck her most was the way she looked in herself – more confident and, importantly, completely different from usual. She put her shoulders back and met her own gaze.

Suddenly, as it sometimes did, grief bubbled up from deep inside her, taking her by surprise. She slumped back down on the bed, her mind racing. Pete. Her Pete had abandoned her. She had lost her house, her business. She was here in France with nobody. Now she was lying, too – to Kitty, the last family member she had in her life in any real sense.

And for the first time in months, she wanted her mother so much she could barely breathe. Just one hug. One smile. One hand to touch her cheek and say it was all OK, to tell her what to do.

It took five minutes to stop the flow of tears, slow her breathing. She'd had her first panic attack at sixteen, but over the years had learned to manage them. Now, while they threatened from time to time, she knew how to keep them in check.

It's OK, she whispered to herself. It would be OK. She could do this and besides, once the house had sold, she'd have options. Not many. But some.

She could do this.

* * *

It was past 2 a.m. when they finally staggered back through the door. Her feet were aching and her dress was rumpled. Her hair had gone beyond 'ruched' and looked more like a mop. But she was laughing; she had been laughing non-stop since they'd left the theatre and gone to the bar, and laughter had carried her home – sore feet and all.

The play had been sombre at best, and so badly acted that it had seemed like a farce. She'd tried to watch it, mirroring the serious expressions of everyone around her. But then she'd caught Odette's eye half an hour in and seen a flicker of recognition. A smile had slipped out, and Odette's face had grinned in response. Then they'd both been taken over by giggles so violent that they were as much pain as pleasure. Henri had remained impassive, but had followed them out obediently when they'd decided to leave.

The bar they'd gone to had been just along the road from the theatre – a small place with a long mahogany serving bar, and several scattered tables. They'd found a bench seat in the corner and sipped white wine from a bottle paid for by Henri. 'That's not fair, you paid for the tickets!' Odette had protested, but he'd insisted.

'Yes, but you girls deserve compensation for that play.'

They'd spoken French for the most part and although Bella had known her tenses weren't always correct, she'd managed to keep up with the pace of the conversation. And gradually, the sense of comradery and influx of alcohol had meant the bubble that Kitty's call had pierced had formed around her again and she'd felt part of things.

It wasn't real, this feeling of belonging. But she'd clung onto it anyway.

Entering the house, the mood was diffused. Odette had fallen asleep in the taxi and looked pale and tired. 'I must go to bed,' she said, giving them both a kiss on the cheek before disappearing into her downstairs room.

'Is she OK?' Bella asked Henri.

'*Oui*, I think she gets a little melancholy sometimes after wine,' he told her. 'She will be fine.'

A silence descended as their eyes met, and for a second she felt a pull of something. She looked at Henri's face – so trouble-free, unlined. Those deep, serious eyes. She reached up without thinking and brushed a little hair from his forehead.

His skin felt electric under her touch and as he reached down and put a hand on each side of her waist, she felt herself almost melt, her legs turn shaky and unstable. Her sex life with Pete had faded to almost nothing over the past year, but even before that she couldn't remember her body responding like this.

When Henri leant down towards her and brushed his lips lightly against hers, she felt it again; that crackle of heat between them.

Then, '*Non*,' he said, almost to himself, and broke away. 'You have been drinking.'

'It's fine! I'm not drunk... I—'

He ran a hand under her chin and tilted her face up to look at his. 'We have all the time in the world,' he told her. And in that moment, she felt it was true.

It was only when she was dropping into sleep, her body

heavy against the mattress, that she heard it. Lifting herself onto her elbows, she pricked her ears like an animal, stilling her breath so that she could tune in to any sound.

And there it was again. The sound of crying. Soft, low, held in, but definitely there. She thought of Odette in the room below. Was it her? Ought she to go and see if her friend was all right? But her body was too heavy, her legs, too wobbly. She tried to swing them out of bed, but it was an effort and she wasn't sure she could manage it.

She'd speak to Odette in the morning, she decided, finally giving up her hold on consciousness and slipping into sleep.

12

2010, ENGLAND

The man – boy really – came up to the counter and plonked down an enormous bottle of shampoo.

Bella looked at him. '£4.99, please.'

As he handed over a five-pound note, Bella glanced at his face. It was bright red. 'Are you OK?'

'Yeah, just—' He cleared his throat and seemed not to notice that she was trying to hand him a penny and a receipt. 'I just wondered if you wanted to get a drink sometime.'

She looked at him, briefly appraising. 'Sorry, I've got a boyfriend,' she said.

Millie looked up from her till as the boy sloped, shame-faced, out of the sliding doors. 'Why did you tell him that?'

'What?'

'You haven't got a boyfriend, have you?'

'Well, no, but—'

'Ah, he was cute! You should have given him a chance!'

Bella shrugged. In truth, she'd panicked, said the first thing she could think of. He *had* been quite cute. She probably should have given him her number or something. But too late now.

'He'll be back,' Millie predicted.

'You reckon? I think that shampoo will probably last him about a year!'

They both laughed.

Working in the pharmacy could be boring, but the other staff were fun and they often found something to giggle about. Sarah had disappeared to uni two years ago and although they kept in touch with the odd email or text, her life had diverged so far from Bella's that it was as if they were two strangers, staying in touch just for the sake of it.

But she'd found a new group of people at work, was trying to make something of herself. Kitty was always at her to get pharmacist training, but it just didn't appeal.

'You know it's not too late to study, to do something different,' Kitty was fond of saying. 'I can help you, and Dad will.'

'Dad doesn't even remember I exist.'

'Come on, that's not fair.'

But even Kitty could probably hear the falseness in her words. Dad was wrapped up in a brand-new family, a brand-new life. Linda had given birth to two boys in quick succession and now they had half-siblings two decades their juniors.

She couldn't explain to Kitty how her life, however small it might seem to her hot-shot lawyer big sister, was big enough. That she might not be stimulated, or particularly fulfilled, but at least she felt safe.

13

NOW

The first thing she felt was a throbbing in her head. Rolling over in the darkened room, she groaned. Something had woken her. Half-awake in the blackness, she tried to focus on her surroundings.

Gradually she tuned in. It was a rhythmical, beeping sound. Her morning alarm. Something fizzed through her – maybe shock, maybe... oh God, it could be vomit.

It *was* vomit.

She pulled herself up to her feet and stumbled, getting her bearings just quickly enough to grab her wastepaper basket and empty what was left of her stomach contents into it.

She crouched by it afterwards, breathing heavily and letting her stomach and head settle, before standing up on slightly wobbly legs and slipping along the corridor to the bathroom. Splashing some cold water over her face, she straightened and looked into the mirror at the fallout of yesterday's still present make-up, the hair that had lost any sense of style and now stood up in an enormous bouffant. The eyes that looked dull and

pinched rather than bright and wide as they might after a
night's sleep.

She was still wearing the yellow dress.

She thought to Kitty's words yesterday, how she should be
prepared for her first day of work. Get an early night. And
regretted just for a moment not having listened to her.

Damn it. Why did the woman always have to be right?

* * *

Bella managed to have what must have been the world's
quickest shower, shoved on an outfit – with no time to worry
about whether it was the right choice – and raced to her train
with her hair half-damp from a half-arsed towel dry.

She had twenty minutes to get herself presentable and pull
herself together before starting. Her hangover had lifted a little
– perhaps the result of the large glass of water she'd gulped
down at the kitchen sink before leaving – and although she was
still exhausted, the relief at having made the train and the
adrenaline from the rush preceding this had given her a kind of
energy boost.

As she tucked her mascara back into her handbag, she tried
to rationalise the events of last night. Yes, it was a bit embarrassing that she'd kissed her housemate. But they hadn't slept
together. She'd been far too drunk to consent, and Henri had
recognised that.

He was a good guy (albeit one who thought she was a fellow
student, not someone a decade older, working a job to make
ends meet). And not one who should be lied to.

She had to come clean, tonight.

But at that moment she caught a glimpse of herself in the
glass of the train window – a ghostly apparition of someone

who looked a bit like her, imposed over the grey of a concrete wall that lined this section of the track. If she told him she'd lied about herself, at the very least he'd probably be pissed off. No more nights out. No more company. Plus, he might tell the landlord. And if they found out she'd lied to get a room there, she could find herself homeless.

It took a few minutes to steady her breathing. But once she'd managed, she knew unequivocally that she had to keep up the façade. It was uncomfortable lying to people who'd offered her friendship, but she just had to get through to pay day and beyond and keep her head down until the house sale went through. How hard could that be?

* * *

The hotel was a ten-minute walk from the station. She'd mapped the route out online but cursed herself for not having made the journey in advance. Things seemed different in reality from on-screen: signs were hard to spot, tall, beautiful, similar-looking buildings sprawled down every back street. If she'd had time to stop and take it all in, she'd have enjoyed the historic architecture, the quaint cafés and antiques shops. But she was in a rush, and it all passed her in a blur.

Finally, she saw it. Nestling between two almost identical structures with a sign painted in italics on wood, only merely legible. The hotel was narrow but four storeys high, with large glass windows on the ground floor, slightly incongruous with the more traditional fixtures and fittings above: the wooden shutters, carved stone faces, high windows, and ornate iron railings whose black paint reflected the sunlight.

'*Come on, you can do it,*' she whispered to herself and stepped forward, pushing the door open.

Inside was a wooden reception desk inlaid with carved rectangles, behind which sat a young girl with blonde hair and a crisp white blouse. There was a door to the right in chequered glass that revealed a café or dining area, and a couple with a battered leather suitcase were standing inspecting a rack of leaflets detailing local attractions.

The girl looked up as Bella approached.

Taking yet another deep breath, Bella tried to smile. 'Hi, I'm, um, Isabella,' she said. 'I believe Claudine is expecting me?'

She was directed to a line of chairs and took an awkward seat as the girl phoned up to find out where to direct her. 'Yves is coming to find you,' she told her eventually and Bella nodded, not entirely sure who this was.

A few minutes later, a small man in navy trousers and a white shirt stepped out and looked in her direction. He was young – probably only twenty or so – and looked nervous. 'Madame,' he said, reaching out his hand. 'It is wonderful to finally meet you. I'm Yves. Claudine's assistant.'

'Oh yes! Good to meet you.'

'*Venez.*' He began to walk along the carpeted corridor and jog lightly up a set of stairs. Bella had to walk faster than was comfortable to keep up with him as they rose through the building, one narrow set of carpeted stairs at a time.

By the time they reached the fourth floor she was embarrassingly out of breath. Yves turned and looked at her, his features suddenly contorting into a look of concern. 'Madame,' he said. 'I hope you are not unwell?'

'I'm fine,' she managed to gasp.

Nodding, he continued to walk at the same relentless pace, but stopped short a few metres on to show her a white-painted wooden door with the word 'Manager' affixed on a bronze plaque. 'This is yours,' he said, turning and pushing it open so she could enter.

'Mine?'

'Yes. Claudine is just a little farther up the corridor.'

'Oh.' She stepped through to find a well-lit room with a white desk, a pencil pot containing a single pen and a white laptop. There was a wheeled chair tucked underneath and a small pot plant in one corner. Otherwise, the room was bare.

Now might be a good opportunity to find out what her actual role would be. 'It says "Manager" on the plaque, but I thought—' she began, yet before she could find the right word, the half-open door was shoved with enough force to propel it against the wall and a woman in a black suit, tightly cinched at the waist, sporting a blue silk top with a slanted neckline, appeared. The chain around her neck looked tough enough to restrain a Rottweiler.

'*Bonjour*,' the woman said, holding out an immaculately manicured hand almost level with Bella's shoulder. 'It's good to meet you, Isabella. I'm Claudine. You'll be working with me for most of the contract.'

Bella looked at the hand, not sure whether Claudine was attempting a handshake or some version of high five that she'd never experienced before, but by the time she raised her own, Claudine's had dropped. Instead, Bella smiled. 'It's good to meet you too.'

Claudine's expression remained stern. 'I will let Yves get you acclimatised, then if you'd like to come to my office for a briefing—?'

'Of course.'

Claudine smiled, rather icily, and then strode back out importantly, pulling the door behind her. When she was gone, Yves relaxed visibly.

'So now you have met Claudine,' he said.

'Yes. I have.'

'I will be honest,' he continued. 'Claudine can be very exacting. We took months to recruit your predecessor but then she got headhunted within a week of starting, so we had to rush the second application process. I was a little worried. But she already seems to like you.'

'She does?' Bella thought of the thrusted hand, the icy smile.

'*Oui*, believe me, she was delighted.'

Bella looked at Yves's face which seemed open and genuine, and decided to take him at his word. 'Well, that's good,' she said. Tentatively she sat in the chair. It creaked a little, but was relatively comfortable. 'So is Claudine the manager?'

'*Non*, the CEO,' he said. 'She owns the hotel. But yes, the manager too, I suppose.'

'So I'm... obviously I'm also a... manager,' she said carefully, not wanting to alert Yves to the fact that she wasn't entirely sure of her job title. 'Is that, uh, my full job title? Just for... just for some forms I need to fill in,' she lied.

Yves looked confused. 'Well of course your full title is Project Manager. As you know, Claudine has big plans for this place and wants to find the right support. I hope that she will find this in you.'

'Oh. Yes. Hopefully!'

'You were the most experienced applicant by far,' Yves said reassuringly. 'You have run many hotels, I understand?'

Bella felt hot. She remembered, as she'd scrolled through application after application, being a little freer with the truth. Nobody seemed to be giving her more than a generic response, so what did she have to lose? She may have substituted 'running a B & B' with 'managing several holiday premises' (there were, after all, several rooms available) or 'managing Pete' with 'managing all on-site staff' (after all, he *had been* the entire staff). But she hadn't thought at the time it would really matter.

'Ah... well, I managed a site. With, um, more than one type of accommodation.'

'*Oui, oui.*' Yves waved his hand dismissively as if it were one and the same. 'For someone like you, this work will be nothing. It is unusual for someone of your experience perhaps to apply for a role like this; as soon as Claudine saw your form, she knew she had to snap you up.'

Her experience? Bella thought again to her late-night applications. Her 'have to secure a job at all costs, so talk up your CV for God's sake' attitude. She remembered saying something about accommodation that was perhaps a little OTT, but had she mentioned multiple sites? By then, after completing what had seemed like hundreds of online applications – and feeling as desperate as she had – anything was possible.

She opened her mouth to correct him, then closed it. This job was her only option, she reminded herself.

'...to see you now,' Yves was saying. He gestured to the door.

'Thank you.'

Straightening, smoothing down her trousers and giving her hair one last ruche for luck, she thanked him and, heart skittering, made her way towards Claudine's office.

14

NOW

'Come in.' Claudine's voice sounded clipped and efficient.

Bella pushed open the door, fixing on a smile. 'Hello again,' she said in careful French.

'Yes, hello, Isabella.'

Claudine smiled and gestured to a chair in front of the desk on which Bella perched, first nervously and then, remembering, in a manner she hoped looked confident and together. She reminded herself that she already had the job – she wanted to impress Claudine, but she wasn't on trial here. Hopefully.

'It is good to meet you properly in person,' Claudine said, arching an eyebrow. 'I'm sorry our call was brief the other day, but given your experience, you will understand that things are very busy in the industry.'

Bella nodded politely, thinking of the B & B rooms in her slightly tumbledown French farmhouse. 'Yes,' she said. 'Busy.'

'OK, well, things have moved on significantly since I first advertised this role, and even since last week. You will be aware that the hotel is being considered for potential "Hotel Club" status.'

Bella was more than familiar with the 'Hotel Club' brand – specially selected hotels linked across Europe, often smaller, boutique places. Presumably becoming affiliated with this brand would mean big business.

'That is one of the reasons we chose to take you on board. A true anglophone with experience in France, you are quite a find. Especially as Hotel Club membership will require some staff to be bilingual.'

Bella made a noise meant to sound like acquiescence, but which sounded more like a strangled cat. She was definitely an anglophone, and had some experience in hospitality. But this sounded way out of her league.

She'd forgotten, when 'being more Juliette', that bigging herself up on a form was one thing. Living up to promises made after a glass of red might be a whole other ball game.

'As you can imagine, having worked here for several years, I have lots of experience in running Hôtel Benjamin! But I have little experience of the wider sector. You will be the ideal person to smooth the way for us. Your knowledge and insight will be invaluable.'

'Insight in—?'

Claudine flapped her hand as if it were not important. 'Hotel Club, as you know, are an exclusive brand, and they like their hotels to offer something extra. Hotels must go above and beyond for guests, in terms of their offering, in order to qualify. And those who do,' she paused, 'can expect their revenue to jump by at least 10 per cent.'

Bella nodded knowingly.

'That is where you come in. I want you to work on developing the brand, adding extra touches and importantly, preparing a presentation for June when two delegates will come to visit and make their recommendation. And if it goes well, there should be a permanent position for you.'

Something prickled over Bella's skin. Because she wasn't just out of her depth – she was swimming above an abyss. She'd imagined she'd be doing a bit of filing, perhaps making a few phone calls. Her mouth felt dry, her teeth too large for it. She opened and closed it like a fish, wondering what to say.

'We discussed salary before, I think. But I wanted to explain a little more,' Claudine continued. 'You will of course receive the salary discussed, but should the hotel succeed in obtaining "Hotel Club" status, then you will receive a bonus.' She slid a piece of paper across the desk like a lawyer offering a settlement to a divorcee.

In the weeks that followed, Bella would come to see this moment as her chance to do the right thing. She could have told Claudine that there had been a mistake. Graciously bowed out of the whole thing. But when she turned over the paper and suppressed a gasp at the amount, she realised that this job might just be her lifeline. The equity in the property was reasonable, but this additional money could help to set her up in something new. It would give her time and space to work out her next steps.

She thought about Kitty, how her sister had always taken life in her stride, had always strived for success. Her impressive achievements, both personal and academic, had always seemed to eclipse anything Bella had accomplished. But maybe this was it – Bella's one chance to prove she had what it took.

People have blagged their way into jobs far above their actual abilities for years and got away with it. Mostly men, admittedly, but still. They seemed to make it work. Plus, if she told Claudine that she'd made a mistake, let someone else take her place, who's to say the person they'd end up recruiting would be any better than her? Perhaps this was just a sign from the universe that she needed to step into her power.

By the time she'd run through all her hypothetical get-out clauses in her head, there were none left in any case, as Claudine was talking about the event she'd need to arrange in three months' time, and about accounts and merchandise and catering and overheads and other things that rattled from her mouth as if they were a third language between French and English that Bella also needed to learn.

She was sweating by the time Claudine had finished. She hadn't thought to take notes, instead spending most of the time wrestling with her conscience. Claudine abruptly stopped talking, and when Bella looked up, she realised her new boss was regarding her intently.

'Is everything all right?' Claudine asked.

'Oh. Yes. Just thinking about getting started!'

Claudine nodded as if confirming to herself once and for all that she had landed a good employee. 'Excellent,' she said. 'Well, Yves is yours for the duration – use him as you will.'

'Um... Thank you.'

There was a brief, awkward silence before Bella realised that this was clearly the end of the meeting. She stood up, straightening the front of her black trousers. 'Well, thank you.'

'No, thank *you*,' Claudine said warmly. 'It was good to meet you, Isabella.'

That name again. Her given name that didn't feel like hers.

She was reminded of a time at school when she'd allowed a teacher to call her Stella for the whole of the first term, too tongue-tied and awkward to correct him. Now, it seemed, she had done it again. But perhaps if she was going to transform herself, this new name could be part of the package. She was

Isabella – the high-flying, executive hotel manager, on course for a large bonus and future success.

'So, you are ready for the tour?' Yves materialised at her side like an apparition, his smile wide.

'Oh. Yes please!'

He nodded and turned on his heel. Once again, she scuttled in his wake, cursing her new high heels. The balls of her feet burned and she began to fantasise about how good it would feel to slip her shoes off under her desk and apply them to the soft carpet as soon as the tour was done.

The corridors of the hotel were pleasingly decorated in a light cream, which was clean and bright if a little impersonal. Yves showed her an example of each of the rooms available: the Superior, with a large king-size bed, a little walnut desk and leather chair, a free-standing bath; the standard room, which was almost identical except for the bed being a little smaller and the bath being replaced by a shower in the en suite. Then the basic room which was decked out with a twin or double bed and small en suite. All rooms were painted in a light, inoffensive cream colour and had prints of Paris on the walls.

It struck Bella that if she'd been a tourist visiting the hotel for the first time, she might have been disappointed. The outside was all Parisian – faded grandeur and carved stone detail. But inside, the hotel, while clean and bright, felt generic. More like a hotel from a chain than something individual.

She didn't know a lot about Hotel Club, but she'd heard of the group and had the impression that the hotels it offered tended to be quirky, original. No wonder Claudine wanted someone on board to add to the offering before the decision was made.

They were just exiting the final room – a standard, but with a view of the street outside – when Yves grabbed her arm and almost pulled her into the wall.

'Wha—' she began, but he put a finger to his lips.

'Shhh,' he hissed. 'Wait.'

He stood with his back to the wall, slightly concealed by a brick pillar as a door halfway down the corridor opened fully. A small woman dressed in a tartan suit complete with hat came out, holding a string of some sort. No, not a string. A lead. She pulled it to reveal a small white dog, the type that looks as if it is permanently scowling, an impression unmitigated by the fact it was sporting a pink bow.

The woman looked up the corridor, almost directly at their location, and Bella watched, confused, as Yves appeared to try to shrink farther into the wall. Then, thankfully, the woman turned and walked towards the lift, disappearing from view.

'What was all that about?' Bella asked, dusting her jacket where she'd leant against the paintwork.

'That,' Yves said, his face looking rather pale, 'is Madame Roux.' He nodded at Bella meaningfully as if she ought to know exactly the significance of the name.

'Who?'

He looked surprised. 'Claudine didn't mention her? Ah, OK. Well,' he leant forward as if imparting a state secret, 'Madame Roux used to be a friend of Claudine's mother when she was young. She fell on hard times a few years back and Claudine offered her a room at the hotel to live in while she sorted herself out. Only Madame Roux misunderstood the length of the offer and now it appears she lives here. Claudine is unable to ask her to leave – or perhaps she doesn't have the heart.'

'Oh. Wow.'

'*Oui*. She is usually harmless, don't worry. But cross her at your peril,' he warned.

'And dogs are allowed in the hotel?'

He shook his head vehemently. '*Non*. Only Coco, Madame Roux's dog. Claudine doesn't speak of this. I think she is lost to know what to do.'

'Right.'

'It is imperative,' he hissed, 'that nobody at Hotel Club finds out about Madame Roux, you understand?'

'Of course.'

Yves, having imparted his secret, seemed to relax. 'Anyway,' he continued, walking normally now. 'You will find the restaurant and breakfast room on the ground floor. And the rest I think you now know. Do you have any questions?'

Back in her office, Bella started by typing in 'Hotel Club' into her laptop, and looking at the various premises. Then, getting up and closing the door, she searched 'presentations' and 'Hotel Club accreditation' and looked at the 'About Us' sections of hotels who'd already made the grade. The hotels accepted for accreditation were beautiful; and although Hôtel Benjamin was a nice place, she could see that in some ways they were worlds apart.

But at least that meant she had some idea of what to do. And she felt a fizz of excitement in her chest – the kind of feeling she'd left behind years ago in Maths class when she'd solved an equation that had proven tricky, or when she'd won first place in the egg and spoon race on sports day. It was unexpected, but welcome.

By the end of the day, she was walking taller. Because although she was still in deep water, uncharted territory, she was managing at least to stay afloat.

And when she popped into the bathroom to wash her hands before going home, she noticed that there was another new 'her' in the mirror. This woman looked older, more confident. She'd tucked her hair behind her ears while working, and even stuck a pen into one of her waves.

Bella looked to all intents and purposes like a woman who had indeed run a chain of hotels, who was more than capable of taking on a large project at her new workplace. The kind of woman who had an assistant, an impressive CV, her own office and a bank account that was destined to have quadruple or quintuple figures in it in the weeks going forward.

She was Isabella – business executive extraordinaire. And it felt good.

d of She'd intended to say no to any invitations out this evening, and even the bar persuasive of her out for a few

15

NOW

She'd intended to say no to any invitations out this evening, but her housemates proved very persuasive and managed to drag her out for a few drinks. The bar a few streets away was lively and vibrant, but Bella's eyelids had started to feel heavy after an hour. 'I'm going to head off soon,' she said, glancing at her watch.

Odette checked the time on her phone. 'But it's only eleven!' she said, seemingly confused.

'Work tomorrow!' Bella finished the last of her wine and made to grab her jacket.

'It is just a temp job,' Henri said, looking at her. 'Does it matter if you are a little tired? It's so early!'

Early for a twenty-year-old, maybe, she thought.

Although her own twenties hadn't looked like this at all. She'd lost her mother at sixteen, her final teen years to grief. Then married young, started a business young. Skipped the years in her twenties that were meant to be about being free and having fun. Maybe this could be her chance to reclaim something she'd thought was long gone?

Odette laughed, filled her glass from the bottle they were sharing. 'Stay a little longer,' she said. 'You are only young once.'

Bella took a breath. 'OK. Actually, I need to tell you something.'

Odette and Henri, perhaps detecting the seriousness of her tone, both looked up from their drinks.

This was the moment. 'I'm actually a thirty-four-year-old divorcee,' she said.

They were silent and the noise of the bar around them seemed to grow to emphasise this. Bella instantly wanted to take the words back. She'd heard what they thought about the 'ancient' landlord, Brad. She'd started to feel as if she might be making friends, real friends; she'd started to feel less alone.

Then Odette glanced at Henri and both turned back to her, grinning.

Henri laughed and raised his glass. 'You are hilarious!'

'Yes, this is what they call the British humour, yes?' Odette said, smiling. 'Where you say something completely ridiculous.'

'I— um...'

But they had clearly decided.

'Imagine!' Odette said, shaking her head as if the idea were completely insane.

Bella remembered being that way when she was twenty. Everyone had seemed old to her then. People turning thirty had seemed utterly decrepit. 'It's true,' she added, sending them into a renewed burst of laughter.

'No, I—' But it was no use. And as they laughed – perhaps not entirely getting the 'joke' but wanting to indulge her quirky British ways – she started to feel glad that they hadn't taken her seriously. Right now, she needed friends. And these were the only people she had. She took a large gulp from her glass and moved the conversation on.

'I'll stay for a bit longer,' she said.

An hour on, the place was buzzing with life and there was a feeling of fun and excitement in the air that seemed to surround the small groups of youngsters getting ready to head on to the clubs to continue their night out.

She had been worried about seeing Henri again, but he hadn't mentioned a thing about the previous night and was acting as if the whole awkward encounter had never happened. She was more than happy to go along with the charade.

'I'm sorry I can't buy a round,' she said as Henri signalled to the waiter to bring another bottle. 'As soon as I get paid, I'll—'

But Henri waved his hand as if batting away the suggestion. '*Non,* it is all on my father in any case. He is pressuring me to help with his business. He says I should be representing the family. I have agreed to involve myself more but,' he shrugged, 'I am not very happy about it.'

'Does he know that, though?' Bella asked. 'I mean, he can't force you, surely.'

'Ha. You haven't met my father.'

'No, but...'

Henri shook his head sadly. 'My father has so much money, and it gives him power. As long as I toe the line, I get to use the credit card,' and he waved the gold plastic card at her. 'If I refuse...' He drew his hand across his throat meaningfully.

'*Oh là là!*' Odette exclaimed in mock horror. 'Your father will kill you!'

'*Non.* Worse. He will cut me off financially, and then I will be working a terrible job at some hotel with Bella.' He tipped his glass at Bella. 'Sorry.'

Bella opened her mouth to correct him, to say that actually, she was a project manager. But it was all too complicated to explain.

'When work is a pleasure, life is a joy. When work is duty, life is slavery,' Henri said dramatically.

'Oh no,' Odette shook her head. 'Please. He is starting to use literary quotes again. It always happens when he drinks.'

Bella laughed. 'Well, he's not wrong.'

'Exactly. So I am a good boy for my father, and it means I keep my money and can continue my studies. But I have to exact my revenge in some ways.'

'And you're doing it by—'

'I have given myself a raise,' Henri said. 'Which means the drinks will always be on me.' He grinned. 'It's a small revenge; my dad is a multimillionaire. But it is something.'

Odette laughed, clinked her glass against Henri's brandished bottle. 'I still don't understand why you don't take the job with your father, though.' She turned to Bella. 'Henri could be an executive, with very little responsibility and lots and lots of money. But he wants to be a professor instead and try to get students to understand Shakespeare and Molière.'

Henri looked serious. 'Money doesn't mean so much to me.'

'That's because you have it.'

'*Touché*,' he nodded. 'Perhaps. But, Odette, I think you are more like me than you imagine. Because working in a bar is not *your* dream. Your dream is to sell your art, to paint for a living, *n'est-ce pas*? So you too prefer to stay away from the "career ladder" and pass time until that happens.'

Odette flushed. 'Maybe.'

'And so I want to live a life with books, to help other people understand and love literature as I do. Sure, there is no money in it and as my father always tells me, it is not a business. But it is important. "A wise person should have money in their head, but not in their heart".'

'Oh God,' Odette said quietly. 'Another quote.'

'I haven't seen much of your art yet.' Bella turned to Odette, changing the subject. 'I adore the seascape in the hall. I'd love to see what you do.'

Odette flushed. 'It is not ready yet. I will show you one day.'

'And are you going to exhibit somewhere? Maybe in a Paris gallery? I'm sure there are lots of opportunities…'

Odette's skin turned almost purple. She sipped her wine and Bella detected a small tremor in her fingers as they gripped the glass. '*Oui*. I am not ready for them though. It is a very private thing.'

'Oh. Sorry.'

Henri laughed. 'Don't be sorry, Bella. Odette is simply teasing us. She graduated from her art degree with *mention très bien* – she was top of her class. And I visited her display even though she told me I must not. It was truly exceptional.'

'Oh wow. Well done!' Bella flashed a smile at Odette who tried to return it but still looked deeply uncomfortable.

'I even bought her painting – the beautiful seascape in the hallway.'

Odette seemed to shrink in her seat.

'Oh, I love that picture!'

'Yes, me too,' Henri said. 'She hates that I display it, but it belongs to me, and I think she should be proud to have it on the wall.'

'Definitely.'

'Then since a year – nothing. I have not seen any more works, there have been no exhibitions.'

'Well, I'm sure good art takes time,' Bella said, trying

desperately to relieve Odette's embarrassment. 'I wouldn't know how to start.'

'Thank you,' Odette said softly, nodding at her. 'Yes, it is hard at the moment.'

There was a silence, amplified somehow by the noisy, happy chatter from the other tables. Bella racked her brain for something interesting to share. 'Well,' she said at last, 'at least neither of you have to compare yourselves to Kitty.'

Henri looked at her, his face creased with confusion. 'You compare yourself to a cat?'

She laughed. 'No. My sister, Kitty. She's four years older than me and she's one of those people who do everything perfectly.'

'You do not get along?' Odette asked.

'Oh, we do. She's great. It's just, it's hard growing up in someone's shadow like that. Every failure I had seemed... worse somehow.'

'But have you failed?' Henri asked, confused. 'Of course, right now you are an intern but it is only temporary. You will have your degree soon. And you are improving your French which is already very good. You live in Versailles! She should be jealous of you!'

Bella smiled. She couldn't explain about the almost decade she'd lived in France already; about the failed marriage, the closed-down business. It was hard, too, to put into words the sense of being less that she'd carried with her all her life. 'Maybe,' she said instead, wishing she'd never brought it up.

* * *

She was not drunk two hours later when they started to walk home, but pleasantly tipsy. Not a fan of red wine, she'd been able to pace herself and although she knew she would be tired tomorrow morning, without the addition of a hangover she'd probably be OK.

They walked from the town, with its old, square-windowed buildings with their flat, white stone fronts, across a cobbled street where the properties seemed less stiff and poised; older, but quainter too. The cobbles were a nightmare with the slight heels on her shoes but just as she stumbled, Henri reached a hand out to grab her arm and steadied her in the nick of time. 'Thank you!' she said, rolling her eyes and embarrassed. 'It's not the wine, it's the cobbles.'

'They take some getting used to,' he said, and held his hand towards her. 'Do you want—?'

She put her hand into his, feeling the soft warmth of his fingers as they closed around hers. Her mind helpfully pulled up a picture of Henri in the shower at this moment, just to ensure that she didn't enjoy this simple offer of help but charged it instead with sexual tension.

Looking up at him smiling at her, she felt a shiver of plea-sure. But of course, it was just the red wine and the fact that she hadn't had sex for over a month, she decided, as they turned the corner onto more sensible paving and her hand was dropped.

She saw Odette looking at her, an eyebrow raised quizzically.

'What?'

'Henri is being quite the gentleman with you,' her new friend said. 'I think he would let me fall onto my face on these stones before he offered me his hand.'

'Oh!'

Odette laughed. 'You have gone quite red.'

Henri turned at this point and looked at them quizzically. 'What are you talking about?'

'Bella was just telling me about life in England,' Odette lied, giving Bella a small wink.

Finally home, Odette once again disappeared to her room, clicking the door shut behind her. Bella realised that she hadn't asked her about last night – the crying she'd heard coming from somewhere in the house. But then, had she heard anything? Her head had been spinning, her mind, active; it had been late – and she'd had a bit to drink. Enough to cloud her judgement at least. Perhaps it had been nothing but her imagination. She looked at Henri. 'Last night,' she said, then realised her mistake. Because the most memorable thing about that to him would probably be the moment they'd shared.

'I am sorry,' he said, stepping towards her. He smelled of wine and expensive cologne, of shampoo and fabric conditioner. 'You had had too much alcohol for me to...' he trailed off, allowing a single finger to trace a line from her shoulder to her elbow.

'Oh. No. Don't worry,' she gabbled. 'I completely... I'm so embarrassed that I—'

'But you have not had so much tonight?' he said, the last word raised in an inflexion.

'No,' she said, looking at him, feeling her skin tingle a little at his touch.

Before she could say anything more, he leant down and brushed his lips against hers. It was a gentle, inquisitive kiss; a question wrapped in an action.

There was a part of her which couldn't believe that this young, ridiculously handsome man was kissing her. But another part of her that wanted to break off and confess that she was actually in the middle of a divorce, that she hadn't exactly been honest with him.

'Henri,' she said, moving her head slightly. 'There are things you don't know. About me. I think you should—'

'*Non*,' he said softly, smoothing back her hair. 'I know everything that I need to know. I can feel you, your spirit. You don't need to say anything.'

'But—'

Then he leant in and kissed her again. And she felt suddenly swept up and desirable and, if she were honest, downright sexy. To be together with someone, even for one night, felt impossible to resist.

16

2012, ENGLAND

Their holiday to France had been, all in all, pretty perfect.

Her first trip away with Pete had been ten days in Spain, taken last October on a late deal. She'd enjoyed relaxing by the pool, cocktails and bingo at happy hour. She'd soaked up the last of the sun, topping up her reserves before the winter.

But this had been a different holiday altogether. Not least because he'd thought to book it himself. He was working now, learning and earning on the building site as well as doing quite a trade as an odd-job man around his estate.

When he'd surprised her with tickets to France, she'd wondered why she hadn't thought to go there since her French school trip six years before. She'd closed her eyes and remembered the sunshine, the simplicity, the slow pace of life. First kisses and morning croissants and above all, the feeling she'd had when she was last there – a simple contentment. Before the clear water of her life had muddied irrevocably.

They'd driven early to the airport and were sitting at the café sipping the last of their coffees before their flight home. It was a sunny day and they'd chosen an outdoor table with a parasol that did nothing to shade them from the sun. But it was raining in England so they'd decided to make the most of their last hours on holiday, top up their tans while waiting for the queue to start forming.

'I could live here, you know,' she'd said.

Pete, leaning back in his chair, eyes closed against the bright morning sunshine, had opened a single eye. 'Yeah?'

'Yeah.'

'Me too,' he'd said, his voice lazy and content.

'No, I mean really.'

The eye opened again. 'Yeah?'

'Yeah. Why not? I'm sick of working at Boots, and you've nearly finished your apprenticeship.'

He shook his head. 'Nah.'

'Give me a good reason why not?'

'Um, I can't speak French?'

'You can a bit.'

'Hardly. And anyway, what would we do?'

But she had the answers for him: they'd stayed in a B & B and paid eighty euros per night; that had seemed like a fortune! Surely, they could do that too? The house prices were low. Dad had given her a bit of cash when he'd moved in with Linda, calling it 'an early inheritance', though they'd both known it was guilt money.

'You're really serious, aren't you?' he'd said when they'd boarded the plane.

She'd shrugged. 'Kind of. Yeah. I mean... I really think I could be happy here, Pete. I feel as if maybe this is *my* place.'

It was exactly a month since she'd arrived in Versailles, and her days had fallen into a pleasant pattern.

She woke up, as always now, in Henri's bed and performed her now customary 'wriggle-from-under-his-arm-without-waking-him' manoeuvre, which involved an undignified slither onto the carpet. Henri was a hugger, and she enjoyed being embraced for most of the night, other than the times when she'd wake from a dream of being suffocated to find his heavy arm draped over her ribcage, but it made getting up without waking him a physical challenge.

Once extracted, she went to the communal bathroom to shower, then to her own room to get dressed and to become Isabella, the alter ego she'd now perfected at work. It had been payday a week ago, meaning she had finally got a bit more in the bank, and she'd splashed out on a few outfits in the boutiques close to work.

Today, she pulled on a belted skirt, teamed with a cotton blouse in pink and grey. She styled her hair and quickly blow-dried it into submission, then put on a flick of eyeliner, a slick of lipstick. She was worlds away from the jeans-clad student wannabe who'd hit the clubs last night with Henri, but dressing the part seemed to help her step out of one identity and into another.

The thought of the lies she'd been telling along the way, or the half-truths she'd allowed people to assume, made her pause – lipstick midway to mouth – as a rush of guilt overcame her. She'd allowed her housemate to assume she was a twenty-something student, her employer to believe she was an experienced hotel manager. She'd built two identities, neither of which was truly her. But then she reassured herself that she *had* tried to tell Henri her real age and circumstances – twice – and that her comments had been laughed at and batted away. And whatever illusion Claudine was under due to her somewhat *enhanced* CV, she was managing to do a good enough job to keep her exacting boss happy. And that was the point, after all.

Plus – and it was hard to admit this in her counterfeit circumstances – she was actually quite happy. Despite Pete. Despite the sale of the B & B. Despite, somehow, everything.

She liked the way she felt about herself with Henri. Liked losing herself in him. After the bruising shock of Pete's departure, the idea of being cherished was exactly what she needed.

She liked the person she was at work, too. Capable, doing a job that somehow suited her more than running the B & B ever had. She'd always been good at the visual side of things, the little touches that made guests feel more welcome or want to return. The practical side of things hadn't been her forte. So the fact that a great deal of her job at present seemed to be improving the offering of the hotel by providing small luxurious touches was exactly in her comfort zone. Hôtel Benjamin was already quirky and bijou, but now customers were treated to locally sourced toiletries, flowers from a grower just outside

Paris, and each room had a basket of complimentary baked goods and chocolates sourced from the nearby patisserie.

The only problem she had – other than the house sale and the lingering problem of the divorce with Pete – was the fact that however wonderful her life felt, she was still carrying around a nagging fear that things could come tumbling down. That her situation couldn't be permanent because the person she was being wasn't entirely 'real.'

Downstairs in the kitchen she picked up a small cardboard box filled with home-made cupcakes for Yves who had been working tirelessly at her side for a month now. She hesitated for a moment, wondering if it might be seen as a bit weird, but shook her head. If there was one thing she knew, it was that there was never a wrong time for a bit of the good stuff.

Then, grabbing her handbag and deciding to risk leaving her coat on its hook – the weather was warmer now with only the occasional shower coming along to spoil things – she began the ten-minute walk to the station.

En route, she pulled out her mobile and made a call.

'What time do you call this?' Kitty's voice was mock angry. 'It's eight o'clock!'

'Yes, but that's seven in England, remember?'

'Well, yes. But you've been up since—?'

'Five.'

'Exactly,' Bella said, making her point.

'OK, you're off the hook.' Kitty laughed. Talking to her had been much more pleasant for Bella recently than it had been directly after the break-up with Pete. It felt as if her sister could see that she was managing and had backed off. She'd certainly stopped suggesting plane tickets and solutions.

'How's Ty?'

'Lively.'

'And Stuart?'

'The opposite.'

Bella laughed. 'So: situation normal?'

'Yes, although I do have some news.'

'Oh?' Bella found she was holding her breath. *Another pregnancy? A house move?*

'I've decided I'm going back to work.'

'You are?'

'Yes! Oh, I know I said I'd be a stay-at-home-mum till Ty was in school. But... if I'm honest, I need it. I don't feel like myself when I'm not working.'

'Of course. Well, good for you.'

'There's actually some talk of my being offered a partnership,' Kitty added as if it were simply an afterthought.

'Oh wow. That's brilliant!' Only for some reason, Bella felt strangely uneasy about her sister's good news. 'Well done.'

'Thanks.'

There was a silence for a second, then, 'Of course, that means I have to find a nanny for Ty, which I'm not looking forward to.'

'Expensive?'

'It's not that. It's the idea of choosing a person who's going to stand in for me every day.'

'Yeah, must be tough.'

'Anyway, forget my boring life. Things are good with you?'

'Yes. Going well.'

'And are you going to tell me any more about this mysterious boyfriend of yours?'

Bella had admitted to being in something of a new relationship the last time Kitty had called, but hadn't divulged any details. Because it would be hard to explain exactly what she was doing with a boy a decade younger than her. Kitty would have her big-sisterly-concern radar activated, might pick holes in the whole idea of her dating a younger man; might even want to meet him. None of these things could happen if Bella was to continue feeling good about how her life was going.

'Not yet,' she said. 'It's not serious.'

Maybe it would become serious, eventually.

Last night at the bar where they seemed to spend most of their evenings, she had felt freer than she had in so many years. Being there with the two of them putting the world to rights, she'd felt her troubles melt away – all the angst that had kept her up at night since she and Pete had split – all the self-recriminations and analysis had seemed not to matter.

Last night, she hadn't been someone who'd taken a wrong turn. She hadn't messed her life up. She wasn't Kitty's younger, more disappointing sister, or Pete's ex-wife. She wasn't even Bella, the youngster who lived in a shared house and had a minimum wage job, or Isabella, the executive manager. She was simply herself, stripped of all the emotional baggage she shouldered every day, and completely present in the moment.

It wasn't the wine either, she thought; she'd only had a couple of drinks – her headache was testament to that – but once she'd entered the bar, the whole atmosphere had lifted her. She hadn't needed any chemical inducement to become part of the joyous whole inside *Le Cocorico*.

She managed to deflect Kitty's questions by claiming to have arrived at the station five minutes before she really did. Once duty call done, she pushed her phone into her bag, and thoughts of subterfuge and younger men out of her brain. Then she stepped onto the train and became Isabella: ready for a day of serious work and poised for success.

* * *

On arrival, she nodded briefly at Mélodie on reception before summoning one of the two lifts. When it arrived, she stepped in; it smelled strongly of the perfume of the last occupant: heady and expensive. On floor one, the doors slid open and to her horror, a diminutive figure in a pink Chanel suit that sported three enormous black buttons on the front hobbled in, a small dog at her heels. The dog looked at Bella with undisguised contempt.

'*Bonjour*,' the woman croaked, not looking up.

'*Bonjour*, Madame Roux,' Bella said, trying to keep her voice bright. In reality, she felt a bit nervous: Yves had seemed terrified of the old woman and so far she'd managed to avoid spending more than a passing moment in her presence. 'And Coco of course,' she added, bending down to make a fuss over the dog, who endured her strokes with stiff suspicion before straightening.

Madame Roux raised her face to Bella's. She was wearing thick make-up, bold red lips. Under her small pink hat, her white hair was pulled back into a bun. 'Oh, so you're the English girl,' she said.

'Yes.'

'I suppose they've told you all about me.'

'Not really.' Bella tried to smile. 'It's nice to meet you.'

'Ha!' the woman laughed. 'Nice to meet me indeed! Now I *know* they can't have told you anything.'

Bella smiled fully at this. Madame Roux seemed completely harmless.

'I'm sure they'd have only said nice things.'

Madame Roux laughed again, a single syllable bark. 'They do not understand me. I try to help. Offer advice. But people are afraid of hearing the truth.'

'Oh, I'm sure that's not true. It sounds as if you are very kind,' Bella said, smiling.

'What's that you're wearing?' The old woman leant forward and inspected Bella's neat black skirt and floral blouse.

'Oh.' Bella looked down. 'Just some... work clothes.'

'I can see that.' Madame Roux looked her up and down carefully. 'You know, that horrible blouse does nothing for you. That colour washes you out. The pattern is ugly. You look dull. You need something red, vibrant.'

'Oh.'

'And the fit,' Madame Roux shook her head as if Bella were completely beyond help. 'It drowns you. And the skirt is too long.' The little dog sniffed Bella's shoe slightly, then also seemed to turn his back as if even her feet hadn't passed muster. 'The whole effect is quite, quite dowdy.'

'Oh well, it's just a work outfit,' she said, tugging self-consciously at her blouse.

There was a silence, then, 'But you are young. You shouldn't be afraid to be bold. Life is too short.'

Bella had actually thought the print on the blouse *was* quite bold, but suddenly it looked drab, formless in the mirrored back wall of the lift.

'Don't be disheartened, *mon petit*,' her companion added. 'You can always go shopping.'

'That's true,' Bella managed to say.

'Well, good day,' Madame Roux said when she exited on the second floor.

'Yes. Thank you.'

Yves was hovering near the lift when it reached the third floor and she turned towards her office, feeling as if every last bit of confidence had been drained from her body.

'*Salut.*' He held out a paper cup from a high-end coffee shop. 'I bought you an Americano. I hope that's OK?'

She smiled. 'Yes. Thank you.'

At least someone seemed to be on her side...

A few moments later, she took her laptop across to Claudine's office and knocked on the door. Inside, Claudine was sitting at a desk that looked completely clear – Bella's was already starting to look messy, she'd have to attend to it later – her porcelain hands knitted together in front of her.

'*Bonjour,* Isabella,' she said in French. 'You are ready?'

'Yes,' Bella replied. 'I've put together some initial ideas for the pitch. I can start making calls after the meeting.'

Claudine nodded approvingly and leant slightly backwards on her wheeled chair, as if somehow a weight were being lifted from her. 'Wonderful,' she said, gesturing to the projector and encouraging Bella to start.

It was as if Bella had stepped outside of her body and was looking at herself with new eyes. Smartly dressed, a little tired around the eyes, confident. She talked about her vision, what they'd need to do – first steps, next steps, final steps. And she could see in Claudine's face that her new boss was impressed.

'*Magnifique!* This is a great start. You definitely have a gift for this industry, Isabella. I am very confident that we will be moving forward brilliantly with you steering the ship.'

Bella realised she was grinning like an idiot, so reined in her smile a little to look more self-assured than flabbergasted. 'Thank you.'

'We will celebrate,' Claudine said. 'Are you free to go for a drink after work?'

Bella thought of her aching limbs, of the fact that she had been hoping to scuttle back on the train and collapse in a few hours' time either in her bed or Henri's. But looking at Claudine, she realised that this was one of those pivotal moments. Her boss was making a gesture of friendship.

There was only one answer she could give. '*Oui!*'

'Wonderful, wonderful.' Claudine leant forward a little over her desk as if imparting a secret. 'You know, it has been a long time since I was able to go out. My husband and I, we separated a few years ago, and it is difficult with such a big job to find someone new. Some of the other staff at the hotel, they go out but – pah! – they are babies. It will be nice to *refaire le monde* with someone on my level.'

Refaire le monde – remodel the world, Bella's brain quickly translated. She smiled, wondering what Claudine might have thought had she seen her the night before in *Le Cocorico*, behaving to all intents and purposes like one of the 'babies' she was describing.

She would have to be careful tonight – not drink too much and definitely not give too much of herself away. But if it was reinvention Claudine was interested in, she was definitely becoming an expert at that.

18

NOW

The bar Claudine had chosen, with its chequered tiles and aesthetically worn leather-clad seating, was exactly the type depicted in films about Paris – traditional, beautiful and full of well-dressed, stylish-looking clients. Seven o'clock and the scattered tables on the street outside were almost all taken, but Claudine managed to commandeer one just as its occupants left, and Bella took the seat opposite her gratefully.

She had been almost superhuman today, existing on barely a wink of sleep, and the last thing she'd wanted to do was step into a taxi and head to a bar. But now, on the street, with the buzz of conversation, surrounded by well-groomed and effortlessly elegant Parisians, she started to perk up a little.

'Cocktail?' Claudine asked, an eyebrow raised quizzically.

Bella nodded, feeling a little like a child being taken somewhere by a glamorous aunt.

A waiter came to take their order and she pointed to carajillo on the menu, hoping that the shot of espresso that it contained would help to keep her alert for long enough to impress her boss before she went home and collapsed.

As they waited for their drinks, a silence fell over them briefly and Bella racked her brain for something to fill it. 'Oh, I've sent out that email to confirm the caterers for the presentation evening.'

Claudine looked amused. 'I am glad to hear it. But let's not talk shop now we are here.'

'Oh.' Bella made a face at her faux pas. 'Sorry.'

'It is just my way,' Claudine said. 'If we let our work come with us into other areas of our life it can become all we are. I like to try to keep it a little separate.'

Bella nodded. 'Makes sense.' She thought of the way the B & B – sharing her home with her business, and her house with strangers – had bled into every facet of her life with Pete. It had meant that they rarely had had time to feel completely at ease and alone. Arguments had been hushed, sex furtive and confined to bedtime hours. Always being on show had meant they'd buried resentments rather than air them. And the resentments had grown.

'Besides, I think it is nice to get to know a person outside of their job,' Claudine continued. 'I already know your work background. But I don't know who you are.'

Bella felt a little start in her chest. Was Claudine on to her? But she realised it was just a turn of phrase. 'Oh, I'm not very interesting, I'm afraid.'

'Pah, nonsense. You do not get to our age without becoming interesting,' Claudine said and leant forward. 'I want to know who Isabella is.'

So would I, she thought. What was it with everyone she met out here assuming she was the same age as them? Claudine looked to be in her early forties, Henri and Odette thought she was in her twenties. Either she was aging like fine wine or a long-forgotten packed lunch left in a school satchel.

'So why you are in Paris? What made you change your occupation?' Claudine waved her hand as if encouraging Bella to speak.

'I'm actually living in Versailles. But I wanted to work in Paris. Who wouldn't?'

'So why not an apartment here in the city?'

'It's only half an hour on the train,' she shrugged, not mentioning the cheap student accommodation she'd had to sign up for. 'I lived in the countryside before. But I wanted a change, I suppose,' she said, then sensing this wouldn't be enough to satisfy Claudine, she added, 'my husband and I also broke up, so...'

'Ah, divorce,' Claudine said, almost with satisfaction. 'Yes, it is a rite of passage for successful women, I find. I have had two,' she held her fingers up in a kind of victory sign. 'Some men, they are threatened by women like us.'

Bella thought about Pete, of their life together in rural France. Of her permanent outfit of jeans and a hoody. Of the fact they'd eat dinner off their knees in front of the TV. She doubted very much that any of her meagre successes had made him feel threatened, or had had much to do with their split. But she nodded, not knowing what else to say.

'And are you heartbroken?' Claudine asked, in a matter-of-fact tone.

'Oh! Well, of course I *was*. It was a shock. Now?' She thought of Pete, their dream, the house, and felt a rush of repressed emotion. 'Maybe a little. But more for the life we could have had than because I still want to be with him.'

Claudine nodded sagely.

The cocktails arrived and Bella sipped from hers gratefully. It was strong – the liquid, bitter in her mouth. But it definitely had a kick. Her stomach churned, reminding her that she'd barely eaten that day.

'And your home in Versailles... You are enjoying life there?'

'Oh yes,' she said, grateful for the chance to be honest.

Claudine nodded. 'It is a nice location. Very expensive of course, like Paris. But then if we cannot have some perks from our success, what is the point?' She took a sip of her own drink – long and cool-looking, blue in colour. 'You have bought an apartment? A house?'

'Oh, I—' Bella wanted to say that she was renting a room, but stopped herself. Would this fit with the executive lifestyle Claudine seemed to have imagined for her? 'A house,' she said, which was, after all, not a lie.

Claudine nodded as if this were what she had expected all along. 'It must be wonderful to have your own space again. I remember when I moved to my first apartment after Gustave – my first husband – and I split. I used to walk naked around my rooms, just feeling free. Having something that is just for you – it is important.'

'Oh!'

Claudine looked amused. 'You should try it. It is very liberating.'

Bella couldn't imagine walking around the rather tatty interior of the shared rental naked, but nodded as if logging the idea for future use.

'Tell me,' Claudine said then, taking another sip of her drink and regarding Bella. 'What is it that brings you to France? I am always intrigued. Of course I love my country,' she put her hand on her chest, 'but England has a lot to commend it too. London is a beautiful city; and for those of us who work in business, there are many opportunities.'

'I've always loved France. I came on a trip here with school years ago and...' She searched for the right words. 'The lifestyle is different, the people, the culture – it's a beautiful place.' It struck her yet again that for the first time in a while, every word that she'd uttered was true. She'd forgotten the initial pull to France that had guided her thinking in the first place.

'And you don't miss your own culture? Your family, perhaps?'

Bella winced slightly. 'I don't really have parents,' she admitted.

'No siblings?'

Bella laughed, took another sip and continued, emboldened. 'If you met my sister, you'd understand why I'd rather be here!'

Claudine seemed to like this comment. Her eyebrow – once again – arched with interest. 'Your sister is not a nice person?'

'Oh. No. I mean, yes. She's a lovely person.' Bella felt her skin prickling as she tried to put her words in order. 'She's lovely. It was a joke, really. Kitty, she's older than me and she's one of these people who— well, people are always comparing us and... I just wanted to get away from that. To be myself. Without the expectations, the comparisons.'

Claudine was nodding again. 'I understand. Your sister is jealous of your success. It is difficult for those who do not fly as we do to truly support us.'

'It's more the other way around,' Bella said before she could stop herself.

'You are jealous of her?'

'Not jealous.' She shook her head. 'I don't want— We have different lives. Want different things. I just always felt as if she was getting everything right and I was getting everything wrong.'

Claudine put her drink down. 'You are a successful project

manager, in charge of a hotel. She must be the Queen of England!'

They ordered another cocktail, and Bella surreptitiously checked her watch. It was 8 p.m. and a new type of clientele had begun to inhabit the bar – couples dressed for a night out on the way to the theatre, groups of twenty-somethings on the way to a meal or club. It was still light, but the air had a duller quality, as if darkness were preparing to enter from the wings.

She'd thought she might get home in time to join Odette and Henri who were off with a student crowd tonight. But in all honesty, she was not disappointed at the thought of missing out. She texted Henri:

BELLA

Will be home late, don't wait for me.

HENRI

OK. See you later.

BELLA

Of course.

They talked more about Claudine – her background in retail, a brief stint on reception at the Ritz before she'd married her second husband, her marriages and divorces, and how she now lived alone in an apartment many of her contemporaries would only dream of being able to afford.

'Some would say that all I need now is a man to complete me,' she said, her eyes twinkling with mischief.

'And do you?'

Claudine laughed. 'Not to complete me, *non*. But I will admit, it would be nice to have a man in my life again.' She looked wistful. 'Someone to talk to. To go through life with. I don't want to end up like Madame Roux.'

'Yes, tell me about her. How long has she lived at the hotel?'

A strange expression crossed Claudine's face. 'Ah, a few years perhaps,' she said. 'She was my mother's friend – did Yves tell you? My mother died when I was quite young.'

'Oh, I'm sorry. Mine too, actually.'

They exchanged a look. 'Then you understand.' Claudine said.

Bella nodded.

'Madame Roux was my mother's friend for many years. She actually helped to sew her wedding dress, I think. She was older than my mother, but they got on famously. Then, a few years ago, Madame Roux's husband got sick...' Claudine shrugged. 'When he died, there was a problem with inheritance. And I offered to help.'

'That was very nice of you.'

'Yes. Perhaps too nice.' Claudine raised an eyebrow. 'She is very good at telling me how to run my hotel, or about the things I'm getting wrong.'

Bella laughed. 'Yes, she's already given me a fashion critique.'

Claudine smiled, almost affectionately. 'I am not surprised. I hope she didn't offend you?'

'Not really.'

'Good. She means well. She was very into her fashions back in the day.'

Bella nodded.

They were silent for a moment.

'So you are single?'

'Not exactly.' Bella made a face. 'I'm with someone new... but he's a bit...'

Claudine leant forward, her eyes lighting up. 'A bit what?'

'Young. He's in his early twenties, so...'

Claudine seemed delighted, throwing her head back and laughing. 'That is perfect!' she said. 'Younger men who are not threatened by older women will not mind your success, will not try to trim your wings. And I am guessing he is good in bed?'

'Oh! Well, yes. He is.' Bella's face felt hot.

'Then I say hold on to him! And when you are bored of him, you can give him my number.'

'Oh!' Bella laughed, then looked at Claudine whose face looked... quite serious. 'Hang on... Do you really—'

But Claudine looked away, signalled to the waiter. 'Now, will you have another cocktail?'

Bella felt disorientated when she finally made it from the train to the front door of the Versailles house three hours later. But it wasn't the effect of the cocktails or the lack of sleep making her feel this way. It was the fact that she had felt completely at home with Claudine. She had felt older, more self-assured. With life experience and mistakes, but purpose and drive. She'd felt, in that moment, like Claudine's true contemporary and travelling back to her student house share was a little like being Cinderella at the stroke of midnight. Everything had looked so promising before, but it had been an illusion. Her horses were rats, her carriage, a pumpkin. Her prince still out on the lash with a group of overgrown kids.

Part of her was enjoying immersing herself in the two different roles life had gifted her right now. Escaping from the Bella who'd moved over to France, giddy in love and confident her life was mapped out assuredly in front of her.

Part of her felt out of her depth.

She slid the key in the lock and opened the door to darkness. Without the others there, the hallway seemed enormous, dark. She snapped on the light and made her way inside, not realising that someone else was in the house with her.

19

2012, ENGLAND

The days had settled into their familiar pattern and France had become a distant dream. November, and the roads were slippery and wet, the skies dark for her journey to and from work. The store had begun to play Christmas music, and she was already sick of its saccharine sentimentality.

The queues to the tills had grown as organised people had begun to tick items off their Christmas shopping lists. Gift boxes of perfume and aftershave; bath sets; make-up advent calendars for those averse to a sweet treat in December.

Bella's mood had soured. The days had become interminable, bleeding into one another. She'd stopped smiling at customers; was doing her job on autopilot.

So she didn't look up when the man came to her counter and plonked down a huge bottle of shampoo. Just rang it up and asked for £6.99.

'Wow, that's increased since last time,' a voice said.

She looked up.

It was Pete.

'Pete! Hello! God, I'm sorry. I just— I wasn't paying attention,' she said, smiling.

He was wearing his on-site gear – a battered pair of jeans with steel-capped boots, a chequered shirt that had seen better days. He looked rugged and dependable and actually pretty good-looking.

She handed him his receipt.

'Hang on,' he said, putting something else on the counter. 'I forgot this.'

'God's sake,' she said, looking at the queue.

But when she turned her attention to what she'd assumed was his other purchase, her mouth dropped open. It was a small velvet box, with an even tinier ring inside. When she had opened it, the people in the queue had gasped in unison.

'Let's do it,' he said.

'Get married?'

'The whole thing. France. Marriage. An adventure.'

She didn't even have to think: 'OK.'

'OK yes?'

'OK yes.'

They'd grinned at each other as Slade had roared out Christmas greetings over the tinny store stereo and the people in the queue had clapped their gloved hands.

When she relayed the tale to Dad and Kitty later, she wouldn't mention the three little words he'd uttered as a proposal had been more of a sports shoe slogan than anything romantic.

Because however you looked at it, all her dreams were going to come true.

20

NOW

She was in the kitchen when she heard it.

Arriving home to an empty house had been a novelty, and she'd just been revelling in the idea of reading in bed, a comparatively early night. Sleep that her thirty-four-year-old body needed even if her twenty-year-old persona might not.

It had been odd opening the door onto the dark hallway, snapping on the light to drive the shadows to the corners of the room. Then walking to the kitchen and doing the same. The slatted kitchen blind had been left open, and she was aware of the darkness outside, broken by the noise of passing traffic, but somehow deep and eerie in a way it had never felt before.

She'd been about to pop on the kettle and make herself a cup of tea to take upstairs when she heard it. Just a couple of notes at first, enough to make her stop and listen, prick her ears, but not enough for her to be sure exactly what it had been or where it had come from.

It was nothing, she told herself. Just some teenager passing by playing music on her phone, or a notification on her mobile from a little-used app.

Then it happened again; single notes plucked on an acoustic guitar, falling together to form an almost haunting melody. Coming from somewhere close by, above her.

Bella was quite a fan of folk guitar. She'd enjoyed listening to performances in her local pub back in the UK, and always stopped to linger when a busker with talent was playing acoustically.

What she wasn't a fan of was haunting, human sounds coming from upstairs in an empty house.

Her heart began to race. She didn't believe in ghosts, didn't think burglars tended to break into people's houses then entertain them with guitars. But there was no good explanation for why the music was softly being played in one of the upper rooms.

She switched off the kettle before it began its pre-boil rattle and crept to the hallway, feeling her whole body tingle on high alert. The music was definitely coming from upstairs.

Any thoughts of it being simply a radio left on dissipated when the playing stopped for a moment – the player coughed – then resumed.

It couldn't be Henri – even if he were unexpectedly back from the bar, she knew he couldn't play anything. His father had apparently paid for lessons on several different instruments during his childhood. He'd regaled them the other evening about a particularly frustrated saxophone teacher who'd ended up grabbing his instrument and whacking it against the wall on finding out his would-be prodigy had failed to practise for the eighth week in a row.

Odette had said something about playing a little piano. But not a guitar.

Whoever it was had no business being in the house.

Bella began to climb the stairs quietly, thinking how she'd

often watched main characters in crime dramas carry out similar investigations and thought how unrealistic it was. In that situation, she would leave the house! Call the police! The only thing missing was the sinister music that would usually accompany this kind of move.

But curiosity overruled anything more sensible. And for some reason, she couldn't imagine someone playing a guitar could have evil intent. Besides, she wouldn't know what to say if she called the police anyway. Someone was playing a guitar upstairs and she didn't know who it was? It sounded ridiculous.

She grabbed hold of a large book as she passed the hall table, just to have something to throw if necessary, and held it slightly in front of herself as if it were a loaded gun that would protect her from anything and anyone. The cover was faded, but she could make out the name 'Proust'. She hoped it wasn't valuable.

Reaching the landing, she cocked her head slightly to one side, trying to hear the music again. To her horror, she realised it was coming from her room.

Somehow, the annoyance she felt at her personal space being invaded made her more angry than afraid. She found herself stepping towards her door. The light hadn't been switched on, but she could see the outline of the gap between the door and its frame due to the street lights outside, perhaps even a little moonlight too.

There was a scent in the air that took her back to her school days, when she'd gathered with fellow rebels behind the bike sheds before they were old enough to realise that rebelling by giving yourself lung cancer wasn't the best form of subterfuge.

Whoever it was, was smoking – *smoking!* – in her room. Taking a breath and relying on something she'd read once about the power of surprise, she switched on the light and flung the door wide open and screeched: '*Que fais-tu dans ma chambre?*' *What are you doing in my room?*

She'd half expected the intruder to leap up, push past her and vanish into the night. Instead, as she stood, brandishing *À La Recherche Du Temps Perdu* above her head, the adrenaline drained from her body, and she became aware of herself. Confronting an intruder, armed only with a book, in a dark, empty house in a strange city. What was she doing?

A man was sitting on her bed – on her *bed!* – with a guitar resting on his knee, his fingers at the strings. His face was rugged and stubbled, his eyes ringed with dark circles. And as he looked up at her, his expression seemed to register a mixture of confusion, annoyance and amusement. She noticed that it wasn't a cigarette she'd smelled after all, but some kind of incense stick in a jar. Which was far less cancer-inducing but no less of an imposition.

'*Je ne*—' he began. '*Je ne*—' He gave a deep sigh and his shoulders slumped. 'Shoot. Sorry, sweetheart, my French has deserted me. Do you speak English?' He spoke with a drawling American accent, slurring his words slightly, clearly more than a little worse for wear.

'Yes!' she said, lowering the book slightly. 'I *am* English.'

'Oh good. In which case,' he paused and fixed his bright blue eyes on her, 'who the fuck are you?'

'Who the fuck am *I*? Who the fuck are *you?!*'

The ridiculousness of the situation didn't escape her. She was in her own home, her own room, and this stranger was sitting on her bed, playing the guitar, drinking whisky or some other spirit whose smell filled the air and asking her who she was. It was like some sort of far-fetched and less child-friendly retelling of Goldilocks. Only if she had been a bear, this guy would have been in real trouble.

All she'd wanted tonight was a nice, strong cup of tea in bed. Not a tall, rugged stranger, an unwelcome dose of burnt perfume and Simon and Garfunkel's greatest hits.

It was ridiculous. It was all too ridiculous. In fact, perhaps it wasn't happening at all? Perhaps she was having a stroke. What were you meant to do in these circumstances? Check if your face has fallen – she remembered that from a TV advert a few years back. She tested her smile, it seemed to be working. Could she touch her fingers to her nose? Worried, she moved her hand sharply and forgetting she was holding a book, hit herself in the face with the Proust.

It hurt and she let out a cry that sounded similar to the noise their family dog had made when it had injured its paw.

'Shit, are you OK?' The man put down his guitar and went to stand closer, peering at her face. 'Looks like it's bleeding.'

She dropped the book and put her hands to her face briefly, then withdrew them. He was right; her nose had started to bleed.

The man stepped farther forward, and she stepped back. 'Don't,' she said, holding up her bloodied hands.

'Sorry.' He held both his hands up in a gesture of surrender. 'Seriously, I'm not going to hurt you.' Then added, 'Seems to me you're more of a danger to yourself than anyone else.' He picked up the box of tissues from the nightstand and held it out. 'Here.'

She grabbed one instinctively.

'Maybe take two, you know, in case you decide to hit your-self in the face again.' He grinned.

Was he laughing at her? Laughing? 'Can you just leave before I call the police?' she managed from behind the crum-pled tissue she was now holding to her nose. 'You're drunk. You've wandered into the wrong house. You don't *seem* like a burglar. And anyway, I haven't got anything of value – unless you're into overpriced high heels and to be honest, you're welcome to them because they are a total mistake and I shouldn't have wasted my money on them. But otherwise, there's nothing... so can you just— Please. Go.'

The man looked confused. 'This is number 12, right?'

'Yes.'

He nodded. 'Thought so. I think it's you who are in the wrong place. Are you feeling OK? Your face looked kind of weird a minute ago. Like twitchy.'

'Of course I'm twitchy! There's a strange man in my room. And anyway, I was testing my movement in case I was having a stroke,' she said, her voice haughty with self-righteousness.

Unless... She couldn't have gone through the wrong front door? These houses probably looked similar inside, but still... She glanced around her room to reassure herself that she wasn't under the influence of the cocktails Claudine had paid for (had they been stronger than she'd thought?) and wasn't wandering into strangers' houses herself.

But then, there was her mirror. Her hairbrush. Her jacket on the back of the chair. And she'd used her key to get in.

All she had wanted was to have a decent rest. Now she had a nosebleed and a drunken intruder. She almost felt like weeping. Then, 'Your incense!' she cried out suddenly, noticing the jar on her nightstand had tipped over, spilling its stinking, smoking contents onto the wood.

'Holy moly!'

Turning and seeing the wooden surface of the nightstand smoking, the intruder grabbed the offending item, scattering burnt embers onto the carpet, the bed. One of the sparks hit the duvet and began to smoulder. He quickly grabbed a glass of water she'd half drunk last night and doused the threatening flame.

Then turned again to her. Clocking her look of horror, he made a face. 'Whoopsie.'

This really *was* the limit.

'Whoopsie? WHOOPSIE? You've burned my bed, soaked it, ruined my nightstand, made a burn mark on the carpet. My room stinks. You're drunk. You're in my house. And all you can say is "whoopsie"?'

Still, the stranger looked amused rather than rattled. Perhaps it was a male privilege thing. He clearly wasn't in any peril from her. All she'd done so far was hit herself in the face.

'It seemed like quite a good word under the circumstances. I could have gone for "dangnabbit", I suppose.' He grinned. 'Or "Holy cow"!'

And now he was joking. How was this situation funny in any way?

The unfairness of it hit her and tears of self-pity welled in her eyes. 'All I wanted,' she managed to sniff, 'was a cup of tea. A cup of fucking tea.'

'Tea?' He cocked his head to one side. 'You're crying over a cup of tea? You British.'

Exhaustion washed over her. 'Look,' she said, removing the tissue from her face, realising the bleeding had stopped. 'Can you just go. Please?'

'I—'

But then, to her relief, there was the sound of a door being opened, laughter. Henri's voice, unmistakable, at the end of an anecdote that Odette had clearly thought was hilarious.

'Henri!' she called out, feeling weak with relief. 'Help! There's an intruder! I need help!'

'I'm coming! *J'arrive!*'

There was a thunderous noise as her would-be knight in shining armour rushed up the stairs and burst into her room.

'Bella?' he said, noticing her bruised face. His eyes went to the stranger. 'Oh,' he said.

'Can you tell him to get out of the house? I think he's a tramp or something,' she said, as quietly as she could. 'He seems OK. I don't think he's dangerous. Just— Well, smelly and a bit worse for wear. I don't know how he got in.'

Henri looked at her. 'I—'

But before he could finish his sentence, the man began to speak. 'Henri, I don't know how you know this chick, but could you help her or something. I think she's— Maybe she's going through something. Unless she's moved in with you. A girl-friend? Which honestly you should have told me about but...' he trailed off.

'Brad, this is *her* room.'

'What?'

'Yes. She is a lodger here. You must know this, surely?'

Brad's brow furrowed. Then, as if a switch had been flicked, it lit up, smoothed out. 'Oh yeah! The English girl.'

'Yes,' Henri nodded. 'The English girl.'

Brad's face contorted as if reliving the events of the last twenty minutes. 'Ah,' he said. 'Shoot.'

'Shoot' indeed.

'So, I think you'll have to take the attic this time?' Henri said, grimacing.

'Jesus. What an idiot.' The man rubbed a hand through his hair, looked at the debris scattered on the bed, the wet patch, the burnt nightstand. 'Sorry. I guess you're... what, Isabella?'

'Bella,' she said weakly. 'And you are...?'

'I'm Brad,' he said, sticking his hand out towards her. 'Your landlord.'

21

NOW

As the alarm trilled to signal yet another day, she groaned and turned over. Henri's arms were still wrapped around her and he pulled her into a warm, soft embrace. It would be so easy to allow sleep to overcome her again, but her phone's beeping was insistent and eventually she tore herself away. 'Sorry.'

Henri moaned and shuffled away from her. He had what he called an 'early class' which meant he had to be up by 9 a.m. and at uni by 9.30 a.m. He always expressed incredulity at her alarm going off at 6 a.m., but then he was a guy, and young and fit enough to get away with rolling out of bed into jeans and sloping to class five minutes before he was due.

Being a woman, and one ten years his senior, meant a lot more work to get to an acceptable standard to be seen in public. There was shaving and plucking and exfoliating and moisturising and hairstyling and make-up application, and all with the hope of looking as if she'd barely bothered and was just naturally gorgeous.

It was exhausting.

Yesterday morning when she'd gone downstairs, she'd been

nervous that she might see Brad. After their embarrassing first encounter it was better for both of them to avoid each other for now, she'd reasoned. But luckily, he seemed to keep a similar schedule to Henri, getting up late and going to bed late. He'd been out when she'd returned from work and other than the odd burst of guitar music – which wasn't unpleasant once she was sure it wasn't being played by a ghost or an intruder – she'd barely been aware of his presence.

'He comes from time to time,' Henri had told her when they'd lain in bed together that night, she still thrumming with anger and embarrassment at the whole thing. 'But usually he calls first and isn't so—'

'Rude?'

He'd laughed. 'I was going to say drunk. But yes, I think rude too. What can I say, he is older and grumpy. Ignore him.'

It hadn't been that reassuring.

Post-shower and clothed in a burgundy shift dress, she made her way down to the kitchen to grab a slice of toast to eat on the walk to the station. But opening the kitchen door she realised that, for once, she was not the only one up.

Brad was standing by the cupboard, holding a box of tea leaves, sniffing the contents. Next to him on the counter was a familiar-looking box, its lid open.

'Oh,' she said, involuntarily.

He turned and looked at her, and she realised for the first time that he was eating. A cookie. One of *her* cookies – the first batch she'd made since moving.

'Hey, it's Bella!' he said, his mouth stretching wide into a chocolatey grin. 'Wanna tea?'

'Do I want one of my own teas?' she said, wondering why she was being quite so arsey. She didn't mind at all who used her tea ordinarily. It was something about the assumption of it.

The fact he'd helped himself to her cookies and stuck his nose in her tin without so much as a by-your-leave.

His face fell. 'Aw, shoot, is that your tea? Henri lets me help myself to his stuff, and I thought— But of course, he's a coffee man. Sorry.'

'No,' she shook her head. 'I'm being— it's fine, actually. And yes please to tea.' Her gaze wandered again to the open box of cookies, Brad's hovering hand.

His eyes followed the same direction. 'Oh man. These are yours too, right?'

She nodded. "Fraid so.'

'Man. I hope you weren't saving them for something important. I just thought—Well, Henri's always got some fancy snacks with that father of his sending hampers and such. I just assumed—'

'It's fine. I can always make more.'

His eyes widened. 'You made these?'

'Yeah,' she shrugged. 'No big deal.'

'Man alive. If I could bake like this, I'd weigh four hundred pounds! You'd have to winch me out of that attic with a frickin' crane!'

Unexpectedly, she found herself laughing. 'Well, I would offer to teach you, but it sounds like I wouldn't be doing you any favours.'

'You'd teach me?'

Oh shit. 'Well, I guess. If you really want to learn.' The last thing she wanted to do was spend more time with Brad. Their first encounter had been less than great, sure. But it was more than that. He was messy, his hair needed a cut, he hadn't bothered to shave for a few days. Forget hairnets, she'd practically have to wrap him from head to toe if they started cooking together. He was probably an OK guy – Henri seemed to like him. But there was something about him that really irritated her.

Only she was in it now, wasn't she?

'Yeah, yeah I do.' He absent-mindedly helped himself to another cookie, closing his eyes as he bit through its crispy outer layer and into its soft centre. 'Mmm mmm.'

'Don't you have, like, work to go to or something?' she asked suddenly. Hadn't Henri said he was some sort of businessman?

'Not right now.' He flapped his hand. 'Let's say I'm taking a bit of time out.'

She nodded. 'OK.'

'One of the perks of working for yourself,' he added, turning towards her with a grin.

She snorted and his brow furrowed.

'What?'

'Sorry. Not you. But I have some… experience of being self-employed, and time out wasn't really a thing I ever got around to taking.' She leant against the counter, then realising that was actually really uncomfortable, went to perch on the kitchen table.

'Oh?' He was looking at her. 'Really? Your own business? Aren't you like at university or something? Or, no, hang on, doing a work placement, right?'

She didn't enjoy this direct questioning. It was one thing having assumptions made about her life and neglecting to correct them. But lying directly felt doubly wrong. 'It's complicated,' she tried.

To her surprise, he seemed to take this as an acceptable answer. 'Gotcha,' he said, nodding sagely.

'So… tea?' She glanced at her watch. She'd have to put it in her thermal mug, sip it on the train.

'Oh. Yeah. Sure.' He turned on the kettle which began to

steam almost immediately, then spooned a rather generous serving of her tea into the pot and poured the water in. The leaves swilled in the hot liquid, creating a delicious aroma. They both stopped and simultaneously sniffed the air like animals tracking a scent. Then caught each other's eye and laughed.

'Can't beat that aroma in the mornings, right?'

She nodded.

Brad gestured towards the oak chairs at the small kitchen table. 'Aren't you going to sit?'

She shook her head, held up her thermos mug. 'Got to caffeinate and run, I'm afraid. Work calls.'

'And you can't be late?'

'Don't want to be.'

'Good for you.' He nodded approvingly. 'You know, in my line of work, it's hard to get folks to turn up on time. Or at all, sometimes. They're lucky to have you.'

She managed to avoid another snort, just. 'Well, maybe.'

'No maybes about it.' He took the thermos mug from her hand, placed it on the counter then filled it with tea. 'Not too strong I hope?'

'No such thing.'

'Well, Bella,' he said after handing it back to her. 'It's nice to have some company in the mornings in this place.'

She smiled. 'Yep.'

'And sorry, you know, for—' He waved his hand slightly as if to fill in the gap.

For burning my bed? For scaring me half to death? The whisky? The near-fire on my nightstand? Luckily, she managed not to say any of these things. Instead, she nodded and turned out of the kitchen.

* * *

In Peyrat, she'd used to love walking to the boulangerie early in the morning to buy viennoiseries for their guests. There had been a freshness in the air – tinged with the scent of pollen and grasses and the rich, earthy smell given off by stone houses after a night of rain.

So far, in Versailles, she hadn't really enjoyed her walk to the station. She'd often been rushing, feeling hungover or tired. And the March and April weather hadn't always been favourable.

But today, slowed by the tea that she sipped as she walked, she noticed for the first time that spring had finally come into itself. The sky was a clear blue peppered with tiny, almost laughable clouds; people had filled their window boxes and hanging baskets with flowers that had started to bud and bloom.

Cars passed her on the road and people walked in various directions on the pavement, looking purposeful. A woman jogged by dressed in running gear, a golden retriever on a lead bounding gleefully at her side. Bella thought of Juliette and Jolie and felt a pang of nostalgia for her old life. But soon, the walk, the tea, the freshness and newness of everything this morning moved her thoughts on to today, her journey to work, her job.

Since moving, she'd been just about hanging on. Worrying about keeping her job, about the house sale that seemed to be ticking along in the background but making very little progress. About Pete and the divorce and whether she was making a complete mess of things.

But she realised in that moment that she had managed to build a life – albeit with a few falsehoods at its foundation –

that she was actually enjoying. Experience or not, she was holding the job down with only a few moments of panic and doubt. She had Henri who despite his youth made her feel safe and secure. She got to go out with people who were young and fun and made her feel better about not having met most of the personal milestones she'd set for herself.

And she was living in Versailles, working in Paris. Two places that many people in the world would kill to visit, and she was immersed in them every day. She looked at the buildings lining her walk to the station – tall and ornate with stone features carved by hands hundreds of years ago. She breathed in the air – tinged with fumes and the scents of the street and far dirtier and less life-affirming than that in Peyrat, but lovely in its own way. It was the smell of life and movement and streets that had been walked on for centuries by people living vibrant, interesting lives.

As she pressed her ticket to the scanner and entered the station, a thought came into her head. Maybe this didn't have to be a stopgap after all. If she could find a way to untangle the lies without ruining everything, maybe this could be her actual life.

22

2013, FRANCE

It was the eleventh house they had looked at.

They'd been in France a week and so far, all the properties they'd viewed had been disappointing. Stone houses described as 'habitable' had been little more than ruins. Gardens had been overgrown and overwhelming. There had been strange annexes and spider webs, mouse droppings or the smell of damp.

On the surface of it, of course, none of this was that important. Pete had reassured Bella that most things could be overcome. 'There's a lot of plastering and pointing needed, but you wait till I've done it,' he'd enthused each time. 'I could transform this place.'

But she hadn't had the feeling she was looking for. The sense that that 'somewhere' would one day become her home.

They'd met the agent at her car just outside her office and she'd insisted on driving them, before ushering them into the back seat of her car. It had felt odd, childish, for them both to be there and they'd grinned at each other when they'd set off, sharing an unspoken joke. It was a relief to be smiling – the

week had been fraught and full of squabbles. Bella had begun
to doubt whether they'd ever find anything they agreed on.

Neither of them had been to Peyrat before; the little village
close to Aubusson was barely a dot on the map. But as they
passed the red-edged sign displaying its name, Bella sat up, a
flicker of excitement in her chest.

They entered the village, driving past a somehow familiar
green of gardens and fields, the light stone of houses. Some had
erected plastic pools for the summer, the water looking blue,
cool and inviting. Others had set out their patio furniture.
Small children played in the garden of a property they passed,
and a dog ran out of a driveway and chased the car, barking
joyfully before giving up and returning home.

'This is really cool,' said Pete, and she nodded in agreement.

And there it was, the house that might one day be their
home. Grey, stone walls, with climbing roses. An iron and glass
canopy set over the front door, painted a deep blue. Enormous
windows with cream-coloured wooden shutters. A garden
stretching forth and crying out for an allotment and chickens
and maybe even a goat or two – the whole French dream. The
possibility of days and days and days of feeling happy at last.

'What do you think?' Pete whispered as they exited the car
onto the stone driveway.

'This is the one.'

The call from reception was unexpected.

'Isabella? There is a visitor for you.'

'Really?' She'd been working on the presentation, something that was drawing ever closer, and had been completely immersed. She checked her watch: midday. 'Are you sure?'

Mélodie sounded amused. '*Oui*, I am sure. There is a gentleman here to see you.'

'Oh?' She couldn't imagine who it might be. Perhaps it was a courier, something to sign. 'I'll be down in a sec.'

To her surprise, when she descended in the lift a few moments later, she found Henri sitting on one of the chairs, engrossed in something on his phone. He looked up as she approached, and his face broke into a smile. 'Hello!' he said. 'Surprise!'

He stood and kissed her on both cheeks. Bella could feel the receptionist's eyes on them. 'Hi,' she said, her voice dropped to almost a whisper. 'What are you— Why are you here?'

'I know you are a busy executive now,' Henri said with mock

seriousness. 'But even the President of France has to eat, *non*? And I am sure he must be busy.'

She checked her watch again. 'That's so nice. But I was kind of in the middle of something...'

'*Vraiment*?' He looked hurt. 'But...' He leant in. 'Surely it can't be that important. You are only an intern.'

'Oh, lunch!' she said, suddenly and loudly, hoping to drown out anything else Henri might say. 'Love to!'

He stepped back at her sudden enthusiasm, but then nodded and took her hand. 'Yes. Let's eat.'

She turned to Mélodie. 'I'll be back in an hour,' she said. 'Take messages if anyone calls.'

'Wow,' Henri said as they exited onto the street. 'They have you doing real work. When my father had interns, he used to say "They are great for coffee, to fetch a sandwich perhaps. But not much more".'

'Oh, I make coffee too,' she lied. Actually, Yves was keeping up such a steady supply of it that she wasn't sure where the nearest café was and she was beginning to develop a twitch by 3 p.m. each afternoon.

She'd had a call planned in an hour with one of the representatives from Hotel Club to finalise some of their requirements for their visit. But she could hardly tell Henri that without giving herself away. Unless... 'Look, it's not exactly an internship. It's more like a job. I'm not... I'm not at uni.' She took a deep breath. It was time to tell him everything. She glanced at him and saw him looking at her with interest. 'And... I'm sorry, but I tried to tell you before. I'm older than you think, too.'

'Ah yes! I like this!' he said. 'The role play, *n'est-ce pas*? You are an executive in your thirties – an older, experienced woman – and maybe I am your husband. And we are both very successful, successful enough to go to GrandCoeur for lunch.'

'No, I really mean it, I—'

'Or perhaps you have a husband at home. He is very rich, but very old and dull. And I am your lover,' said Henri, warming to the idea.

'No. Henri. You're not listening. I'm the project manager at that hotel. I'm actually working on an important assignment—'

'*Oui*, I know,' he said, winking elaborately.

'But—' She felt exhausted. What was she meant to do? Make him read her birth certificate? Chop a limb off and have him count the number of rings? Or perhaps that was just a tree thing.

'Ah, here it is. Not GrandCoeur, but maybe next time, huh?' he said, grinning.

Her stomach growled as if to say *Look, you tried. You're off the hook. Now eat!*

He pushed open the door of a glass-fronted seafood restaurant she'd noticed a couple of times on her walk to work. It was set in a white, rather smartly renovated building with a bright blue and white awning and decorative brickwork. 'Welcome to *La Cabane*,' he said. 'The best fish restaurant in France.'

Inside, the room was lit with low, yellow light. Small circular tables with white linen napkins were scattered throughout, half of them filled, the other half set with plates and cutlery, ready for further guests.

They were shown to a table by a waiter who seemed to know Henri on sight, and after a moment or two she felt herself relax. She'd been intending to work through lunch, get as much done as possible so she could leave on time, or as close to 'on time' as possible. But although Henri didn't know the full facts, he was right. It was important to have a break.

They ordered seafood – a *plateau de fruits de mer* – the platter edged with shrimp and mussels surrounding an enormous red lobster split open on the plate, shelled crab and smoked salmon. Nestled between the delicacies were slices of lemon and fresh lettuce leaves. Henri ordered a sparkling white wine, despite her protestations about work, and as they picked at their feast, first carefully and then with more abandon, she started to enjoy herself. She was in Paris! Eating at a gorgeous restaurant with her handsome boyfriend. Surely the type of thing that people dream of.

'This is delicious,' she said, tipping a mussel into her mouth and closing her eyes for a moment.

'*You* are delicious.'

She looked up into blue eyes filled with mischief and passion and felt a rush of affection for this man who had given her a sense of being on stable ground once again. She wondered whether to say something reciprocal, or thank him for whisking her away from her desk. Or maybe something about how he was dressed – in a snug white shirt and grey trousers that fit him so well it was hard to look away. Instead, she found herself saying 'Pah!' and metaphorically flicking away his compliment with a flap of her hand.

Did she always have to be so fricking British? What was it with this desire to undermine all compliments at any cost? She felt annoyed at herself for batting his words away. This new, improved version of herself should know how to take a compliment. She'd seen someone comment on Claudine's new lipstick the other day and she'd enthused about it too, rather than saying '*Oh, this old thing*' as Bella probably would have done.

But after at least a year with a husband who'd stopped complimenting her, stopped seeing her, the idea of her being delicious or attractive felt false and a little ridiculous. She didn't feel delicious. Most of the time she felt as sexy as a lump of gone-off Brie.

She reached for another prawn, and jumped a little as Henri's phone started to ring. He looked at the screen and his face fell. 'I'm sorry,' he mouthed, then answered. '*Bonjour, Papa,*' he said in a completely different voice, rolling his eyes at her over the table. He grabbed a shrimp then stood, making his way across the restaurant to the door, opening it and standing outside in view of the window, having what looked like a heated conversation.

It was odd seeing him like this. Her happy-go-lucky lover suddenly looking hunched and angry. A completely different version of himself.

Ten minutes later, he re-entered, his face flushed. 'I am so sorry.' He sat down across from her. 'It was my father. I didn't mean to be away for so long.'

'It's OK,' she replied. 'Although the food went cold.'

He looked confused. 'But it is seafood...' Then he realised and laughed. 'It is true,' he said. 'I am sure it is quite ruined.' He sipped from his wine. There was still an aura of tension around him; a prickle in the air.

'Everything all right?'

He ran a hand through his hair, leaving it in disarray. '*Oui.* Just my father, he always knows how to ruin the moment.'

'Yeah?' she enquired, not wanting to probe, but actually very much wanting ALL the details.

'*Oui.* Ah, it is just a business thing. He is tired of me being a student. He thinks I'm avoiding real life. Tired of my studies, if I'm honest. Does not even want me to complete my course.'

'Oh, that seems harsh.' She made a sad face. 'What did you tell him?'

'That if real life is putting on a suit and sitting in a meeting room with lots of people, I am very keen to avoid it for as long as possible.'

She laughed. 'That sounds perfectly reasonable to me! Plus, it's *your* life, right?'

'Yes. But he is old-fashioned. He wants his only son to take the reins of the business for him. It is his dream.'

She nodded. 'What's *your* dream though?' she asked softly.

He leant forward on his elbows, 'Is it OK if I am not yet sure? I know I want to do something with words, with literature. But I am not sure whether teaching is for me, or whether I want to write. Or maybe direct.' He looked thoughtful. 'Maybe my father is right; maybe I am just avoiding real life.'

'Yeah, but you're so young. It's OK not to know yet.' She put her hand on his and he put a second one on top and smiled at her gently.

Great. Now she was his mother.

'We are *both* so young.'

She lifted her glass to take another sip but realised it was empty. Obligingly, Henri lifted the bottle and filled it up again. 'It's not really his decision. If you don't want to, you shouldn't have to,' she added.

He nodded. 'I agree. Only my father is the one with all the money. So he is used to getting his own way. The money gives him power and he knows it.'

'But couldn't you—' she stopped herself.

'What?'

'No. It's none of my business.'

'No, tell me.'

'Well, do you need his money? I know it's difficult, but you could... get a job maybe?'

He laughed. 'Yes. You have found my flaw. I am very, very lazy.'

'There are worse things.'

'*Oui*, it is true.'

'Can I ask you something,' she paused, wondering how to put this into words. 'Do you ever feel bad?'

'Bad?'

'Yes, for letting your father believe you're going to join him one day.' She looked at him, her eyes searching his face.

There was a silence. 'Yes,' he admitted. 'A little. But sometimes if lies do not truly hurt another person, perhaps they are necessary.'

'Maybe.'

He reached for her hand again, and she was surprised, as she always was, how much his skin made hers tingle at the slightest touch. She half felt like suggesting they forget dessert and go home. But she couldn't – there was so much work to do.

'But for now, I am trapped in this gilded cage,' he added.

'What, the house share? Not really "gilded" is it.' She wrinkled her nose. 'More like a standard cage. Or a cave, maybe.'

He laughed, throwing his head back in a way that felt gratifying. '*Oui*, it is not so gilded there. But my father gives me a generous allowance. And I am too frightened of losing it right now.'

'So he still thinks you're going to join the business eventually?'

He grimaced. 'It is too hard to say no to him. He has put me on the board. I have to go to meetings sometimes. But nothing much. Only, yes, he believes that when I have my doctorate, I will be joining the company. And that when he dies, I will step into his shoes.'

'Is he dying?'

'No, he is as healthy as a flea! But one day...'

'You know, you really should tell him. You might find that he's more understanding than you think.'

Henri made a face. 'If you met my father, you might not be so sure.'

'He's not a nice guy?'

'Oh, he's nice, he's just very traditional. In fact, my sister would quite like to run the business I think, but he has a fixed idea that it should be his son. It is a man's job, apparently.' He made a muscle and laughed.

'Your poor sister!'

'Yes. Once, we planned that when I get the business, I will take her on as a partner and then leave. But I think this might kill my papa.' He shrugged. 'Sometimes people are set in their ways, and you know there is nothing you can do about it.'

'Has he got any idea? About you? About your sister? Any of it?'

He shook his head. 'My father is not the easiest man to talk to.'

She nodded. 'Families can be difficult.'

'*Oui*,' he said raising his glass. 'And you are very wise.'

Assuming he was raising his glass for a clink, she thrust hers forward. But instead, he lifted his to his lips. Unable to stop the motion, she ended up sloshing wine onto his sleeve. 'Oh God. Sorry.' She picked a napkin from the table and began to dab at the spill, her cheeks flushing.

A waiter, eyes wide, rushed over with a large linen napkin and began dabbing too, muttering under his breath.

'*Non*, it is OK, it is OK,' Henri said.

The waiter retreated, looking troubled. Clearly they were not used to customers slinging wine around during meals.

But it was hard to take it all seriously, especially after a lunchtime drink, and Bella found herself grinning. Looking at her, Henri laughed. 'Why do I find myself laughing so much when I am with you?'

'I don't know. Because I'm an utter disaster.' His white shirt now had a damp stain which would probably dry yellow.

He looked at her with earnest eyes. 'But you are the opposite of this. You are so refreshing. In my world – my father's world I suppose – everyone has an image to maintain. Everyone is serious and businesslike and they only show part of themselves to others. But you? You are not complicated like this.'

'I'm not?'

'*Non*, Bella. With you, I know exactly where I am. You are honest. It is refreshing.'

'Right,' she said with a thin-lipped smile.

'Maybe I also see a future with you,' he said softly. 'One day, when we are grown up.'

'You do?'

He nodded, all seriousness.

It was a knife to the heart. Things were working right now because she'd told herself it was just a fling. He didn't need to know the truth about her.

But if he was imagining a future, she could no longer pretend to herself that what she was doing was harmless.

He probably wanted to travel, live his life. Have kids, but not yet. Her biological clock was beginning to tick, and she'd have to make the decision about her own fertility sooner rather than later. It wasn't fair to keep him in the dark if they weren't on the same page.

She didn't want to think about shrivelling ovaries or broken hearts. Not today at least. And not while eating a seafood platter that looked fresh enough to be released back into the wild.

But she would have to soon, she thought, looking at Henri's hopeful face. Because one thing was for sure: he didn't deserve to be hurt.

24

NOW

To: Isabella Baker
From: Claudine Dupont
Re: Bio approval

Dear Isabella,
    As promised, please see below the bio for the text that will be used on materials relating to the presentation, including a biography and your credentials. Please could you provide a recent head shot to accompany?
    Let me know if there are any errors.
    Cordialement,
    Claudine

Isabella opened the attachment marked with her name and read through the text:

Isabella Baker joined Hôtel Benjamin earlier this year after a prestigious career in the hospitality industry, during which she managed a hotel complex in England, overseeing the running of several sites. Since joining Hôtel Benjamin she has been working with CEO Claudine Dupont on improving the overall offering to guests, streamlining processes and ensuring that Hôtel Benjamin offers that something extra required of hotels in the Hotel Club family.

So there they were, in black and white. Her lies. She could barely remember her application – had she really said all that? Somehow seeing it written made it all seem too real. But she could hardly back out now.

'It looks good,' she replied finally, which was true. The design of the leaflet was on point, with gold embellishments and pictures from the hotel brochure edged in black. It looked chic and contemporary and on-brand.

But whatever she might tell herself about staying on the side of truth, she had now crossed a line. She had accepted a write-up about herself that contained something completely false. And it was going to be distributed as part of the package when they presented to Hotel Club in a few weeks' time. After which it would be out in the world, together with her picture, and it would no longer be containable.

She was supposed to be going through some designs for new room-service menus, but the various options sent through by the graphic designer seemed to all blur into one. Her concentration was shot.

Her heart seemed to be racing and sweat was forming on her brow. She knew she needed to calm down to stop this escalating. She had to distract herself. She forced herself to look at the designs and for a moment it felt as if she were winning.

But as her concentration broke, the sweat came again, this time more intensely. She needed air, she needed to breathe.

Pushing back her chair, she walked quickly out of the office

down the thankfully empty corridor and to the lift. She pressed
the button for the ground floor and, as soon as the doors
opened after the lift's descent, she sped through the glass front
door before anyone could question her. And she was out. She
was free.

It was times like this when she wondered whether she'd be
better off being a smoker. Nobody questioned you going to
stand outside a building for a while if you were addicted to
nicotine. As it was, she'd noticed Mélodie's head snap up and
watch her as she stepped out. She'd have to come up with some
reason for her hasty exit, grab a coffee to bring back as an alibi.

Trying to regulate her breathing, she drew out her phone
and called Juliette.

'*Oui*, hello?'

'Juliette,' she managed. Her voice came out in almost a gasp.

'Bella, is that you?'

'Yes.'

'What is it? What's happened? Are you ill?'

'No. I'm OK. I'm just— Oh Juliette, I've got myself into a
situation.'

'Tell me everything.'

She felt weak as she opened her mouth. 'OK,' she said. 'But
you have to promise not to hate me.'

'I don't understand,' her friend admitted a few minutes later,
once she'd relayed her lies and how they'd come about. 'Why
didn't you correct them at your interview? They would still have
been impressed, I am sure. Perhaps when you said you
managed a *chambre d'hôtes* they misread it or something?'

Bella had been walking during her confession, her pace fast,
matching her breathing. Now, spent, she made her way to a
pavement café and slipped into a chair at an empty table. 'It's
not quite that, Juliette. I mean, I was trying to— well, make

myself sound better than I was. I suppose... I may have caused the confusion with my— with how I described things.'

'So you lied?'

'Well, yes. No. Sort of. I made it... I left things open to misinterpretation.'

There was a silence. 'But why would you do that?'

'Juliette. You know. I couldn't get a job. Nobody wanted me.' Bella felt her eyes fill. 'I was running out of time, out of money. And I just thought, *what would Juliette do*?'

'Me? You think I am a liar?'

'No. No. But you project confidence. You're so sure of yourself. And I suppose I took it too far. But I mean, half the applications I'd written just got ignored anyway. I wasn't to know... and then when they got in touch... I needed a job.'

There was another silence. She could hear Juliette's fingernails tapping against a hard surface, something she did when thinking. 'OK,' Juliette said. 'Well, what is done is done. But you need to come clean, Bella. With work, but also with Henri. It is not fair on him that he thinks he is dating someone who is not what they seem.'

'I can't.'

'But you must,' Juliette said softly. 'People are kind. They will understand.'

'But they won't want me any more,' she found herself saying. A waiter came over, raised an inquisitive eyebrow, so she pointed to coffee on the menu. He nodded and disappeared. People streamed past, all wrapped up in their own worlds; chatting, checking phones, wandering with cameras. Around her at the other tables, people sat in pairs and trios. She was the only person who was completely alone.

'They might be angry, yes, but...'

'It's not that. Juliette, there's a reason I lied in the first place.

I've wasted eight years running a B & B and it's all for nothing. I have no experience in anything else, no credentials. I just— I ruined my life. Lying was my only hope.'

'You—'

'And what about Henri? He won't want some old, unemployed divorcee. He's with me because he doesn't know who I am. Not really.'

'Bella!' Juliette sounded shocked. 'How can you talk about yourself like this?'

'It's true.'

'*Non.* It is an interpretation. One that even an enemy might not come up with. You are beautiful. You are young. You have a history, sure. But who doesn't? I cannot say whether Henri will want you or not, or that work will be OK or not. But you, you will be OK. You will find work, and you will find people who love you for you.'

Bella shook her head. The waiter appeared and set her coffee on the table. She gave him a small, watery smile before breaking eye contact. 'No, Juliette. I'll be *alone*. Henri will leave me, I'm sure. Claudine will fire me. Odette won't want to know me either after she finds out I've lied. I'll probably be thrown out of the house share for lying too. I'll have nothing. And I'll be alone. I just— it's too much.'

'You will have me.'

Bella paused, wiped her eyes, picked up a small, white-wrapped packet of sugar and began to tear off the corner. 'Thank you. But I can't— You're wonderful but it's not enough. I need people here, now. I need this job.'

'OK. OK. So breathe.' Juliette's voice sounded concerned. 'It's OK. Just concentrate on that for a moment.'

'OK,' Bella said a moment later. 'I'm OK.'

'So. Let me ask you. Can you do this job?'

'Yes. I really can. I think.'

'And you say that there is this big presentation, a meeting?'

'Yes – for potential Hotel Club status.'

'So perhaps it is not fair to leave before this anyway,' Juliette said gently. 'If you feel you cannot say, perhaps just do your best work, and then tell them once they secure the status. If you have been instrumental, perhaps they will see beyond the... the misunderstanding.'

'You think?'

'It is possible. But Bella, you must still tell Henri.'

'OK,' she breathed. 'I'll try.' But as soon as she hung up, any resolve she had dissipated. Henri was one of the few bright things in her life right now. Being held by him, kissed by him. Having someone at home waiting for her when she got in. She wasn't sure if she was ready to give that up.

She sipped her coffee, feeling the warm liquid flood her mouth. Everything in her life was balanced on a lie, but she wasn't ready to let it tumble just yet.

25

Kitty's house was, as always, immaculate. From the polished wood floors and the cream sofa to the antique and carefully sourced furniture. Whenever Bella mentioned anything about it, Kitty was careful to remind her that house prices had been cheaper in the early noughties when she'd first bought, and that she and Stu had combined their equity when they'd married – clearly keen to make Bella feel better.

But for the first time, Bella didn't feel envious. Because she was now set to be a homeowner too. And not one in boring Hertfordshire but in France, somewhere brand new and time-less all at once.

'Come in,' her sister said. She was dressed in jeans and a T-shirt, a flash of stomach just visible when she moved. Her hair was loose and fell in a way she'd never allow it to usually, in slight untamed waves. But it suited her.

Bella walked through the perfect living room to the kitchen where white cabinets were set against black granite, and took her seat at the breakfast bar. Kitty's home had been a second home to her for years, even more so since Linda had appeared on the scene. She thought for a moment how she might feel about not having her sister within a stone's throw and felt a well of something painful, but swallowed it down.

'Coffee?' Kitty offered, reaching for the percolator.

'Just instant will be fine.' Bella found she couldn't wait another moment to break the news; the length of time it would take for Kitty to brew one of her trademark delicious coffees was just too great.

'So,' her sister said, moments later, sitting down opposite her, cradling her own cup. 'What's up?'

'Well, obviously you know I love France—'

'Understatement of the century,' Kitty grinned. 'Yes.'

'Well...' Bella took a breath. 'You know we've been looking at houses, but what you don't know is that we've found one. And the mortgage has been approved!'

Kitty set her cup down heavily on the granite, making a sharp clicking sound. A little coffee spilled onto the counter. 'Sorry, you're— I mean, I knew you were having a look at things. But you're actually going to do it?'

'Well, yeah.'

'Oh God, Bella.' She reached out a hand. 'I didn't think— I never thought. Are you sure?'

'I'm not a baby, you know. I'm twenty-six.'

'I know. But—' Kitty's head had dropped slightly to the side. 'Bella, this is huge.'

'It's exciting!'

'Well, yes. And I'm happy for you. But—'

'But what?'

'I know you're twenty-six, you're engaged. You're all grown up. But Bella, you're still so young. You don't realise—'

'Don't do that.'

'Do what?'

'Mother me.'

The word silenced them both for a second.

Kitty eyed her, as if trying to work out her next move. 'Just hear me out, OK? You're young, you— I realise you haven't had much fun in your career so far. But what you're doing is— It's a huge thing, Bella.'

'I am aware.'

'And Pete's on board? He's up for quitting his job? Really?'

'He's excited too.'

'Right.'

Bella looked at Kitty. 'What?'

'What do you mean, "what"?'

'Why say that about Pete?'

Kitty sighed. 'I'm just worried, that's all. You know me.'

'Yes, but why? I don't get it. I really think I can make a brilliant life in France, Kitty. Why don't you want me to do that?'

'It's not that... I just— I suppose I thought it was one of those things people say but don't really ever get around to. It's great. Impressive, actually. But I just worry.'

'I know you do.'

'And you're sure Pete is the one?'

'Well, yeah. If nothing else, the fact he's willing to move to France for me should tell you something! We're in love.'

'Well, good. Wonderful. Congratulations.'

'You don't sound very sincere.'

Kitty sighed. 'I'm sorry, Bella. I am honestly happy for you. But I can't help being worried too. It's my job.'

'You don't have to, you know. Worry about me, I mean. I'm OK.'

'I know.'

Their eyes met for a long, gentle moment.

'I'll miss you, you know.'

'Then you'd better make sure your passport is up to date, because I plan to have a spare room just for you.'

26

NOW

Tonight, when she reached the house, the front door was slightly ajar and music was playing softly from the kitchen. She wondered whether Brad had brought his guitar downstairs, but when she opened the door, she found Henri and Odette with a collection of other youngsters, milling around the central table. One of them had Brad's guitar in his hands, although Brad himself wasn't there. Henri looked up and gave her a grin.

Six days had passed since Brad's arrival, but he seemed to have spent most of his time holed up in his room. Sometimes she heard the sound of soft, beautiful guitar music playing; other times it was silent and she wasn't sure whether he was at home or out somewhere, conducting whatever business he was here to conduct.

'Bella!' Odette said, sounding inordinately pleased to see her. 'You're home.'

'Yes.' She accepted the glass of wine that was already being shoved into her hand.

'I didn't realise they would keep you so late.'

In reality, she'd chosen to stay late to get her desk in order, to prepare what she could for the next day. But she smiled and said, 'Yes, everything got really busy.'

'We've been waiting for you!'

They had? She racked her brain, trying to figure out why that might be, but couldn't for the life of her work it out. She definitely didn't remember agreeing to go anywhere this evening. 'Thanks,' she said at last then, 'Does Brad know that guy has his guitar?'

Odette shrugged. 'Brad was here when we arrived, but he disappeared into his room. He left his guitar so—'

'Yeah, but surely someone should ask before they play it?'

'I don't think he'd mind?' Odette said, the last part raised in an inflexion which suggested she hadn't considered this possibility before. 'We asked him to keep playing, but he is very private about it. He seemed almost angry when we turned up.'

'Oh. So, you waited for me?' she prompted, changing the subject.

'Well of course! We couldn't go to Pigalle without taking you, after you said you'd never been!' Odette said, laughing. 'Now go change.'

Bella suddenly realised that her attire was very different from that of the others in the kitchen. The women – girls – were dressed in short dresses made of shiny material, the men – boys – in jeans and shirts that were fitted and open-necked. She glanced at her own plain work outfit and realised that she looked like their chaperone rather than a friend.

'Oh, tonight?' she said, thinking longingly of the bath and the fact that when the house emptied it would be so very wonderfully quiet. 'I think I might prefer to—'

'Nonsense!' Odette interrupted. 'You will love it.' She

grabbed Bella's hand. 'Come on, I will lend you something. We are only young once, after all.'

Bella allowed herself to be taken along the corridor to Odette's room. Odette disappeared inside, and Bella made to follow her, only to have the door – abruptly – closed in her face. She stood back, surprised, and was about to knock and say something when Odette emerged, smiling, with a black dress edged with sequins. It was made of some sort of silky material. While beautiful, it wasn't something Bella would usually consider wearing.

'Put it on,' Odette commanded.

'I honestly don't mind not going,' Bella said. But she obediently made her way up to her room. Inside, she slipped off her day wear and pulled the dress over her head. Odette followed her in, unfazed by her near nudity. 'Wow, you look great!'

'It's been quite a day at work, and they want me in early tomorrow so—' Bella continued.

'Pah! What does it matter?' Odette asked. 'They don't own your soul, just a few of your hours. You are interning, not running the place!'

Bella was about to protest, when Odette spun her around towards a full-length mirror propped against the wall. Seeing herself, Bella gasped. Gone was the corporate, efficient, possibly forty-year-old businesswoman, and in her place was a young woman who looked vibrant, confident. Ready for a night out.

She resisted the urge to tug at the hem of the dress to make it a bit longer and instead turned to Odette. 'You really think I can get away with this? It's quite short?'

Odette scoffed. 'It is perfect for you. Now, come.'

Something about seeing herself on the cusp of a night out, being pulled along by a new friend. Something about the comradery of the group in the kitchen and the fact that they'd waited for her – as if she actually mattered to their night out – drove Bella forward.

Her fatigue lifted slightly by the time they piled into a couple of Ubers and asked to be taken to Pigalle. 'What's at Pigalle again?' she asked Odette who was squeezed next to her on the seat.

'Oh, you will see,' her friend grinned. 'You will soon see.'

After half an hour, the taxis pulled up at the entrance to a cobbled alleyway behind a busy street full of people dressed to the nines heading out for the night, and sombrely dressed workers heading home. Bella's eye was caught by the vibrant red of a windmill attached to a building, so lit up it seemed like a beacon. 'Is that the Moulin Rouge?' she asked, and Odette looked at her and laughed.

'Have you not been to Paris before?' she joked.

'Not this area.' Bella wondered why she and Pete had never made the regular trips to Paris they'd thought they might on moving to France. The city had only been a few hours away on the train, but running the business and paying the overheads had meant that both free time and money had been in short supply.

They exited the Ubers and the group of them walked towards a rather shabby-looking building and joined a queue. Things moved fast and soon they were in, twenty euros poorer and a drink in hand, and in a completely different Paris from anything she'd imagined.

The club was packed, people drinking and talking and dancing. Couples and groups crowded the dance floor, arms in the air, lost in the music. There was a raised platform where a DJ was mixing tracks, something Bella didn't recognise, with a thumping tempo that seemed to reverberate through her whole body.

She felt herself swept up into the pulse of the night, giving into her body's urge to move and surrender to the beat. She knew from experience that she wasn't a good dancer but somehow, being on this packed floor with nobody really paying attention, she was able to find some sort of rhythm. She sang along to the odd lyric she recognised, took a swig from her plastic cup and, for once, felt completely part of things as she moved – Henri to one side of her, Odette to the other, completely given in to the important task of having a bloody good time.

And despite her worries about Henri, as he moved closer and leant down to kiss her, she found herself kissing him back. He smelled of aniseed and cigarettes and some sort of spice – a weirdly exotic, intoxicating mix – and his kiss sent shivers of electricity through her. It was the proximity of him, the lights, the sound, but also the feeling of being desired.

Intimacy had begun to fizzle out between her and Pete a couple of years ago and although they'd enjoyed cuddles on the sofa, the passion had definitely gone. 'It's what happens in a marriage,' Kitty had said when she'd mentioned it. 'It's a natural part of settling down.'

Bella had accepted this, and over time had learned not to miss the passion that had come at the start of their relationship. But with Henri, her body was responding in ways she'd forgotten it could; and she wondered how she'd let that part of her go, allowing it to slip away almost unnoticed.

But suddenly there was dizziness, a feeling of disorientation. Smiling faces seemed to leer, bodies dancing close felt suffocating. The music started pounding, the lights were a blur of nightmarish colour. She pushed past Henri and rushed for the stairs.

* * *

The air was unseasonably chilly when she exited onto the street, Henri behind her, but felt fresh; welcome. She breathed deeply and leant against the wall until her head stopped spinning.

'Are you OK?' he asked, concerned.

'Yes. I think so. Just... tired, I think. Bit too much to drink.' She smiled at him, still feeling slightly wobbly. Now, in the alley which smelled unpleasant but at least was out in the open, she felt a little better. She checked her watch: midnight. 'I think I'd better go home.'

Henri nodded, his eyes still concerned. 'Will you be OK?'

'Yeah, I think so.'

'OK,' he leant in and kissed her lightly. 'See you later.'

'See me— What?'

He had already turned and was disappearing into the club, leaving her feeling wobbly and a little annoyed. Surely he should at least have seen her to a car? He hadn't thought to see her home, let alone go home with her.

There was nothing else for it but to get herself a taxi. She straightened her shoulders and made her way to the main road, tapping in her phone to request an Uber and telling herself that it was fine – Henri had left her because he knew she was more than capable.

Despite this, when she finally and gratefully slipped into the back of the car, she felt a little tearful. And for the first time in a long time, she found herself wondering what Pete was doing. Then she thought of Kitty and how after a night out they'd used to sit in the kitchen with a cup of tea and put the world to rights. And of Juliette, who had always been nearby if she'd needed her.

These people, even Pete, felt like home in a way her friends in Versailles still didn't. And she had a longing for her own place, for being herself, for feeling on solid ground rather than out of her depth. She turned her head to look at the streets as they travelled so that the driver wouldn't notice her tears.

27

NOW

The alarm on her phone made her gasp awake, and she was tempted to throw the thing out of the window. Instead, she sat up, let her heart rate return to normal levels then, with a groan, slid her legs out from beneath the duvet and wobbled to her feet.

After showering she stood in a towel and opened her wardrobe, then made a face at the contents, wondering what Madame Roux would make of them. Hanging, still with its tag, was a silk blouse she'd bought on a recent shopping trip, and a fitted pair of black trousers. She'd avoided the blouse so far – it was scarlet and every time she'd put it on, she'd worried she looked too bright. But she was behind on her washing so it was the last piece of office-ready clothing she had. And perhaps Madame Roux was right – maybe she should be bold.

She slipped it on and looked at herself. If anything, the vibrant material made her skin look paler, more washed out. She added a slick of red lipstick to see if she could create some balance. It helped a bit.

But no. She looked too... obvious. Too noticeable.

Sighing, she grabbed her white blouse from the laundry basket. It would do for today.

Henri hadn't made it back to her bed last night and in all honesty she was relieved. She'd felt a mixture of sadness and anger at his abandonment last night, and might well have had a go at him. Today she felt more Zen. She'd worried that he was getting too serious. Well, here was the proof that she didn't matter that much to him. It had felt bad, but it was actually a good thing.

Anyway, there was no time to muse about her love life. Buttoning up the last of the delicate silver buttons on the front of the blouse, she grabbed her handbag and made her way to the kitchen for a coffee.

There was no Brad this morning to brew her a cup, and she was surprised to feel a little disappointed. Still, she spooned some of Henri's expensive brand into the cafetière and poured hot water over the grounds, watching them dance and settle in the water as it turned from clear to deep and dark. Then she pushed down the plunger, watching the grounds gather together in a black solid clump at the bottom of the pot, leaving rich brown coffee above. Sighing as the rich aroma drifted up to meet her, she reached for a large mug and poured herself a generous serving.

As she lifted it to her lips, her hand jerked slightly and a little coffee leapt out of the top of the mug and splashed onto the floor – missing her white blouse by an inch. Thank God, she thought – that could have been a disaster.

Then her phone rang. The sound was so shrill and unexpected that she jerked her arm, sending half a cup of boiling coffee onto her chest. With a sound that was somewhere between a gasp and a scream, she ripped the blouse from her body and rushed to the sink to splash cold water over herself.

Thankfully, other than a reddish patch on her skin, she was unharmed. Sighing, and damp, she stood for a moment, arms stretched out against the sink, dropping her head to her chest.

A great start to the day.

The blouse was ruined and now she'd have to fish something out of the dirty laundry to wear to work, or brave that bright red beacon of a blouse.

She was just making her way to the stairs, hoping not to bump into anyone in her slightly stained bra, when she thought of asking Odette. Her friend seemed to have an endless supply of clothing and was always offering Bella the chance to try stuff. She made her way to Odette's door and lifted her hand to knock.

But it was early. She checked her watch: only seven o'clock. And Odette still hadn't been home when Bella had finally made it to bed around 2 a.m. last night. She tried the handle and, finding the room unlocked, decided to sneak in rather than wake her.

She'd explain everything later. Or simply wash and return whatever she borrowed. Odette seemed particularly conscious of her privacy and hadn't let her through her door so far, but Bella wouldn't pry, she'd simply make her way to the wardrobe, choose something quickly and scuttle off to work. Surely Odette wouldn't mind that?

She pushed the door open and stepped inside. It was darker in here than the hallway; curtains hung at the windows and although the light was shining through them, it was muted, throwing the room into a kind of dusky half-light. Eyes still adjusting, Bella started to take in her surroundings. And as she did, something in her tensed up, as if she'd stumbled across a crime scene or been caught with her hand in the cookie jar.

Because something was wrong. Odette was sleeping in a bed

in the corner, her arms thrown across the pillow, snoring lightly. But how she even got to her bed was a mystery. Every last space in this room was covered. An easel stood near the bed, with a palette stained with blobs of dried paint. A few brushes were next to it in a jar.

Next to these, a toolbox full of artist materials spewed pencils and pens and rubbers across the floor. But these were all things she might have expected to see in an artist's room.

What she hadn't expected was that, aside from a few piles of clothes – clean and dirty – and the occasional bag, trinket or photograph, every inch of the place was taken up by canvases. Propped together against walls, laid out on a table to dry, stacked on the floor.

From what Bella could see, all the visible canvases were finished. And actually, utterly beautiful: scenes she recognised from Versailles; the palace, milling tourists, a couple sipping coffee at the café down the street from here. But rather than filling her with joy, the sight of piles of paintings and materials, the sheer volume of it all, made Bella shiver. Why was Odette living like this? Why so many canvases piled up as if they were rubbish? And why didn't she want anyone to see them?

She'd talk to her later, she resolved, and stepped forward towards the wardrobe which she hoped would not be filled with paint pots and art paper, but with tops suitable for someone high up in hotel management. Only in the half-light, it was hard to avoid hazards, especially as there were so many. As she moved, her foot came into contact with a jar being used to soak some dirty brushes. It wobbled teasingly before falling over and spilling its contents across the corner of a canvas.

'Damn!' Bella grabbed some rags and tried to soak up as much as she could. The liquid was some sort of chemical and the fumes stung her eyes, lodged in the back of her throat. Her feeble attempts with the rag were not soaking up as much as she'd have liked. And she was nowhere nearer having anything to wear to work today.

It was only when she heard a gasp that she realised Odette had woken. Not only woken but was standing by the bed, a look of horror on her face. She was wearing an enormous T-shirt which swamped her tiny frame, her hair was in disarray and her mouth an oval. 'What are you doing in my room?' she cried, her voice sounding deeper, angrier than Bella had ever heard it.

'I'm so sorry. I ruined my top, and I know you have—' Bella straightened then, aware that she was standing there in her bra and trousers, and covered her front with the chemical-soaked rag.

'You came to take my things?'

'No! No. Of course not! Well... I was just going to borrow something. You've been so generous with your clothes, and I thought you wouldn't mind. I didn't want to wake you and...'

'You came into my room!'

'Well. Yes.' There didn't seem to be much point in denying this obvious fact.

'And you know that I hate people doing this!'

'I'm sorry. I thought you were just—'

'Just *what*?' Odette's eyes narrowed.

Bella took a breath. 'I thought you were probably just a bit messy. That maybe you didn't want me to see your room because you were embarrassed. I didn't realise—' She gestured vaguely at the stacked canvases, the pure chaos with which Odette had surrounded herself.

Odette took a step forward. Despite her tiny frame, Bella found herself trying to step back. But there was a pile of canvases behind her: she was trapped.

'You didn't realise *what*?' Odette's voice was louder than

before, her eyes flashing. 'That I am mad? That I live in a room full of pictures that nobody wants? That I am not messy but crazy?'

'No. No! Not at all.' Bella waved her hands in a gesture of surrender. 'Just—'

Odette took another step and for a moment Bella worried that her housemate was going to lunge forward and hit her. But then, as if someone had clicked a switch, Odette's shoulders slumped, and the life seemed to drain out of her. 'Well,' she said. 'Now you know my secret. I can paint, I can produce work. But I cannot let people see it. I cannot bring myself to show anyone.'

'I don't understand. They're beautiful, you should—'

Odette looked at her, her eyes dull. 'Yes, perhaps. But are they good enough for a Parisian gallery? Curators, they can be very exacting. I cannot bear—'

'They're—'

Odette's expression seemed to harden. 'What do you know of art? And in any case, you should not have come into my room. Perhaps you think I am strange, that I am living strangely. But you had no right.' It was hard to tell whether the moisture shining in Odette's eyes was the result of sadness or anger.

'I'm sorry. I'm really sorry.'

Odette sat on the floor, folding herself seamlessly into a cross-legged position like a child in a school assembly. 'Just go. Please.'

'But you're not— We can talk... and—'

'No. Please. Please just go.'

Bella looked at Odette, at her little crumpled form, and felt a strong urge to go over and hug her. But instead, she nodded. 'OK,' she said. 'Sorry.'

Odette shrugged as if it no longer mattered.

'I really am,' Bella added as she reached the door and turned. 'And you know, if you need some help with... with this, or just someone to talk to, I'm here.'

Odette nodded almost imperceptibly.

There was nothing else for it but to leave. Bella twisted the handle and let herself into the cool hallway. For a moment, she rested her back on the door, head looking to the heavens, wondering if she should go back in; should talk more.

In the end, instead, she climbed the stairs and steeling herself, slipped into the scarlet blouse.

Feeling a little shaken up from an unexpected early morning argument, she decided to pop into Henri's room for a little sleepy sympathy before she left for work – and maybe an opinion on her attire. She knocked lightly on the door, then, not waiting for a response, turned the handle.

Inside, in the half-light, she could just make out a tousled duvet, a pillow on the floor. His leg sticking out on the left-hand side. She traced the outline of his body then gently lifted the duvet from his sleeping face. 'Wakey-wakey!' she said.

Only it wasn't Henri under the duvet. Instead, she saw the face of a sleeping woman, the remnants of lipstick still smudged across her face.

She let the duvet fall back into place and, without a sound, turned from the room.

28

2016, FRANCE

'It's Dad.' Kitty handed Bella the phone.

The pair of them exchanged a long, knowing look before Bella finally put the handset to her ear. 'Hi, Dad,' she said.

'How's my bride-to-be?'

'Yeah, I'm good. Thanks. Nervous.'

'It'll be great.'

A silence bloomed between them, filling the gaps where the conversation should have been. 'So,' Bella said at last, her stomach contracting. 'All ready for the flight?'

'Yeah, about that, sweetheart.' Her dad's voice was heavy with awkwardness. 'I'm not going to be able to make it, I'm afraid.'

'Dad, it's my wedding!'

'I know. I know, honey. And I want to be there, believe me I do. It's just things are a bit hectic here. You know how it is.'

'But it's my wedding... I know things are— I realise you have a lot going on there, but you said you'd be here, Dad. I mean we booked the tickets six months ago. And you know I said Linda and the boys were welcome too.'

'I know. It's just a bit too much. Tom's got flu and Linda can't take any more time off. Come on, you'll have all your friends there, all of Pete's family. You won't even notice I'm not there.'

'I will. Of course I will.'

'Now, Bella,' he said, his voice firmer. 'You're all grown up now. You have to understand that Tom and Lucas, they're just little. They have to be my priority. You don't need your dad there to have a great day. And I'll come visit you later in the year maybe, if we can figure out the time off work.'

She was silent.

'Bella? I've put some money across into your account. Buy yourself something pretty for the day. And I'd love to see some pictures, you know? I'm sure you'll look beautiful.'

'OK,' she managed.

'Atta girl. Now I'd better let you get on with preparing for the big day!' he said, his voice generous and jovial again.

'OK.'

'So, bye then!'

'Bye, Dad.'

As she hung up, Bella's eyes met her sister's and saw they were full of rage.

'He promised he'd come,' Kitty said.

'It's OK.'

'No, it's not. You know it's not.'

'I guess he's right. I suppose we're grown up now. We should stop— We don't need him like we used to.'

Kitty shook her head. 'I tell you what, when I have kids—' She didn't finish the sentence. But Bella knew. She reached forward and squeezed her hand.

'Same.'

29

NOW

Somehow, she'd made it to the train, but she was still filled with indignant adrenaline, her hands shaking.

So she'd left him alone for what – an hour? – in the club and he'd managed to pull someone else. And he'd had the audacity to bring her home. Bella's horror at what she'd seen had given way to sadness, but even that had very soon been jostled aside by anger.

'Good night?' she texted him pointedly, then slipped her phone back into her bag.

She stepped off the train into the May sunshine, feeling the warm rays caress her skin; she loved this time of year when the spring weather brought with it the possibility of summer. But today it was as if the sun was mocking her. Far too upbeat and jaunty for her liking.

Reaching Hôtel Benjamin, she pushed open the glass door and said a cheery hello to Mélodie, before pressing the button for the lift. As she waited, she felt a sudden presence at her side and glancing over, realised that Madame Roux was standing beside her, Coco waiting patiently on a lead at her feet.

The old woman had excelled herself today – was dressed in a buttercup-yellow suit, with matching shoes. No hat, but her hair was tied up in a yellow scarf. The only thing about her that wasn't all sunshine and happiness was her face, which remained pinched; her eyes darting and sharp.

'*Bonjour*, Madame Roux,' Bella said, trying to smile.

Madame Roux nodded and as the lift doors opened, stepped in first, leaving Bella to slip through the doors before they closed, with no offer of holding them open.

A silence descended over them as the lift doors whirred. But next to her, Bella felt Madame Roux turn, sensed that she was being looked at with sharp eyes. 'Better,' Madame Roux said at last.

'Sorry, what?'

'Better.' Madame Roux nodded sharply in the direction of Bella's blouse. 'The colour. It brings out your eyes.'

'Oh! Thank you. Actually, it's been in my wardrobe for a few weeks, but I haven't felt brave enough to wear it!'

Madame Roux snorted. 'But you were brave enough to leave the house looking like a rag doll?' she asked. 'I do not understand this. What about looking good requires one to be brave?'

She had a point, Bella supposed. Although she wasn't too flattered by the rag doll analogy.

'I'm not sure,' she said, at last. 'I suppose I just don't like attention.'

This also seemed to confuse Madame Roux. 'You are in the prime of life!' she said. 'If you do not make the most of yourself now, then when? When you are old like me? No. You must express yourself however you want.'

'Thank you.'

The old woman nodded almost curtly, as if to signal the end of the conversation.

On the second floor, the doors slid open and Madame Roux hobbled out, Coco at her heels. They began to whirr back into place, but suddenly the old woman put out a foot adorned in bright yellow leather and stopped them.

'You know,' she said, looking at Bella with interest, 'not many people listen to me. Not since I—' she shrugged, unable to put what she meant into words. 'But you did!'

'Yes,' said Bella, too embarrassed to admit the blouse was more a result of spilled coffee and late laundry.

'I wasn't always old, invisible. Did you know that when I was young, I used to work for Gaultier?'

'Jean-Paul Gaultier?' Bella said, impressed.

'Do you know any other Gaultiers?'

'Well, no. Wow. That's amazing.'

'Yes, perhaps. My point is that I know one or two things about fashion. And colour. And hotels, for that matter.'

'Oh, yes. Of course.'

'In my heyday, I would travel often to shows. And I have stayed in many, many hotels. Some were terrible, but others were fabulous. And I learned to recognise the difference.'

'Right.' Bella nodded.

Madame Roux looked amused. 'And you do not want to know what I think of the hotel?'

'Oh. Well, yes. I do. Please.' Bella said, flustered.

'It is plain,' the old woman said, spitting out the word as if it were the worst possible insult.

'Oh.'

Madame Roux raised an eyebrow. 'It is not just people who need to be well dressed,' she said, letting the door slide shut.

When they slid open again Bella was on the fourth floor. She walked to her office, bemused, Yves at her side. 'You look different today,' he said.

'Thank you.'

'New hair?'

'Something like that.'

Bella couldn't get her mind off Madame Roux's words. *Was the hotel plain?* Was plain bad? She knew from her own experience that she liked neat, clean hotel rooms when she stayed away. Nothing dust-gathering or historical or overly ornate.

But what were the people going to Hotel Club hotels looking for? Something bijou or quirky or individual. Something with that little bit extra.

It was silly. How could a conversation about a blouse unnerve her? Still, she couldn't shake the feeling that something wasn't right.

This wasn't helped when, the moment she reached her office, Claudine appeared looking pinched and pale.

'Hi, Claudine, everything all right?' she asked.

'Let's sit,' her boss said. She perched on the chair in the corner, so Bella walked around the desk and sat in her usual chair.

'So, are you satisfied with the preparations?' Claudine asked her, head askance.

'Yes. Oh, definitely,' Bella said, trying to keep her voice upbeat. 'Let's see. We have the brochures ready, caterers booked. I've kept the Superior rooms free for the two delegates. Fresh flowers in all of the rooms, and a huge display for reception. Oh, and I'm working on the welcome trays, but I think you'll be pleased.'

Claudine nodded. 'That's good. Only I spoke to my friend – she's in the industry; her hotel has the status – and she asked me what our theme was. The USP that Hotel Club will be looking for. And I realized you hadn't yet discussed this with me.'

'Oh.'

'You have a theme, of course?'

'I...' Bella felt something inside her flip over. 'Of course! I'm — I'm just working on a few... uh, extra touches. Shall we, um, schedule a meeting to go through the more detailed plans?'

'Excellent, excellent,' Claudine said, clapping her hands. 'I knew you would have it all under control.'

Moments later, she left, and Bella finally let her face fall. She was tempted to get up, race after Claudine and tell her the truth. That she simply wasn't up to the job. She hadn't even thought to build in a theme, and Claudine's confidence in her had meant she hadn't questioned any of the progress so far. And now, she had no idea how to proceed. She should tell her, then leave. Walk away.

But if she did leave, what would Claudine do with just a month to go? There was no way she'd be able to engage someone else and get them up to speed. No. Bella would have to find a way to make things work, put together some ideas for tomorrow, ones that could be actioned in a tight time frame.

She put her head on her desk and groaned. Because she suddenly knew why she'd been feeling so uneasy. At first, her entire goal had been to keep up the pretence, to be 'Isabella', the highly qualified manager whom Claudine thought she'd employed. And she'd felt all the while that if things went wrong, she could just cut and run.

But things had changed. In the almost two months she'd been there, Claudine had become a friend. The people here – she'd begun to care about them. And she realised, suddenly, the enormity of the task that lay ahead. And how much it mattered.

30

NOW

What she'd want to do ordinarily was go home and let Henri wrap his arms around her, make all the worry and stress go away. Only after this morning she would be going home to either his confessing and breaking up with her, or her accusing him of having an affair.

She stayed late at the office in the hope that he'd be out and she could put things off until tomorrow. This morning she'd been fizzing with anger, but now she was simply exhausted.

But when she arrived home, she pushed open the front door only to find him inside, waiting for her. 'My love!' he said, opening his arms. 'I did not see you since last night. I hope that you got home OK?'

It was so, so tempting to just fall into those arms, just for now. But she held firm. 'You didn't seem too concerned this morning,' she said in a tone she hoped sounded icy.

He looked confused. 'We spoke this morning?'

'No. But I came in to see you. And I saw that you weren't alone.'

He nodded now, his face uncertain. 'You saw—?'

'I saw... her. In bed. With you.'

He flinched. 'Oh. But Bella, she meant nothing. I was drunk. She was from the club. I was going to tell you of course.'

'Were you?'

'You should have woken me! Spoken to me! I could have explained!'

'Henri, there was another woman in your bed.'

He nodded as if waiting for her to finish the sentence.

'Naked!'

Another nod.

'I caught you. In the act! Well, not in the act itself but you know what I mean. After the act. The act was definitely involved at some point.'

He looked confused. 'The act?'

She felt her temperature begin to rise. Was he actually serious? 'You had sex with another woman. How could you have explained that?'

He reached for her, but she flinched. 'Bella, please. It was a mistake of course. I was very drunk. It was a moment of madness!'

'How could you do that to me?' she asked, her voice suddenly small.

'*Ma chérie*, I didn't realise you would be so hurt,' he said. 'Please, let me make it up to you.'

'I'm not sure you—'

But he bent down and kissed her softly on the lips. 'I have to go. But I will make things right, I promise.' He kissed her again softly before opening the door and disappearing into the bright evening air.

'But—' she was left saying. 'But—' Then, 'Aaargh.' She stamped her foot and let out a cry of frustration. Had he really been so blasé about it? And why had she let him kiss her after what he'd done?

Odette's door opened and her friend poked her head through the gap. She looked at Bella, her brow furrowed. 'Did you scream?' Her voice sounded concerned, but there was a flatness to it, a remnant of this morning's anger.

'No, it's just—' She paused. 'Well, this morning Henri was in bed with a woman.'

'Oh!'

'Naked!'

'Ah, he is thoughtless. I am sorry.'

'More than thoughtless. He cheated on me.' Bella felt unexpected tears well.

Odette tilted her head. 'I am sorry, you seem very upset. I didn't realise that you and Henri were serious?'

'Well, we're not... but...'

'So you didn't agree to be faithful just to each other?' Odette looked confused. 'Perhaps it is an English thing,' Odette said. 'But to me, this does not sound too serious. Not when you are so newly together.'

'Really?'

'Yes. Maybe the English are more old-fashioned. Like the old days when the woman and man must be faithful to each other and do not sleep with other people from the beginning.'

In Bella's mind, the words 'old days' meant last century, or the 1800s where the most sex people seemed to indulge in – if you believed Jane Austen – was rubbing up against each other at an organised dance. Not— Was Odette calling the noughties 'the old days'?

'Perhaps it was a misunderstanding.'

'He is still a shit for bringing her here,' Odette offered.

Bella found herself smiling, momentarily. 'I feel so lost

sometimes,' she admitted. 'I suppose I made assumptions. I'll talk to him.'

Odette looked at her strangely. 'So you are all right?'

Bella nodded.

Odette withdrew her head from the gap, shutting the door with a click, leaving Bella more confused than she had been before.

She hated the idea of anyone she was dating seeing other people too – and couldn't imagine ever having the energy to do so herself. But maybe if she was going to start seeing people again, she'd have to get up to speed with modern dating norms in France.

In the kitchen, she grabbed a sandwich and a cup of almost ridiculously strong tea, then took them upstairs. She was exhausted and some time alone, followed by an early night, would be exactly what the doctor ordered.

* * *

She couldn't sleep. Thoughts of Henri, and naked women, and Odette, and Madame Roux, and the Hotel Club representatives, and Claudine had been buzzing around her head since she laid it on the pillow.

1.45 a.m. In five hours, she'd be up again, getting ready for another day at work. And rather than the buzz she'd started to feel at the prospect of going in, she felt a vague sense of dread.

Sick of trying, she got up and went downstairs. Pushing open the door to the kitchen, she made her way to the cupboard and took out a tall glass, then walking over to the sink she ran the tap until the water ran cold and filled it up.

It was only when she turned, glass half drunk, that she realised she was not alone. Sitting at the table in the near darkness was a man, his face in shadow. In front of him, a bottle of what looked to be whisky and a half-empty glass.

She screamed, dropping her glass which shattered spectacularly on the terracotta tiles, sending shards of itself as far as each of the walls.

'Crap!' the man said, standing up. 'What in God's name—?' Brad.

'Sorry. Sorry.' She dropped into a crouch and began sweeping the glass into a pile with her hands.

'Stop!' he said, and his voice was so loud, so forceful that she froze. 'You'll cut yourself. Here.' He slid his hands gently under her arms and helped her into a standing position, then pulled another of the chairs out and guided her into it. Then, 'Right!' he said, and flicked on the light.

They both blinked like nocturnal creatures in an artificial environment. Then he took her hand in his and for a moment she thought he was going to lift it to his mouth in an old-fashioned greeting. But no, he was inspecting it for glass. Brushing off a couple of tiny pieces, he dropped it, satisfied. 'No damage done.'

'Thank you,' she said, her words feeling thick in her mouth. Her heart was still thundering from the shock of seeing someone sitting in the dark kitchen, the sound of her own scream and the crash of glass on tile. She started to stand. 'I'll get the dustpan and brush.'

'No. You stay there,' he said firmly. 'You're barefoot.' He reached into the cupboard under the sink and extracted the rather worn plastic ensemble, then, crouching, swept the glass shards into it, the brush becoming wet with water residue. Tipping it into the bin, he reached for a cloth and wiped the remaining water from the floor. 'There,' he said. 'Better.'

'You didn't have to do that, you know. It was my mess.'

He laughed. 'Feels more like it was my fault, scaring you like that. Again! Although,' he touched his chest, 'that scream scared the hell out of me!'

She made a face. 'Sorry.'

'Honestly, no need.' He slid back into a chair and looked at her, his blue eyes kind. 'It's probably the first time I've been up past eleven since I arrived.'

'Pretty much.' She smiled weakly.

'Can't sleep?'

She let out a short laugh. 'Not exactly.'

He poured a small measure of whisky into a glass and slid it towards her. 'Need one of these?'

She didn't, actually, but politeness forced her to thank him and take a small sip. Looking at her face, he chuckled softly.

'What?'

'Not a whisky fan, huh?'

'Oh.' She felt her skin prickle with embarrassment. 'Well, no. Not exactly.'

He took the glass back from where she'd set it on the table. 'Yeah, I figured when I saw your face.' He screwed up his eyes and turned down his mouth in imitation. She should probably have been insulted, but there was something so open, so non-judgemental about the way he was teasing her.

'Hey!' she said with mock indignation.

He shrugged and took a sip from the glass he'd given her. 'I'd do the same with Prosecco, if that helps. So what's up?'

'Ah nothing. Just stressed, I think.'

'You sure?'

'Yeah. Why?'

'It's just,' he touched his own face below the eyes, and ran a finger down his cheek, tracing an imaginary tear. 'You got that panda thing going on,' he explained.

'Oh!' She stood up and glanced in the glass of the door. Her reflection wavered, but she could make out the darkness around her eyes. 'You got me,' she said.

He laughed, but there was sympathy in the sound. 'Yeah?'

'Yeah.' She sighed. 'I'm shattered from work, I think. Just... hard not to think about it.'

'Amen to that,' he tilted the whisky glass slightly as if giving cheers then took another sip. 'These students don't know what's going to hit them in a few years, am I right?'

'Definitely.'

'Ah, can't help envying them that.'

'So, you're here for work?' she asked, changing the subject.

He made a face. 'Kinda taking a bit of time to think strategy.' He took another sip.

'God, I wish *I* had a strategy. If I'm honest, it's more like I'm drowning!' She grinned, but almost instantly felt the corners of her mouth waver. *Don't cry. Do Not Cry.*

'Yeah? How so? You're like an intern, right? You're not meant to know everything,' he said kindly.

She wanted to nod. Tell him she was being stupid. Play the 'I must just be hormonal' card to get him to back off. But she was so, so tired. And so, so sad. 'Not exactly,' she said.

'Hey,' he said, shifting his chair a little closer. 'You can tell me anything. Honestly. I can keep a secret.'

And somehow she managed to explain to this virtual stranger exactly what had gone on in her life. The misunderstandings that had occurred. The fact that she'd talked her way into a job that was way out of her league; that her money situation had made her feel obligated to play the part.

'And I'm not twenty-anything. I'm thirty-four,' she sobbed. 'I lied about that too, here. Because I needed to get somewhere cheap to live. I'm... I'm getting divorced, my business has closed.

I don't have anything. But at work, I'm like this executive. They think I'm an experienced hotel manager. They even think I own this place!' she said, gesturing around. 'But in reality, I'm renting a room, I haven't got any qualifications, I have no idea what I'm doing. And to top it all, Henri's sleeping with other women, but apparently I'm the one who's got a problem, because I mind.'

'OK, slow down, slow down.'

'Sorry.'

'Right,' he said, nudging a box of tissues towards her. 'I know this seems a lot. But none of it is unfixable, OK?'

'OK.'

'First things first, what's up with the job?' He seemed completely invested.

She wiped her eyes. 'Hotel Club,' she said. 'It's my job to get the hotel over the line and win accreditation. And I'm just going to fail.' And she explained about feeling out of her depth – the fact that, if she were honest, she'd probably fallen behind because she'd been going out too much. 'I don't want to fool them,' she said. 'I really thought I could do it. But now I... I guess Claudine, Yves, Madame Roux, they've become real people to me. I don't want to let them down. It feels more important than it did at the start.'

'And then I started seeing Henri – and I really like him. He's fun. But last night he brought someone else home. And apparently, it's what people do in France, so I'm not allowed to be mad.'

Brad's eyes widened and he nodded. 'Can I ask you something?'

'OK.'

'Are you sure Henri's right for you?' His eyes searched her face.

She shrugged. 'I don't know. I suppose in some ways he was just... there. And it's nice, isn't it, having someone.'

'But he cheated on you.'

'Apparently, it's not cheating.'

'Oh.'

'And do you need the job right now?'

'Well, yes and no. I need *a* job.'

'I guess my overall question is: do you need to be here?'

'Sorry, what?'

'Hear me out. You have family back home, right? Mom and dad? Siblings?'

'No mum. She... she died when I was sixteen. No dad really. But yes, I have Kitty. My sister. She's... she's great. Why?'

'It seems to me that you need to think about what you really want. I mean, this job, it doesn't sound like it's for you. Henri's a nice kid, but no offense, way too young for you. Why not go home for a bit? Figure out what you really want. You're young.'

'I'm thirty—'

'That is young.' He looked at her. 'Hell, I'm forty and I still haven't got it all figured out. Why not go easy on yourself. Take some time.'

She shook her head. 'I can't.'

He looked at her, as if waiting for her to finish.

'I just can't leave Claudine in the lurch. I want to fix things. And I can't leave France! Coming here was my dream. *Is* my dream. I've wanted this ever since I was a teenager. If I leave, I'll be giving up on a part of myself, you know? I want to make it work. I mean, haven't you ever had a dream?'

Brad made a noise somewhere between a laugh and an exhale. 'Sure. I wanted to play guitar when I was younger.'

'You *do* play guitar.'

'Yeah.' He looked at her. 'You ever see me play in front of anyone?'

'Not— I suppose not,' she said, thinking of the night they'd met. 'At least, not on purpose.'

'Exactly. Because I can't.'

It was her turn to look at him, confused.

'Oh, I know I seem confident and the whole thing seems stupid. But as a kid, for years it's all I wanted to do. And then, I don't know. I got a big chance, at a festival. Me and a couple of others. And I just froze.'

'Oh.'

'I thought maybe it was a one-off. Only after that, I couldn't even play in front of my friends, let alone strangers.' He shrugged. 'Twenty years ago, and I'm still chicken.'

'But can't you—'

'Ah, it don't matter,' he said. 'I've got the businesses now. It's fine. I can play for myself. It's cool. But yeah, I get it. I get having a dream.'

Brad sat back, leaning on two legs of the chair in a way that would have driven Bella's mother mad, took a thoughtful sip of whisky. Then, just when she was about to excuse herself and scuttle off – embarrassed that she'd bared her soul and wondering how she was going to continue to live with someone who now knew what an utter fraud she was – he pitched himself forward, the front legs of the chair clicking against the tiles.

'Got it,' he said.

'Got what?'

He set his glass down. 'Look, I know what it's like out there. It's a fucking jungle.'

'It is?'

'Are you kidding me? It's impossible to get a job, let alone a good one right now. Whenever I recruited anyone, I'd get like fifty applications for each role. And these are shitty roles. People just want to be given a chance.' He looked at her, his blue eyes filled with something she couldn't read. 'You know?'

She nodded.

'And most people like me – people who own companies or whatever – we're usually only where we are because of luck. Tons of hard work too, right? But you check anyone's back story and there's always this moment where someone gave them a break, or a shot. And that's the thing that opens the rest of the doors.' He took another sip and she watched silently. 'I was maybe twenty-five when I started this business. It was going OK. But then I got this goddamn tax bill. I was naïve; didn't realise how much I'd have to pay. My folks couldn't help. I was going to have to fold the whole thing up. Not that it was much back then anyways.'

He was staring off into the middle distance. 'Then this guy – he was an uncle of one of my friends, he'd trained me in baseball when I was about ten – he offered to lend me like ten grand. Not give me. Lend. And he saved me.'

She was nodding now. 'That was kind of him.'

'Yeah. And you know what the kindest part was? That he didn't *give* me the money. He was loaded. He wouldn't have missed it. But he lent it to me, made sure I agreed to pay it back. And then I knew...'

'Knew what?'

'That he believed I could do it. That I could clear my debt but then go on to make a success of things. I could make the money back. He felt confident and something in that— it changed everything for me.'

Bella wondered suddenly if he was going to offer her money. She started searching in her mind for ways in which to gently turn him down. In any case, what good would money do her? Yes, it would mean that if she quit her job she wouldn't be instantly destitute. But she wanted to fix things, not run.

'Maybe I can be that guy for you,' he said.

'I don't get it?'

'I'm a businessman, right? Businessperson. Whatever. I've done tons of hospitality things. I know the sector inside out – don't mean to boast.'

He smiled broadly, almost triumphant.

'I'm sorry. But… I'm not quite sure what you're saying.'

'Bella,' he said. 'I can help you. Get yourself off the Internet and start tapping into this thing.' He tapped the side of his head. 'It's got everything you need.'

'Oh. I couldn't…'

'You can. Look. You've got the goods. You're clever. And more than that, I can see – I know we've only just met, but honestly – that you want this. That you have that drive. That's rare nowadays. That passion. You just need someone who believes in you.' He prodded his chest with his thumb. 'And I'm it.'

31

NOW

'Where are you going?' Henri moaned, turning over and reaching for her.

She'd slept in her own bed again last night, not quite ready to completely forgive him. Then this morning, she'd woken early and crept into his room – half expecting he might have company. But he'd been alone. She'd sat on the edge of his bed. 'I have to go out,' she whispered. 'Work stuff.'

'But it's Saturday!' He sounded a little like a petulant child.

'Yes. But you know I have this important presentation coming up. I have to put in some extra hours.'

He groaned. 'I feel like I never see you.'

'I know,' she said, softening. 'We're like' – she lapsed into English, unable to find a suitable French saying – 'ships passing in the night?'

Henri lifted himself up on his elbows. 'Why would you say that?'

'It's an English saying. You know, that we don't see each other properly.'

'You English are strange,' he said. 'Why would you want to compare us to excrement?'

'What?'

'Yes, shits passing in the night. It is not very romantic, *n'est-ce pas?*'

'Not shits! Ships!' she said, 'like with a "p".'

'A pee? So we are piss and shit?' he said, confused. 'It is not very romantic to say that.'

'No, *ships*,' she said, half laughing, half frustrated. 'Like, boats!'

'Oh!' He was silent for a moment. 'So we pass each other but we do not meet.'

'Exactly.' She grinned.

'And nobody is going to flush us away?' He was grinning too now.

'We can only hope.'

They smiled at each other and she realised, despite finding him a bit frustrating at times, that she really did like Henri. He was cute; easy-going. She leant down and gave him a kiss on the forehead, and he grabbed hold of her arm. 'Stay with me. I am sorry for what I did.'

'I really can't. I'm sorry.'

He narrowed his eyes in mock annoyance. 'OK, but tell your boss if she makes you work too hard, I will hunt her down like a dog.'

She smiled. 'Yes. I'd expect nothing less. Although probably not at 7 a.m. on a Saturday?'

'*Non.* I keep my vengeance for the afternoons. You don't get to be as good-looking as me without beauty sleep.'

* * *

Brad was waiting when she came down the stairs, standing by the front door, his arms folded in front of him, looking up as she descended. It was like a low-budget version of a grand 'prom' entrance: he, the nervous date, she, the beauty, gliding down in her best gown.

Except, obviously, they were both dressed casually, there were no parents waiting expectantly to see them off. And of course this wasn't a date.

'Thanks for this,' she said in a near-whisper, not wanting to wake Odette.

'Pleasure.'

They walked the short distance to what Brad told her was his favourite Versailles café, a small, single-windowed building with a wooden door and window surround. Italic letters spelled out 'Café' across the wood, faded with age. It was quaint, albeit a little run-down.

'This looks nice,' she said.

He laughed. 'Don't worry, the coffee here is amazing, even if the place looks a bit... crappy. I used to come here when I was a kid with my grandmother, and the signage was exactly the same. The proprietor too, only he was younger back then, obviously.'

'You went for coffee as a kid?'

'They do milkshakes.'

'Fair enough.'

They sat at a corner table in the already quite busy space, filled with people who looked to be on their way to work in the service sector – dressed in uniforms of local hotels and restaurants. A pair of gendarmes sat near the window talking earnestly and sipping espresso. The room was filled with the rumble of quiet conversation and the gorgeous aroma of coffee and freshly baked bread.

Brad went to the counter as she sat and opened her laptop on the table. She noticed that, despite the fact this was a busy café, she was the only one who'd brought a device with her. One woman looked at her almost with admonishment as if her computer had no place in a café, and Bella quickly looked away.

When Brad returned with two large cups of black coffee, each with a tiny pastry nestling on the saucer, she had already pulled up her plans. He sat, placing her hot drink next to her carefully, then taking a sip from his own. 'Mmm.'

She also lifted her cup to her lips, the rich aroma meeting her before the beverage even made it to her mouth. It was rich and delicious. 'You're right,' she said. 'Great coffee.'

He nodded. 'Still do milkshakes too, but my gut can't take it these days.' He smacked his stomach. 'Anyway, enough of the small talk. Hit me with it.'

She laughed. 'I assume we're talking metaphorically?'

'Well, think I'd probably be more help without concussion,' he replied, 'but hey, go ahead if it'll help your stress levels.'

She pushed the laptop in front of him. 'Here's what I've done so far,' she said. 'But I didn't realise Claudine was expecting more. You know, creating a unified look for the hotel, a theme – I hadn't realised how important that was.'

'OK,' he read through the list, his tongue just visible at the edge of his lips as he concentrated. 'Right,' he said at last, pushing the laptop back towards her.

'Right?'

'It's OK.' He nodded. 'These things you've done, they're pretty cool.'

'Right? But?'

He looked at her. 'Well, I was having a look at Hotel Club stuff last night, after you went to bed. And I looked at your place too – it's pretty cute.'

'Thank you.'

'And you know, you might just make it. There's nothing wrong with it as far as I can see. Plus the home-baked goods – that's a great touch. Especially if they're anything like the ones I ate yesterday.'

'Last week.'

'What?'

'You ate my cookies last week.'

'Ah. Well, sorry. I also ate some yesterday.'

'Brad! Those were for the launch!' But she wasn't angry, not really. 'I was practising.'

'Sorry. They're just too good. And I guess they help.'

'Help with what? Your aim to develop diabetes before you're fifty?'

He gave a small, breathy laugh. 'Nah. Just... I guess I feel a bit down sometimes is all.'

'Oh.' It was hard to know what to say. 'Well, in that case, feel free.'

'Thanks.'

He pulled a tattered notebook from the inner pocket of his jacket. 'Anyway, I wrote down a few ideas – you know, quick fixes that you can turn around in a few weeks. Just things maybe I'd do in your position.' He shrugged as if it were no big deal.

She took the notebook from him, noticing the scribbled 'Lyrics' on the cover. 'You write songs?'

He shook his head. 'Not for a while.'

Bella read through his suggestions; they seemed obvious now, written in black and white, and she felt a little foolish she hadn't thought of them herself. New bedding, curtains, rugs for the rooms to knit the theme together. Some original art or sculpture, with a theme. Maybe a band or quartet for the party where she'd make her presentation, to play while the guests milled around. Her cakes (he'd drawn a smiley face next to this entry) and specialist coffees, mini cafetières for each of the rooms.

'So, like you say, each of the Hotel Club places seems to have something that draws them together. You need to find a theme, then we can create a showroom – something that really shows it off.'

'Maybe the theme could be Paris?'

He shook his head. 'Too dull. I mean, maybe if the hotel weren't in Paris, it would be kind of cute. But they have Paris already.'

'Yeah, I see what you mean. I'll have to think.' She looked at him. 'Thanks, though. This is great.'

'It's nothing, really.'

'It is to me. I was— just stuck, I guess. Panicked.'

'It's nothing you couldn't have come up with.'

'Maybe, but not under pressure. Seriously, I owe you big time.'

'Ah, just buy me another coffee,' he said, draining his cup.

'Brad...' she said.

'Sorry.' He held his hands up. 'I'll take an enormous cheque too. Or, you know. A snack.'

She went up to the counter and came back shortly with another coffee and a muffin.

'Will this cover your costs?' she joked.

He laughed, looking at the chocolate muffin in its dark brown paper. 'Ah, I think that'll just about do. Although I usually charge two muffins an hour.'

'Two muffins an hour!' she said, slipping into the chair opposite and lifting her own fresh coffee from the tray. 'Things really are expensive over here.'

The two hours they'd spent together had flown by.

It was only 10 a.m. but she already felt lighter than she had, as if she might be able to relax this weekend, safe in the knowledge that she would cope – maybe even thrive – on Monday. She took a bite out of her muffin – it was freshly baked and crumbled deliciously in her mouth. She let out an audible 'Mmm.'

'That good?'

'Yeah, just a bit.'

'You're not going to go all Meg Ryan on me?' He raised an eyebrow.

'It's not *that* good.'

There was an awkward moment in which they both pictured the famous scene from *When Harry Met Sally*.

Then, 'So what business are you actually in? I know you have premises here? Or offices? But I have no idea what you actually do,' she said.

He took a sip of his drink, regarding her over the top, then set it down as if suddenly the mug were heavier than it had been before. 'Ah,' he said. 'You got me there.'

'What do you mean?'

'Ah, nothing.' His shoulders slumped slightly and he let out a breath, looked at her. 'Look, I was going to give you the usual bullshit. But I guess we're all about truth here, right?'

She nodded.

'The others, they probably said I'm some sort of hotshot CEO, right?'

'Yeah, something like that.'

'Well, that was true once. Only things changed last year, and I never got around to... updating them.'

'Oh?'

'Yeah, so I moved permanently to France when I got

married, like fifteen years ago now. And I started up this little
café near the beach in Nice. It did OK. So I opened another.
Soon I had, like, five of these cafés. I was making some real
money too.'

'Right?'

'But then I started to do more. So I got a couple of little
restaurants, nothing fancy. And things kept building and building. I was getting more and more hands off, just organising
things. Overseeing it all, I guess. It was kinda dull, but kinda
exciting too because I was making good money. For a bit it was
like I had the golden touch or something.'

Bella waited for him to continue.

'But you know, I got kinda greedy too. I felt like I had something special. A good eye for business or whatever. So I began to
invest in different things. Then last year I ended up putting a
load of my money into this little start-up – two friends, nerdy
dudes, starting their own software company. I thought I'd be
able to retire once they launched their product.'

'But...?'

'But here I am!' He opened his arms as if illustrating. 'The
thing went bust and I lost thousands. Hundreds of thousands.'

The idea of losing so much made her go cold. 'What did
you do?'

'I had to sell the cafés, most of my property – I had quite a
good portfolio by then. Kept the Versailles house though,
because of my grandma. Closed everything else down.'

'Oh no!'

'It's OK,' he shrugged. 'I've got a couple of assets to tide me
over. I'm doing OK, I guess. Looking to start again. Hardly a
success story though.'

'But it's great you're picking yourself back up.'

He grabbed a packet of sugar, ripped it open and emptied

half into his coffee. 'I wouldn't say I've quite picked myself up yet.' His eyes had developed a sheen that threatened to become something more. He wiped a hand roughly across his face. 'Stupid fool. Split up with my wife too, did I tell you that?'

'Oh. No.'

'Yeah.'

'Well, if she split with you because of money then she's not wor—'

'Nah. It was before. A mutual thing. We'd kinda grown apart. Probably my fault. But you know, even though we both wanted it, it still made me feel kinda... rejected.'

She gave him a sympathetic smile.

'And I guess lonely?' He looked at her. 'That's why I came to Versailles. Ah, I know I don't exactly hang out with you guys, but it's nice knowing someone else is in the house.'

She nodded. 'I'm like that too. In Peyrat, you know, my old place. Sleeping there alone. It felt— I mean I'm more or less alone now too, but nearer people. It's nice. I get it.'

'You've got Henri, too.'

She made a face. 'I guess.'

'Can't get over the cheating?'

'Something like that.'

He tipped his cup to drink the last of his coffee. 'I'm not sure why I told you all that,' he admitted. 'It makes me look like a bit of a loser.'

'A loser? Have you *met* me?'

He smiled. 'I love that about you.'

'What?'

'That you're willing to say that stuff about yourself. I don't mean it's cool to run yourself down. I mean... I guess you're humble. So many of the people I've worked with, they're full of it, you know. They think they're Richard Branson or Jeff Bezos.

The next big thing. And they ain't got shit. And you...' He looked at her and she almost had to turn away. 'You've got the goods, Bella. But you're modest.'

She made a play of opening the tiny ginger biscuit in its individual packet on her saucer. 'It's not modesty. I genuinely mean what I say about being out of my depth. In fact, I *know* I am.'

Brad shook his head. 'But you're not. Nah, sorry to say. But you're the real deal.' She looked up and saw his blue eyes fixed on her, full of warmth and kindness. The intensity of it made her feel out of her depth in a whole new way.

'Brad,' she leant forward, lowering her voice in case they were overheard. 'I am literally only in my job because I exaggerated – lied even – on my CV. I have no idea what I'm doing.'

He reached up and tucked a stray hair behind her ear. There was something tender in the movement. His fingertips brushed her skin, and she felt a strange sense of recognition. As if her body had been somehow waiting for his touch. It was unlike anything she'd experienced before. As if they'd always known each other. No longer out of her depth; more of a feeling of coming home. She tried to concentrate.

'You can deflect all you like,' he said. 'But your ideas are pretty good. And you might not be... Isabella, corporate genius or whatever. But you did run your own place for eight years.'

She was momentarily silenced. Around them the café buzzed with noise, life, movement. But at their table, everything was quiet and still. 'You think?' she said at last.

'Bella, if I were running a hotel, well, I'd be headhunting you immediately!'

'As a cleaner?'

He laughed. 'Yeah, as a bathroom cleaner, obviously.'

'So, what are you going to do?' she asked at last. 'About your businesses, I mean? Get back into the café trade?'

He shrugged. 'Not sure yet. I've got a bit to live off. I need to think about what I want.'

'Sounds sensible.'

He looked at her, his blue eyes earnest. 'I guess I'm still not being completely honest. It's not just about what I want. It's about... well, you know how it is when you've been burnt by something.'

She nodded.

'See, when I made my investments before, I was young. Stupid maybe. Whatever it was stopped me from worrying about it too much. Now... well, I'm older. The stakes are higher. I don't want to lose again. Can't. So I kind of— I just can't work out where to start. And I'm not sure I've got it in me.' He flushed, cleared his throat.

'You'll get there.'

He looked out of the window. 'Anyway, there are worse places to lose your mind than Versailles, right? Fancy doing the tourist thing today?'

'The tourist thing?'

'Yeah. Ah, the others, they're used to this place. But for us foreigners, it's all new. Maybe we should forget hotels and divorces and lost investments and business chat and just go look at the palace. Pretend we're on holiday, you know?'

Bella thought of Henri back at home. They had vague plans for tonight, but she'd earmarked the day to catch up with work, thinking it might take hours. But they'd done all they could for now, and it would feel great to step away.

'Sure,' she said, draining the rest of her cup. 'Why not?'

32

NOW

'Oh man, we should never have come on a Saturday,' Brad moaned as they joined the long queue at the palace.

She laughed. 'Come on, it's not so bad. Anyway, I'm British. We love queuing.'

'Yeah, I never really understood that.'

'Me neither. I don't think any of us actually do, if that makes you feel any better. We just put up with it better than most.'

He grinned. 'Well, looks like you'll have to put up with it for quite a while today.'

He wasn't wrong. The popularity of the palace, particularly on a sunny Saturday, meant they waited for entry for over an hour. But finally they paid, and suddenly they were in a decadent building she'd only read about before.

Versailles Palace was even more astonishing than she'd imagined: there was so much gold – on statues, the cornices, edging the ceilings – that each room seemed to glow with decadence. She marvelled, looking up at the elaborately painted ceilings, almost stumbling as she took in the scene: angels and gods in brilliant blue skies depicting scenes of battle, or of royal dignitaries on elaborate thrones.

'Pretty impressive, right?' Brad said. 'No wonder they called him the king of kings.'

'Louis XIV?'

'Yeah. He liked things luxurious, right?'

'Just a bit.' She moved around a woman with a camera to avoid ruining her picture.

'You know a lot of this was just distraction,' he said.

'What was?'

'All this.' Brad waved his arm. 'Apparently he was distracting the nobles with luxury and God-knows-what, so he could get on with ruling France without them bothering him.'

She laughed. 'Pretty good strategy. Might try that sometime.'

'Ah, we all still do it to ourselves,' he said. 'You know. Distraction. Drinking, going out, late nights. It means we don't have to think about anything too much.'

Bella felt her neck prickle. 'Like I do, you mean?'

'Woah, no. Don't get me wrong. I was talking about me. Not so much going out these days, but I know I'm getting through a little too much whisky at the moment.'

'And me, on the wine,' she admitted. Was Brad right? Was the *going out and having fun* she'd been participating in more of a way of forgetting her reality? Probably.

He smiled. 'Still, must have been harder, right, in those days? No TV.'

She laughed. 'You should become a tour guide here.'

'Yeah?' He seemed genuinely complimented and she felt a little mean.

'Yeah, you know. Speculating on the lack of TV in the eighteenth century. How these days it'd be Netflix on the ceiling rather than paintings.'

'Very funny.'

They walked on, down the famous Hall of Mirrors which reflected so much light against the already sparkling decor that it was almost blinding. Bella saw her reflection as they passed; mirror after mirror, each one somehow reflecting a different version of her as the angle of the light changed. Isabella the executive, Bella the pretend student, Pete's wife, Henri's girlfriend. And someone else. Someone who looked happier than all of them – the way she felt today. When had she last taken a proper day off, she thought? Got away from it all?

'This has got to be my favourite room,' Brad remarked as they reached the end of the Hall.

'Why's that?'

'Ah, probably because the dudes in the pictures are all so goddam handsome.'

'They're mirrors... oh.' She grinned. 'Got to love your confidence. Have you been here many times before?'

'Oh God. Thousands, probably.' He shrugged. 'What can I say? They don't have anything like this in the States. It's all concrete and modernity. And my grandmother used to bring me here as a kid.'

'You don't get bored?'

He shook his head. 'Never. There's so much here. So much to look at.' He pointed at a painting. 'Like that fella. I mean, I know fashions have changed. But he's actually wearing white pantyhose and pumps.'

'That's the king,' she said, looking at the picture of King Louis in ceremonial robes spread decadently around him, his legs exposed in – yes, it did seem to be an ensemble of white tights and slightly heeled shoes.

'I know, right? I bet you're glad your British king doesn't go in for that sort of thing.'

She imagined King Charles making an appearance in enormous pantaloons, tights and heeled shoes, and let out a brief, barking laugh that reverberated around the high-ceilinged room, breaking through the buzz of chatter. Several people glanced in their direction.

Brad laughed. 'What was that?'

'A laugh. My laugh.'

He nodded. 'Interesting. Are you by any chance related to a farm animal?'

* * *

An hour later, they were in the café; an incongruous mixture of high ceilings and rich decor, with the rather ordinary café tables and counter, drinking coffee. Bella's feet hummed from standing and walking for such a long time, and she was grateful to give them a break from gravity.

Brad staggered over with a tray: he'd bought them two enormous sandwiches on French bread, alongside the coffee he'd promised.

She was about to say that she hadn't asked for any food; admonish him for spending his money when it was her who had a debt of gratitude to pay. But then her stomach grumbled loudly enough for them both to hear and she had to admit defeat: she was starving.

Biting into the baguette, her mouth was flooded with a sweet and savoury flavour – not the simple cheese she'd imagined. 'What is it?' she asked, her mouth full.

He looked at her. 'Did your mother never teach you table manners?' he said, shaking his head in mock reproach. Then, 'It's goat's cheese and honey.'

'Oh.' She swallowed. 'Oh. Wow. Well, it's nice. Weird, but nice.'

'Yeah.' He looked at his dubiously. 'I kind of panicked when I got to the front of the queue, and the other fillings seemed a bit boring, considering where we are.'

'What were they?'

'Cheese and ham. I mean, we're in a palace, right?'

'Right.' She took another bite. 'Well, this is nice. There're nuts in it too, right?'

'Yeah, I think it said walnuts.'

They chewed in silence for a minute or two, letting the hum of other people's conversation settle around them. Bella thought briefly about work – something that had dominated her thoughts every day for ages – and it was a shock to realise that it was the first time since they came out that she'd thought about it at all. Progress.

Her phone pinged with a message.

HENRI
Where are you?

BELLA
Just out. With Brad.

HENRI
OK. Still coming out later?

BELLA
Probably.

He gave a thumbs up and she wasn't sure whether that was a passive-aggressive move or not. Emojis seemed so loaded these days – apparently skulls were now a sign of humour and the droplets she texted to Kitty last time she went swimming were actually meant to symbolise some sort of bodily secretion.

Thinking of Kitty gave her the familiar pang of guilt. She would ring her as soon as she got home, she resolved.

'All OK?' Brad had abandoned his sandwich and was eating a piece of cheese he'd pulled from its centre.

'Yeah, sorry.' She turned her phone over to give him her full attention.

'Henri?' he asked. 'Need to head back?'

'No. He knows I'm busy.'

'Right. And you're on a date later?'

'Not sure. What about you?' she found herself asking. 'Are you dating anyone?' Her cheeks flushed as she heard the words aloud.

'Nah. Not right now. Need to take a bit of "me" time.'

'That sounds so sensible.'

'It does, don't it!' He grinned and rolled his eyes. 'If I'm honest it's not so much a decision but something that's happened. I've kinda forgotten how to do it.'

'Do what?' She raised her eyebrows suggestively.

They made brief, humorous eye contact and she was surprised to see his cheeks redden.

'Dating,' he said. 'Not, um, the other thing. I mean, the rules have all changed. Have you seen the dating app stuff?'

'No. Well, not really.'

'And there's all this— There's these rules,' he said. 'Like having a date, which is different from actually dating, then being official, and BF and GF and exclusive and... I mean, what happened to just going on a date and liking someone?'

'It is a minefield.'

'Definitely.'

'You know,' she said. 'I didn't feel at all old until I started to try to act younger than I am.'

Brad laughed.

'I mean it! There's nothing worse than realising you no longer understand how the world works.'

'How the world of Gen Z works, you mean.' Brad jabbed his thumb against his chest. 'I'm a proud Millennial like you.'

'Remember when we used to be seen as the complicated ones? The ones with all the newfangled ideas.'

He laughed again. 'Ah, those were the days, right?'

They finished their coffees and Brad returned their tray. Then they made their way out into the day again. It was two o'clock and the air felt hot after the cool of the palace rooms.

'Want to check out the gardens?' Brad asked.

She checked the time. 'Yeah, why not?'

Despite the heat, walking the orderly paths next to lush green bushes and plants was cooling – both the plants themselves and the shadows they cast gave relief from the intensity of the sun. She found herself breathing deeply – the air, still full of city scents, smelled cleaner here, fresher somehow.

'I think I like the garden better than the house,' she admitted. 'It's gorgeous, isn't it.'

'Yeah. That it is.'

'It's amazing really that all this is here. That you could walk ten minutes and be on city streets, take a bus ride and be in Paris. It's like someone has managed to bring the country into the city; I could imagine I was miles away from anywhere.'

He was looking at her. 'I like that,' he said. 'Like a reprieve from city living. An oasis.'

'That's it!' She grabbed his arm and he looked around, alarmed, as if worried about a possible ambush. 'The theme! I could bring the countryside to Hôtel Benjamin. Not the Paris theme – like you said, the guests are already in Paris. But something greener, bluer, more natural. Water, woods, wildlife. People could step through the door and feel like they've escaped all the noise and the dirt and the artificial light.'

He was still watching her face, nodding. 'I love it!' he said.

'Thank you.' She rummaged in her pocket and pulled out her phone. 'I'm just going to note it down before I forget it.'

'Good idea.' He was silent for a moment as she typed. Then, when she slipped her phone back into her pocket: 'You know, when you had that idea, you looked kinda—'

'What? Wild?'

'Nah. Kind of luminous. Like you were all lit up.'

She felt a prickle of embarrassment. 'Oh.'

'It was good. You know, you've been kinda sad recently. Not just when we spoke, but before. I noticed it. In your energy, I guess. But now...' He looked at her. 'I feel like I can see you, do you know what I mean?'

She looked at him; their eyes locked briefly. 'Yes,' she said. 'I think I do.'

* * *

Henri was on the sofa in the living room when she got back, scrolling on his phone. He was wearing black, but this time with the print of a band she didn't recognise on his T-shirt. He looked up at her and smiled. 'Hello.'

'Hi.' She felt suddenly shy as she sat down next to him.

'Did you have a good day?'

'Yeah. It was lovely actually.'

'And you are coming tonight? There is a new club and Odette—'

She shook her head. 'I don't think so.'

Henri looked confused. 'But it is Saturday,' he said as if this explained everything.

'I know,' she smiled. 'I'm just tired, I suppose. And... don't get me wrong, I like a drink, but I think I've been drowning my sorrows too much recently.'

He nodded. 'OK. You're not sick?'

'No. Just... old.'

He laughed. 'Now I know you are lying!'

She touched his hand, squeezed it. For a moment, they both looked down at their joined hands. There seemed to be something unspoken between them.

'Can I ask you something?'

'Of course.' Henri looked at her, his eyes bright, searching her face.

'Might you— Do you think you might bring someone back? You know, like before?'

'Do you want me to?'

'No! I mean, it's up to you, I suppose. I... guess that I'm just not that comfortable with the idea.'

He shifted towards her. 'You want that I become your boyfriend officially?'

She paused. 'I don't think so.'

'I'm sorry. I don't understand.' He looked at her. 'I feel as if you are saying goodbye.'

'Not goodbye exactly. I'm just— I suppose I think we want different things.'

'But we have so much fun!'

'We do. Most of the time.'

He looked at her. He was astonishingly good-looking. She was suddenly aware of his proximity. An image of their nights together flashed in her mind. But it was too complicated. There were too many lies. And although he was a nice person, she could see now that he wasn't the right person. Her person.

'Just— After what happened... I suppose it made me realise that we're not... not on the same page?'

'But when we make love...'

'Well, yeah.' She looked at him. 'But it's not enough, really. Not enough to— for a relationship.'

He made a face, perhaps considering this. 'Perhaps. But does it have to be a relationship? Can it not be two friends having fun?'

She shook her head. 'Maybe that's what you need right now,' she said softly. 'But I'm looking for something more than that. I'm—' She paused, looked at him. And thought, *if not now, when?* 'Like I said before, I'm a little bit older than you think I am.'

He frowned. 'What do you mean?'

She looked at her hands, there was a little chocolate powder wedged under her thumbnail and she brushed it against her jeans to try to dislodge it. 'Look, when I came, when I first arrived, I just wanted you guys to like me...'

She paused, looked up, saw his eyes were fixed on her, looked down again.

'I didn't— I didn't actually lie. I— but I let you believe that I was twenty-something and single when I'm actually— I'm thirty-four. And I'm sort of married.'

'You are married!' Henri looked horrified. 'And old!'

'Separated. And not old. Old-*ER*.'

'How old did you say again?' he said, looking her up and down as if suspecting she might whip out a walking stick or bus pass and admit to being his grandmother's age.

'Oh. Only thirty-four!'

'*Bon Dieu*,' Henri looked quite pale. 'I have been having an affair with a married woman. An *older* woman.'

'I just wanted—'

'But I do not understand how you could lie. How you could let me believe you were someone different?'

'It wasn't like that, it just sort of... happened. I did try to tell you. And Odette. You thought I was joking.'

'Still,' he shrugged huffily. 'I feel you could have tried harder.'

'Sorry.'

He sighed, shook his head. 'It is OK. I have had my heart broken before. I will survive.' He put his hand to his chest:

> *When you depart from me, sorrow abides and happiness takes his leave.*

She looked at him. 'Isn't that—'

'What?'

'Well, a teeny bit dramatic.'

He coloured. 'It was Shakespeare.'

'Oh.'

'Perhaps a little bit dramatic,' he admitted. 'But I think I could have loved you – maybe I did a little.'

'I know. Me too. But, I suppose, as they say, if you love someone, set them free.'

'Shakespeare?' he asked.

'Sting.'

'Bloody hell, you're alive!' Kitty said dramatically again on answering.

'Why do you always say that?'

'Oh, I don't know. Because sometimes you take so long to get back to me I think you're either dead or have been abducted by aliens or something.'

'Oh, come on, I haven't been that bad recently, have I?' Bella asked, making a face that her sister couldn't see.

'I think an average of two text messages a week has got to be classed as pretty poor communication,' her sister said. But there was a smile in her voice. 'It's good to hear from you.'

'Sorry for being crap.'

'What, recently? Or throughout your entire life?'

'Ha ha, very funny.' Bella wondered, actually, why she hadn't called Kitty much over the last couple of months. Just hearing her sister's voice was somehow reassuring, grounding. It had just been hectic, and confusing. And she wasn't sure which parts of her life would pass the 'Kitty test' and which would earn her big-sisterly disapproval.

'So. Tell me everything,' Kitty said, and there was a familiar creak as she sat down on her leather couch.

'Um. Well, it's all going OK,' Bella started, hesitantly.

'Work going well? What exactly is your job again?'

'Yeah,' she said carefully. 'Work is going well.'

'And what's the house like, now you've settled in? Getting to know your housemates a bit?'

Bella thought of Henri; the nights they'd spent twisted in his expensive Egyptian cotton sheets. The fact they now barely saw each other. She thought of Odette and her cluttered room, the confrontation which neither of them had mentioned since. And Brad, with his easy-going attitude and the fact that he'd sort of rescued her from a difficult predicament at work. And the feeling that she got when he was around that she couldn't quite explain. 'Yeah, they're fine,' she said at last.

There was silence on the line then Kitty said, 'You would tell me, wouldn't you, if you weren't OK?'

'Of course!'

'Because I worry about you; you know I do.'

'I know. But you needn't, Kitty. I'm actually fine. Better than fine, really.'

'Good. Well, good.'

'How are *you* anyway?'

There was a pause. 'Yeah, I'm OK. Ty's being a little rascal and refusing to sleep through the night, just when we thought we had that cracked, so we're trying to survive on a ridiculously small amount of sleep. But otherwise, yeah.'

Bella thought of her own broken nights, but she wasn't sure nights made short by clubbing, or sex, or worry that you're pretending to be someone you're not, quite compared to having to wake up for an infant. 'Hope it gets better.'

'Me too.'

There was another pause. The conversation was stilted and neither of them seemed to be able to find a way through. Bella racked her brain but there was nothing much she could say. In the end they finished the call, with Bella promising to catch up again midweek. Once the presentation was over and they'd got Hotel Club status, she would come clean – until then she couldn't face the fallout.

She lay back on her bed for a while, then seconds later had to jerk herself from the edge of sleep. If she didn't do something she'd fall back into slumber and lose half the day. And Sundays were precious things – not to be wasted. She had work to do, and washing, and she probably ought to get some food into the cupboards. *Well, Bella,* she thought to herself as she got up and pulled on yesterday's outfit, *you really are living the dream.*

* * *

The doorbell made her jump. She was in the kitchen, sipping a black coffee and scrolling the news on her phone when it happened, and for a moment she waited to see if anyone else would make the effort to answer it. It wouldn't be for her, obviously. Unless it was some sort of delivery she'd forgotten about.

The other bedroom doors remained resolutely shut so on the second ring she sighed, got to her feet and trudged to the front door, flinging it wide. Then she gasped. On the doorstep, almost unrecognisable in some sort of workout gear, earbud in one ear, the other removed in her hand, stood Claudine.

'Oh. Hello!' Bella said, trying to hide her shock. 'What do I — I didn't expect—What— Why are you here?'

Claudine smiled. 'I am jogging,' she answered, as if that explained everything. 'I am training for the marathon next year.

I set myself a challenge each Sunday. Did you know it's only sixteen kilometres from Paris to Versailles?'

'*Only* sixteen kilometres?'

Claudine shrugged. 'I like to push myself.'

'Did you plan to run... here? To see me?'

Claudine laughed. '*Non*! I am not stalking you, don't worry. But it is a long run, I wanted a break, then remembered you lived here and thought it would be fun to say hello!'

'Oh,' said Bella. 'Well, hello! Do you want to go grab a coffee? There's a lovely café...'

'No,' Claudine shook her head and for a moment Bella thought she was simply going to – literally – jog on. But then: 'I can just have one here. If that's OK with you of course? We talked about your place that time at the bar and I'd love to see it.'

'Oh, it's a bit of a mess, really...'

Claudine's face reddened. 'If I'm honest,' she said, in more of a whisper, 'I really need to pee. All this running. And hydrating. I...'

'Oh! Of course!' Bella found herself stepping back, inviting Claudine in. As she did so, her stomach, which had already sunk as a result of opening the door to find her boss on the doorstep on a Sunday morning, dropped to a new low. Because of course, Claudine thought the house was hers; that she was inhabiting it solo. She didn't know that 'Isabella' was a tenant in a down at heel student house.

Probably, Claudine wouldn't judge her on her living circumstances. But she might judge her for lying. Bella gestured towards the kitchen, trying desperately to remember what kind of state it was in.

In her own place, Bella had tried to keep things tidy, and mostly she'd succeeded. But here, something about having no stake in a place and living with multiple occupants, had brought out her inner sloth. She often left washing up to the last moment, mugs on the side. There was always an unspoken battle amongst them all, about whose turn it was to empty the bin, and it was often left piled high until one of them cracked.

Sure enough, the kitchen was in a state; Bella, looking at it with new eyes, was suddenly ashamed. 'Sorry about the mess,' she said. 'I have— There are housemates.'

'Oh, you are renting rooms to others! Of course!' Claudine exclaimed. 'Always the businesswoman.' She pulled out a chair at the small wooden table, lifted a magazine from its seat then slid into it. Bella quickly cleared the debris from the table's surface and flicked it over with a cloth.

'Please do not go to any trouble,' Claudine said. 'I am just sorry that your housemates are so slovenly.'

'Um. Yes,' Bella said, boiling the kettle and locating the good coffee pot – the one without the chip. 'I'm meaning to speak to them about the mess they leave. This is my home after all.'

Claudine nodded sagely. 'Very wise.' Her nose crinkled slightly as she glanced around the room. 'The kitchen is very quaint though. I can see without the mess it would be quite cute. You will have to give me a tour! I would love to see the rest of it.'

Bella made a sound that was a little like a laugh, but ever so slightly like a squeak of fear. 'Of course,' she said. 'I'd love to show you around.' She poured water onto the coffee grounds then set the pot on the table. 'Let's have a coffee first though, eh!'

Once the coffee was served, Claudine seemed to relax a little. She stretched out her legs and sighed as she sipped from her mug. 'Ah, I try not to drink too much coffee, but sometimes it is exactly what I need.'

'Definitely. Do you run often then?'

Claudine shrugged. 'I find it helps with stress. I've been— It's a challenging time. Running clears my mind, helps me sleep.'

Claudine hadn't struck her as someone who'd ever experienced stress. Somehow her work persona was all hard edges and efficiency. But seeing her now, in her stretchy running gear, looking tired, she seemed different, more human.

In other circumstances, she and Claudine might have become proper friends. But Claudine was her boss, and one who believed Bella had a different background, a different life. It was odd how the lies she'd told to get herself accepted, both here and at work, were the things actually creating a barrier between her and the people around her now.

Her lies – or the places where she'd allowed assumptions to grow without countering misunderstandings – were stacked like a game of Jenga. If Claudine found out that she was renting, or that her housemates thought she was an intern, the rest of it would likely tumble down as well.

But it was still early – just nine o'clock – and she hoped that the others would simply sleep for the next hour as they often did and she'd be able to send Claudine on her way without anything terrible happening.

'So,' Claudine said after a few sips of coffee. 'The tour?'

Reluctantly, Bella led her through to the living room which, while cleaner than the kitchen, had all the marks of a student let: second-hand sofas with worn covers, a line of wine corks displayed proudly on the mantelpiece. There was a rug that had seen better days, a pile of unopened post on a coffee table. The curtains were old-fashioned, with coral flowers twisting their length – probably left by a previous owner.

Bella had no idea what Claudine's place was like, but she

imagined it being all glass and granite and polished, shiny surfaces. She looked at Claudine's face, trying to gauge how she might react.

'Oh, it is lovely!' Claudine suddenly exclaimed, clapping her hands together like a delighted toddler.

'It is?'

'Yes. So homely. Oh, I get so tired of all the clean lines in my apartment. This reminds me more of coming home to my mother's. You have recreated the look perfectly. The curtains! The vintage couches, even the corks – I love how everything is repurposed and you haven't wasted anything. You must be very environmentally conscious.'

Bella tried to smile. 'Well, yes. But also I'll be changing it a little when my divorce goes through and I'm able to buy—'

'No.' Claudine put a hand on her arm and looked at her, all seriousness. 'You must not change a thing. It is perfect.' She set her drained coffee cup down on the table.

It was odd. But Bella decided she'd take the compliment. Perhaps now she'd be able to guide Claudine to the door and on her way without being discovered.

As if malevolent fate could read her thoughts, at this moment the door opened and Henri wandered in, wearing just a pair of tiny tight briefs, through which he was sporting the beginnings of an erection. His hair was tousled, he was yawning, his eyes were almost closed.

He looked at Bella then at Claudine, then down at himself and abruptly turned and left the room.

Claudine looked at Bella, raising an eyebrow. 'Was this your lover, Henri?'

'Yes, that was Henri, but we're not—'

'Oh my! I must go. I will let you lovers carry on with your day.' Claudine tipped her head knowingly and Bella got the impression she had now gone up several points in Claudine's estimation. She walked her boss through to the hall, her heart rate slowing a little. Relieved that despite a few near-misses she'd managed to keep up appearances.

Seeming to be in no hurry, Claudine paused in the hallway and began to carefully appraise Odette's seascape.

'I love your painting!' She leant to inspect it more closely. 'Is it a Soraya French?'

'Oh. No. It's my— it's Odette's. She's one of the... tenants.'

'She lives here?' Claudine was almost reverent. 'Well, if she is one of the messy tenants, I understand you forgiving her slovenliness. If she can produce art like this, she can live how she wants!'

'I didn't know you liked art?'

'Oh, *oui*. My family— My father was an artist. And my sister owns a gallery and knows lots of curators. I have grown up learning to appreciate good work. But then who could not love this?' Claudine gestured at the seascape. 'Give her my compliments, won't you?'

'I will,' Bella said, stepping towards the door in the hope that Claudine might follow. She didn't want to be rude, but the longer her boss stayed, the more likely she'd slip up.

'Well, see you tomorrow!' Claudine said, stretching her legs on the front doorstep.

'Yes. Bye!'

And she was off, disappearing around the corner and leaving Bella weak with relief.

34

2016, FRANCE

They'd completed the formalities at the *maire*'s office earlier that day, but this unofficial ceremony felt more like a real wedding. Simple, beautiful, and held in the garden of their new house. Bella had booked an English celebrant, mainly so the guests could understand what was happening, and they'd fashioned an aisle from mismatched chairs, each tied with a cream-coloured ribbon.

There were fifteen guests in total. Kitty and Stu, Pete's parents and sister, two new friends from Peyrat they'd asked along and a few friends who'd made the trip over. Still, the morning had been difficult. Bella had hoped that having the wedding so far from her childhood home would mean she didn't feel her mum's absence so deeply on the day itself.

Everything, from having her hair pulled into an updo, small tendrils curling around her head, to slipping on her dress, had felt somehow devastating without Mum by her side. Worse, perhaps, because she knew that if her mum had had anything to do with it, she'd have been there. Yet Dad seemed not to want to know.

Kitty made a fuss of her, and fluffed her dress and handed her champagne and tissues. But she still felt the wrench of loss every time she realised that on this pivotal day, she was effectively an orphan.

The string quartet struck up a rendition of the Beatles' 'Something' and she stepped forward on the grass, holding a small bouquet of white roses. Pete turned, his face splitting into a smile as she approached.

A small breeze was buffeting the longer grass that surrounded the part of the garden they'd prepared for the wedding site, and as she walked she saw it: a single white feather, softly travelling along the uneven ground, moved gently by the wind. Noticing it, Kitty moved forward and quickly picked it up, tucking it into Bella's bouquet.

For some reason it felt comforting.

I promise to love you every day, to share each adventure with you. To always be around and never leave your side – unless you're sick of me! Pete's vows caused a ripple of laughter at this point, and he grinned, pleased. *To hold you when you need to be held, to listen when you need to talk. To be your rock from now until the day I die.*

Couples in the audience gripped each other's hands more tightly. Kitty and Stu looked at one another, and he winked.

Then it was Bella's turn:

Thank you, Pete, for being the person I need – to laugh with, cry with, experience joy and pain with. I promise that I'll always love and cherish you. And that from this day, neither of us will ever feel abandoned, alone or afraid. Because we'll have each other and that will be enough.

Moments later the celebrant finally pronounced them husband and wife. And Bella smiled as she felt her future unfurl in front of her. With this new life, in this new place, where she could start again on her terms with a person who would never let her down.

The Bonus Name Store

could it from places with this story. He is the best place where she could she light for her office with a lover who would need little down.

35

NOW

'You really think I'm the best person for the job?' Bella asked Brad, tapping the card against the kitchen table. It was the fourth evening in a row they'd spent working together on Bella's plans. But however helpful he'd been with those, he clearly wasn't going to step in when it came to giving this business card to Odette.

When Claudine had pressed the business card into Bella's hand earlier that day and told her it was for her 'lodger', she'd thought Claudine had meant Henri; that she'd wanted her to set up a date or something. She'd been just about to say that Henri was just out of a relationship and wasn't ready to date yet – although she wasn't sure whether this was true or not – when she'd looked and realised that the card belonged to a woman named Marie Fontaine, a curator at a Parisian art gallery.

'For Odette?' she'd asked.

'For the one who painted that beautiful seascape,' Claudine had said. 'I can't remember her name, I'm sorry.'

'No, that's fine. Wow, thank you.'

'Marie is a friend of my sister's,' Claudine had added. 'I

cannot make any promises, but I think she would be interested to see some of your friend's work.'

Bella had felt quite excited at the prospect of being able to help Odette to the next stage of her career, until, on the train, she'd wondered whether Odette was ready to make the most of this opportunity. Her friend had been distant since their argument and while she still chatted about this and that when in the kitchen, she now always locked her door after disappearing back into her room.

'Ah, she's just embarrassed,' Brad had said when she'd told him. 'She had this problem – this fear – and she didn't want anyone to know. You've kind of seen inside of her and she can't figure out how to talk to you.'

They'd spent most of the evening writing down names of potential suppliers; making lists of people that Bella would need to contact. In truth, she was exhausted – working all day and then all evening felt like a lot. But she was excited, too, at the progress they seemed to be making. She'd already booked decorators – an amazing feat at such short notice, but Brad *knew a guy who knew a guy* – to paint the two Superior rooms in a soft, muted green, and had managed to source some furniture from a maker who created solid-wood pieces in antique designs.

'You know, I think you're going to land this, and the job,' Brad had said. 'The Hotel Club folks are going to love it, and you'll get that permanent position.'

She'd screwed up her nose. 'You think? I mean, that would be great. But most of all, I don't want to let Claudine down. She put a lot of faith in me, and I guess it was misplaced. I want to... I just want to do what I promised I would.'

Bella spent a lot of time wishing she'd been more honest. Of course, now she was earning, she had cash in the bank; it was natural to look back and not fully understand her actions beforehand. But that was because she didn't feel the urgency, the fear she had then. It was like having a full belly and wondering why anyone would stuff themselves with chips.

She looked at the card again, black with gold embossed words. 'Don't you think it might be better coming from you? You know, she'll feel she has to listen to you at least, being her landlord and all.'

He shook his head. 'You got this for her, it should be you. And besides, I want her to really want this, not say yes to it just because I own the house she lives in.'

Sighing, but accepting he was right, Bella got up from the table.

It was ten o'clock and while it was still light, the evening air had a muted quality, a dullness to its edges. Then again, even in the darkest night, light still streamed into the Versailles kitchen from other houses, apartments, street lights. In Peyrat, she knew, the night sky was thicker, darker, like a blanket. But the darkness made it easier to look at the stars.

She knocked on Odette's door and heard movement inside. 'Yes?'

'I'm just— Odette, can I talk to you for a second?' she said, trying to keep her voice breezy.

There was an audible sigh, and a creak as her friend stood up. Then the sound of paper crinkling and floorboards creaking as she walked to open the door. Bella hoped that Odette wasn't treading on the beautiful canvases as she made her way.

The door opened a crack. Odette looked at her with a smile that was wide, but clearly forced. '*Bonjour*, Bella,' she said. 'Henri's gone out I think, if you're looking for him.'

Since their break-up, Henri had been out most nights. Bella wasn't sure whether he was just trying to stay out of her way.

Odette seemed to have stopped going out altogether; she went to her work in the bar four afternoons a week but seemed to want to spend the rest of the time in her room.

Bella was doubly relieved that Brad was here – a friendly face to speak to over coffee, and someone who was willing to help her make the grade at work. Someone who wasn't avoiding her or pretending she didn't exist.

'No, actually, I wanted to speak to you. You know, my boss, Claudine – she popped in the other day?'

Odette's brow furrowed. 'Yes, you told me I think?'

'Well,' Bella tried to cover her misgivings with a smile. 'She wanted me to give you this.'

Odette took the small card, turned it over, read the name. 'Marie Fontaine? Why – why would she give me this?'

'My boss loved your painting. The seascape. Really loved it. And she knows her stuff. Her sister's a curator, or an artist or something. Her dad was in the industry too. I can't remember all the details, but anyway, she has this connection and thought it would be worth you approaching her with some of your work!'

Odette's eyes were still focused on the card. Then, '*Non,*' she said, handing the card back.

'What do you mean? Surely – I mean I know it's daunting – but this is a great opportunity, right?' Bella didn't raise her hand to take the proffered card and the two stayed in some sort of stalemate.

'*Non.* I am not ready,' Odette said, pushing the card at her more forcefully.

'Yes, you are!' Bella gently pushed the card back, so that Odette's arm folded in a little closer to her body. 'Your paintings are amazing. And you have— well, you have a lot of paintings in there.'

'*Non.*'

'Seriously, Odette. If not now, then when? I know this is your dream. I know you've lost your confidence, but if this Madame Fontaine would be willing to look at your work, surely that's an opportunity you shouldn't miss out on?'

Odette scowled.

Sometimes Bella wondered why she'd ever thought she had anything in common with her housemates. The more she lived here, the more she noticed remnants of the children they had once been, still evident in some of their behaviour. They were in that weird phase of not-childhood but not-yet-adulthood.

'Come on,' she said. 'At least think about it.'

'OK, I will think about it. Happy?'

'Thank you.'

Odette closed the door rather abruptly and Bella was left standing in a hall full of shadows.

There was nothing else she could do.

She made her way back to the kitchen where Brad was still sitting at the table, papers spread out, laptop flickering. He'd switched on the lamps; the room was bathed in a warm, yellow light, and the kettle was just coming to a boil. He looked up at her expectantly. 'And?'

She shook her head. 'Not keen.'

'But she took the card?' he said, noticing that she wasn't holding anything.

'Yep, she took the card.'

'So we'll see.' He grinned.

She felt suddenly grateful for this man who'd come from nowhere and was now dedicating his evenings to helping her, and doing it with such enthusiasm and kindness. 'Want a cup of tea?'

'You bet.'

Bella made her way to the kettle. 'Thanks for this. You don't have to.'

'I know. But when I—'

'Let me guess,' she said, turning and grinning. 'When you were younger, people helped you. You may have already mentioned this once or twice.'

Her tone made it clear she was teasing, so she was surprised to see him fixing her with a steady gaze. 'Actually, I was going to say that when I'm with you, it's like all my own problems fade away.'

'Because it keeps your mind busy?' she said, spooning loose tea into the pot and wondering why her hand was trembling slightly.

'No. Well, maybe. But actually, I think it's you. I enjoy spending time with you.' She looked at him and their eyes locked.

'Oh,' she said. The odd thing was that although she hadn't expected him to say those words, she didn't feel surprised.

She'd come to value these evenings together, how the conversation flowed. The proximity of him.

It was different from what she'd felt for Henri, she realised. That desperate, needy feeling of lust and wanting to be rescued all at once that had burned bright, but had burned out.

When she was with Brad, things seemed so easy, so natural. He wasn't her landlord, her mentor. He was her friend. A friend she thought about on and off for most of the day, and looked forward to seeing every evening.

But before she could say anything else, there was a loud banging sound from the hallway. A key turned in the lock and, as they looked through the open kitchen door, Henri stumbled through, looking more than a little worse for wear.

He looked at them together in the kitchen, smiled and staggered through. 'Bella,' he said, standing and swaying slightly on his trainered feet. His laces, she noticed, were untied and had almost definitely been soaked in a puddle on the way home. 'Oh, *salut,* Brad!'

'Hey, man. Seems like you've had a bit to drink.'

'I am drowning my sorrows. My broken heart.' He clutched his chest dramatically.

'Henri! Seriously?' Bella said.

'The heart wants what it wants,' he lyricized.

'In his case,' Brad said quietly in her ear, 'the heart seems to have wanted a LOT of tequila.'

She tried not to laugh.

'Come on, dude, let's get you to bed,' Brad said, standing up, putting his arm under Henri's and helping him walk.

As they disappeared from the room, Bella realised that she'd missed her chance to respond, to say that she liked spending time with Brad too; that part of her wished this project would never end.

36

2017, FRANCE

'I can't believe it,' she said to Pete. 'Our first guests!'

'Well, don't stand at the door – it looks a bit desperate.'

Their advert had gone live on Airbnb and they'd had a flurry of bookings almost instantly. They'd only just readied the guest rooms in time and now they were poised, waiting for the first clients to descend.

'It's going to work,' she said. 'I can feel it.'

He'd kissed her. 'It'd better, after all this.'

It was true that it had taken more than they'd expected to get the B & B ready for guests. The stone house was charming but solid as it was, had needed more work than they'd planned for. Ancient, creaking plumbing had had to be replaced; loose tiles had had to be refitted. Every job they'd accounted for seemed to have had another, messier job beneath it: plaster had crumbled, removed light fittings had revealed dodgy wiring, the septic tank had had to be drained.

It hadn't been the romantic image that Bella had been searching for.

Only all that was behind her now.

As she watched, a car signalled then turned into the drive and she shut the door abruptly, almost squealing. 'They're here! They're here!'

Pete looked at her, shaking his head affectionately. 'Yes, they are. Maybe letting them in would be a good idea.'

And, smiling, she unclicked the latch again, throwing open the door to what she hoped would be a bright future.

'Green is very this season.'

Bella, leaning against the door-frame and admiring the freshly painted room, looked to see who was talking to her. Madame Roux was standing there, still bundled up in a winter suit despite the heat, nodding approvingly.

'You like it?'

'Does it matter?'

'Yes. Of course!'

Madame Roux nodded. 'It's good.'

'Thank you.'

She smiled. It was nice to have someone's approval. Especially someone whose good opinion was hard-won.

Since Henri had interrupted their heart-to-heart in the kitchen the previous week, Bella had felt a distance between her and Brad. Something about the intimacy they'd experienced during that week of work together had dissipated.

Or perhaps she'd misread the signs completely.

At least the hotel seemed to be coming together. She'd finished writing the presentation, the two Superior rooms were painted, and she'd managed to source some artwork from a local gallery to hang on the walls.

Each room had a king-size bed with new linen in a complementary colour to the walls: rich greens and blues, creating a calming feel. The art depicted forests and trees – and she had named each room too. '*La forêt*' and '*Le bord de mer*'. The idea was that Hôtel Benjamin would become a retreat – a place to escape from the hustle and bustle of Paris, yet still be present in the heart of the city. Outside: Paris; inside: Peyrat.

These rooms would be showcased on the night, but she'd made sure that prints of suitable artwork had been put up in the others, that bedding and soft furnishings had been changed to reflect the mood of the hotel. In time, they would upgrade the rest but hopefully the theme, and the idea, would be enough to convince the Hotel Club representatives that Hôtel Benjamin was a suitable match for their brand.

The entrance to the hotel had been altered too. She'd managed to source an old, carved reception desk, with cupboards behind that had once been used in an apothecary's. The wood was worn and authentic-looking and created a charming contrast to the smart, white plastered walls. The seating had been changed too, replaced with mismatched vintage chairs – all solid and in good condition. Finally, she'd managed to find a company who could create 'living pictures' with foliage and fauna growing out of specially made frames. Stepping into the space did feel worlds away from the street outside.

None of this would have happened without Brad. Sure, a lot of the ideas had come from her, and she'd fleshed them out and made them work. But it was his explanation, his structure, his calm measure of the problem that had got her off the starting blocks. She'd invited him to the presentation the following week, but wasn't sure whether he was going to come.

In fact, for the first time in months, she was feeling quite alone.

Despite everything seemingly going well in her professional life, her personal life was once again in tatters.

Henri, after his performance, had distanced himself from her – perhaps embarrassed – and seemed to have started dating someone else. Odette hadn't mentioned the business card. Brad didn't seem to be fully present when he was with her. She still didn't talk much to Kitty or Juliette, unable to face what might be their incredulity at her situation.

It was nice to have someone speaking to her, even if it was Madame Roux, even if she knew that Claudine thought of her as a nuisance.

Coco snuffled at her feet, and she bent down and tried to stroke it. The dog snarled a little, baring her teeth.

'Oh, don't mind Coco, she's very friendly once you get to know her,' Madame Roux said, looking at her little dog with as much love as a mother gazing at her newborn.

'Sure.' Bella straightened, feeling quite lucky to still have her fingers.

'Well, good luck. I doubt I'll see you again.' Madame Roux turned and gave a small wave of her hand.

A surge of nauseous anxiety rose inside Bella's chest. 'I'm sorry, what do you mean?' Did Madame Roux know something about her prospects that she didn't? Surely that would all be decided after the Hotel Club visit in any case.

Madame Roux turned. 'Claudine hasn't told you?'

'Told me what?'

'I'm going. She's found a home for me. For old people. One

that will let me take Coco. I've no business living in a hotel for so long.'

'Oh. That's— I mean, that's good. Is it?'

Madame Roux lifted a shoulder and let it fall. 'We all get old,' she said. 'But the real age comes when we lose our independence.'

'But—'

'Oh, I know,' the old lady continued, batting away what she imagined Bella was about to say. 'I realise that living in a hotel is not exactly independence. But it was a way of living...' she sighed. 'A way of living a life that I wanted. Of living alone but not being alone, do you see? But Claudine, she thinks I need nurses. Care. And it is her hotel, so...'

Madame Roux let the last words fade away as she continued her walk along the carpeted corridor.

'Madame Roux?' she found herself calling.

'*Oui?*'

'Does she know? Claudine, I mean?'

'Know what?' The woman turned, looked at her.

'How you feel?'

'I don't think that really matters, *mon petit*.'

'I'm sure it would.'

Madame Roux laughed. 'That's because you are young. When you get to my age you realise that people stop seeing you as a person. They start seeing you as a problem. Claudine is a lovely girl, she has given me so much. But she doesn't really see me. She cares, in her own way. But to her I am simply an old lady she is responsible for. Not someone who is entitled to wants and needs and... Not someone who can add value.'

'Oh, but you—'

There it was again, the flick of a hand. 'Goodbye, dear,' Madame Roux said firmly. 'Good luck with your rooms.'

'Thank you.'

As Madame Roux disappeared around the corner, Bella turned towards Claudine's office. It was none of her business, but then her problems at work had been none of Brad's business, yet he had helped her. Saved her, really. Maybe she could help Madame Roux in some way?

But before she could make her way to Claudine, one of the younger office staff turned up, almost breathless. 'The artwork has arrived,' she said. 'Shall I send it up?'

'Oh. Yes please,' she said, excited to see the paintings she had chosen in situ.

Soon, a man and a woman, both casually dressed, appeared, carrying a large box. Alongside them was a woman dressed more formally in a black trouser suit. 'Where do you want them?' she asked. Bella explained and the couple took the box into the first of the hotel rooms, carefully unwrapping the first painting and securing it onto the wall.

It was the forest painting – oil on canvas displaying such a mixture of greens and blues that looking at it made you feel as if your mind were being washed clean by nature. It was impressionist in style, and here, from her position in the hall, Bella could see clearly the wood of the trees, the light sparkling through the branches. Yet as she approached, she knew she would see individual blobs, brush-strokes that somehow together gave the illusion of space and light and trees and nature.

It was amazing how something that seemed so chaotic and messy could look so together and beautiful from a distance.

Back in her office an hour later, she ran through the list of things she'd tasked herself to prepare. The caterers were booked, the key rooms for Hotel Club associates and delegates reserved. There was a string quartet booked to play in the corner of the room before the presentation as everyone mingled and introduced themselves. The leaflets she'd had produced looked professional and on point.

And for a moment she felt that she was Isabella. Someone capable and ready and professional. Someone who would help this hotel get the recognition it deserved. Not Bella, who'd turned up terrified and had had to lie to get her foot in the door. But someone brand new.

Smiling, she decided to check her emails one more time before leaving for the day. She pulled up her work inbox, but there was nothing new. Then she checked her personal emails to see if Juliette or Kitty had been in touch.

And there it was. A message from Pete.

Suddenly her breathing became erratic. Her hands felt tingly and not fully part of her body. She clicked on the message to read:

The notaire wants us to go to Peyrat to sign the contract. I thought maybe we could go together, sort out the last of the furniture before the house clearance people come. It would be nice to catch up. I've missed you!

It was as if someone had reached through and popped the bubble she'd formed around herself. Letting the past back in. The feelings she'd had when Pete had left her resurfaced and she had to work hard not to sob. Why after weeks, months, of no contact would Pete get in touch now? They'd been working through the *notaire* until this moment and, while it made her sad to know that the B & B would soon no longer be theirs, she'd had no intention of visiting Peyrat again before the sale.

Looking at their house, stripped of its personality, knowing that some of their favourite pieces would be cleared and probably sold for a song, or placed in storage by a remover recommended by their estate agent, would be like identifying the body of a loved one after they'd died.

It wouldn't be the home they'd loved, that had so much history for them. It would be an impersonal stone shell, ready for the next person to create a life.

And what on earth was Pete saying. That he missed her? Was it a casual comment, or more meaningful? She'd worked hard to put him out of her mind. But the thought of him came now, fresh and urgent. Pete had been her rock for so many years, her family when her own had deserted her. The person she'd confided in and relied upon and built a life with.

She had been so lonely.

But she'd started to build herself up now without his help. To find her way.

She simply couldn't let him come into her life again and risk his tearing it all down. She replied at last:

BELLA

Sorry Pete. I'm really busy at work. I'll just sign electronically if that's OK. All the best.

PETE

OK. Fair enough. But I would still like to see you. Kitty told me you're in Versailles? I'm over for a bit, sorting some stuff out. Can I pop over and see you?

Thanks, Kitty.

BELLA

Maybe at some point. Look, I'm in the middle of something right now. I'll be in touch in a few weeks, OK?

She pressed 'Send' and watched the email disappear from her screen. Any traces of the high she'd felt from the thought of a job well done had disappeared with Pete's words. Another email from him quickly appeared in her inbox but she couldn't bring herself to open it. Instead, she deleted it and after a moment, blocked his address.

She would be back in touch. She would be friendly. They could catch up if that's what he wanted. Just not right now. She had more important things to do first.

'Ta-da!' she said, opening the door and gesturing enthusiastically with her arms.

Claudine gave her a puzzled look, which could be interpreted as 'What is the crazy English woman doing now?' but stepped inside the completed Superior room.

Bella was reminded of the nineties home makeover programmes where the host would show the owner into their newly decorated room and the audience would hold their breath, waiting to find out if they'd like it or burst into tears.

Claudine's hands flew to her mouth and for a moment Bella felt more sympathy for Laurence Llewelyn-Bowen than she'd thought possible. She'd been sure that Claudine was going to fall in love with the renewed decor as quickly as she had, but the pause was more unbearable: the kind of long silence usually reserved for judges' verdicts on TV talent shows.

Claudine had approved the mood boards, she'd seen the linen samples and pictures of the artwork. She'd even had a sniff of the scented candles that Bella had put on the beautifully varnished chest of drawers. But she hadn't seen the combination of them all together: the curtains hung, the cushions scattered, the painting adorning the wall and the candles' flickering flames.

'Do you like it?' Bella asked at last, timidly, looking at her boss's back as she toured the room, inspecting the painting, the walls, the newly acquired bed linen.

Claudine turned to her, eyes shining. 'It's beautiful!' she said. 'Oh, it's amazing. When they see what we can offer our guests in the Superior rooms and hear our plans to roll out the design even more, I am sure they will be thrilled!'

'Thank you.'

Claudine smiled. 'So, what's next? What is left to do?'

The four Hotel Club delegates would arrive in a week's time, and be shown to the Superior rooms. They'd do a tour of the hotel as a whole, with Madame Roux squirreled away somewhere no doubt. They'd eat at the hotel restaurant, then there'd be the meeting, the presentation and presumably some time after that, the verdict.

Bella had a fizz of excitement inside her, similar to that she'd had at school before her GCSEs. Part of it was nerves, fear. But part was a feeling that things were going to go well, that she had finally proven that, qualifications or not, poor choices or not, she was good enough. She could succeed.

She beamed at Claudine. 'Well, we have a photographer coming later to take some pictures of the new rooms for the presentation, so I'm going to leave them dressed like this, welcome trays and all.'

Claudine nodded.

'Then it's a case of rehearsal and checking on suppliers' arrival times, that sort of thing. But I think, I *think*, we're pretty much there!'

Claudine made a noise that from a more frivolous woman would have been described as a squeal, but was so out of character that they were both momentarily stunned. Then, rather than leave the room or whip out her phone and schedule in times for a rehearsal, she sank suddenly to the bed – almost as if her legs no longer had strength to hold her.

Her hands went to her face again, this time covering her eyes, nose and mouth entirely.

It was only when her shoulders started to shake that Bella realised what was happening.

Claudine was crying. Sobbing, actually, would be more of an apt description.

'Claudine?' she said, floored for a moment. Claudine was not the sort of person to show much emotion, especially at work.

Bella instantly began to worry that this was a delayed reaction to her design. Perhaps she'd overdone it on the colour? The theme? Had she missed quirky and gone straight to tacky or overdone?

Nervously, she perched on the bed next to her boss and put an arm around her shaking shoulders. 'Claudine,' she said, feeling sick. 'What's wrong?'

Claudine raised her face from her hands. Her eyes were red-rimmed, her cheeks were wet. Her hair, usually so neatly scraped back, had escaped from its chignon and some strands stuck straight out around her face. It should have made her look awful, but somehow, she looked younger, vulnerable in a way that Bella had never seen before.

'Nothing,' she said. 'Nothing is wrong.'

Bella looked at her, waiting for some sort of explanation.

'Ah, I suppose I can tell you now, as we are friends as well as colleagues?' Claudine looked at Bella for confirmation.

'Of course.'

'Well,' Claudine sighed, as if she were expelling breath she'd held onto for some time. 'OK. So, when I took you on, I wasn't 100 per cent honest with you.'

'Oh?'

'Yes. I told you that the hotel wanted to achieve Hotel Club accreditation to get to the next stage, to be a bigger player, *n'est-ce pas*?'

'Yes. And... I mean, the Hotel Club people are coming... so...?'

Claudine nodded. 'Oh, yes. It is very much something we want. But it is not so much to get the hotel to the next stage, but to save it.'

'Oh?'

Claudine looked at her hands, turning them over as if they might hold some sort of answer. 'When my husband left me, I had been away from work for a time,' she said. 'We had hoped for children but... well, never mind. That is a story for another time.'

'OK?'

'The hotel was one of his assets. He was quite successful in business. And I acquired it in the divorce. I think, although I didn't know it at the time, he tricked me a little. Because it was not in as good a state as he said. There were problems with the building, things that needed to be corrected.'

Bella nodded, encouraging Claudine to continue.

'I think he thought in any case that I would just sell it. But I had worked in hospitality some years before, and I had no other skills. So I decided to run it, to try to make it work.'

'Right.'

'This was five years ago. And it has been a difficult time. There are many things in this industry that I was not aware of.

Difficulties, overheads. Staff. And of course we had to close for a time for some renovations. There was damp.'

'So...?'

'Since then, we have done OK. Better than OK, perhaps. Especially with a novice leading the way. But because of the costs of the renovations, because of the time we spent closed... the hotel has lost a lot of money, and we are not making enough to correct the balance.' She looked at Bella, her eyes wide. 'I can tell you this now that we are nearly there, but without this accreditation, the extra money and custom it will bring, I was afraid I would have to close.'

Bella felt sick. So much had been resting on her doing a good job. In some ways she was glad she hadn't realised that before. *All I'd thought about was myself, how I was going to manage,* she thought. She'd assumed that Claudine was experienced, that if she had done a bad job her boss would have picked up on it. But it seemed, actually, that they were both a little in the dark – only Claudine, as the owner, had the right to be.

But it was OK, she reassured herself. They'd made it. She'd made it. The job she'd done for Claudine may have started off being a bit rudimentary, but she'd learned along the way and now they were ready to impress the executives. It would be OK.

Claudine wiped her eyes then decisively slapped her hands on her legs before standing up. 'Well,' she said. 'Enough of that. Time to be the big boss again.' She gave Bella a little wink. 'Your secret is safe with me.'

When she was gone, Bella plumped the pillows and straightened the bedding. She went to stand in the doorway as she had before to take in the whole of the room. Surely it would be enough. It had to be.

Quietly she closed the door and made her way to her office.

She had two hours to kill before the photographer arrived and wanted more than ever to be sure she was ready for the presentation.

At her desk, she answered a few emails before checking her spam. There was a note from an unknown email address that she would have left alone had it not been for the title 'Urgent.'

She opened it, and realised that it was from Pete. She'd blocked his email address but he'd written it from a second one.

Bella, my messages don't seem to be getting through. Are you OK? I told you that I need to speak to you, and I know you said you're busy, but I really think that you're going to want to hear what I have to say. Please reply to this urgently so I know you're all right. I'm at the Peyrat house for a day or so more, but I can be with you in a few hours, whenever you're ready. Pete.

She simply couldn't deal with this now. She'd had an update from the *agent immobilier* and knew that the house sale was due to complete in three weeks' time, so it couldn't be anything about that. She'd yet to speak to a solicitor about their divorce, but it was early days in their separation, and she wasn't in a rush to get that particular ball rolling. Not until she'd sorted everything here at work. One crisis at a time.

He must have suspected she'd blocked him; otherwise, why use the separate address? If she replied to this email, she'd just be confirming the fact. Better, surely, to give it a couple of days, wait until the Hotel Club executives had left and then reply to his original email, citing problems with her PC.

She closed the email and left it in spam.

Back in her inbox, there was a new email. This one from an address she did recognise. Juliette's.

Hello,

You mentioned you had an important event at work, and I am at a loose end this week, so I thought I could come and stay in your hotel and offer you moral support. What do you think?

J

Hi Juliette,

That would be amazing. I'd love to see you. Maybe we can go out after to celebrate (fingers crossed). I'll book you a room with my staff discount. It won't be one of the Superior rooms I'm afraid (the ones I've worked on the most) but I'm getting some photos taken this afternoon and...

Before she could write more, an almost deafening sound began to reverberate around the building. Seconds later her door flew open and Yves burst in. 'It's the fire alarm!' he said. 'We need to evacuate!'

'Oh my God, is there a fire?'

'It might be one of the guests activating it in error,' he admitted as they jogged down the stairs. 'Sometimes it happens. But it's important we get everyone out safely. You need to assemble in the car park – can you get there OK? I'm going to check the rooms for guests.'

'Are you sure I can't help?'

He shook his head. 'It is protocol,' he said, 'don't worry.'

She nodded. At least she had some time before the photographer arrived and work wasn't too hectic, or she'd have cursed being away from her desk like this. She wondered whether the fire alarm had been set off deliberately, or whether someone had stumbled against one of the red fire points or something. Yves was right, it was more than likely a false alarm.

It was only when she passed the entrance to the second floor that she was sure for a moment that she could smell smoke.

'What's happening?' she asked breathlessly, standing next to Claudine on the small, tarmacked area just behind the hotel.

Before Claudine could answer, Mélodie ran up, phone clamped to her ear. 'It's Yves. Everyone is out,' she confirmed. The guests were grouped together in the corner of the car park; there were about thirty in all. Among them, Madame Roux, somehow still immaculately dressed, with Coco on a lead sniffing at her boots. She caught Bella's eye and shook her head impatiently. A small collection of staff – cleaners, the kitchen workers, and one or two Bella didn't recognise – were grouped nearby.

'Is it a false alarm?' Bella enquired.

'No.'

For the first time, Bella looked properly at her boss. The woman's face was pale, her eyes, glassy.

'Don't worry,' Mélodie said. 'Yves has said it was contained in only two rooms. Very small fires. He was able to use the fire extinguisher. And of course there were the sprinklers.' She smiled, clearly delighted the crisis was averted.

But the juxtaposition of Claudine's pale face next to Mélodie's untroubled one meant that Bella couldn't relax. Something had happened. Had Claudine been burnt in some way? Was it shock?

Yves appeared at the corner of the building and Mélodie began to walk quickly in his direction. Bella turned to Claudine.

'Do you need to sit down?' she asked.

'*Non*. I do not need to sit down!' Claudine snapped.

'Oh. I'm sorry... I just—'

'I can't believe that this has happened. A week before the presentation! It is the worst luck. Or perhaps the worst judgement.' She gave Bella a look. Gone was the friendliness that she'd had in her eyes when she'd confided in her just an hour or so ago. Instead, her expression was fixed, cold.

'But everything's OK, the fire's out. Mélodie said—'

'Ah, Mélodie. She is a fool. She doesn't know!'

'Know...?'

'How important it is! How important the rooms were.'

'The rooms?'

Claudine looked at her. 'Yes, the rooms. You did not think to ask which rooms have been burnt and sprayed with foam and watered from above? You did not think that they might be important rooms, perhaps?'

An icy hand gripped Bella's heart. 'Oh. Oh no.'

Claudine nodded. 'And have you considered perhaps how the fire started?'

Her look was so fixed, so accusatory that Bella was taken aback. She had been nowhere near the rooms when the alarm had been raised. In fact, the last time she'd entered the rooms had been earlier when she'd been with Claudine. She'd only stayed afterwards to fluff a couple of pillows, check everything was in place for the photographer.

Then something inside her sank as rapidly as if she'd plunged downward on a fairground ride. The candles. She'd lit the scented candles to impress Claudine, to showcase the overall effect of the room. But she hadn't thought, as she'd closed the door feeling so pleased with herself, to blow the candles out, relight them later. Then again, they were in glass jars; they should have been OK.

'The candles?' she said.

'Yes. They were placed on the bedside tables, *non*? Very near the curtains? Of course, the damage from burning is minimal. The smoke alarm and Yves's quick thinking saw to this. But the water damage, the foam...' Claudine's voice was devoid of emotion. 'The rooms are quite ruined.'

Bella felt the blood drain from her face. She'd put the candles there for ambiance, to throw light on the curtains and highlight the embroidery, the slight sheen on the material. It had been a momentary decision; she hadn't thought.

'We can delay Hotel Club, we can—'

Claudine shook her head. 'Everything has been paid for up front, the air tickets. Everything. Yes, we can cancel but...' she shrugged. 'I am not sure we will be able to afford to start again. Besides, Hotel Club have a one year waiting list...'

* * *

It was an hour before they were allowed back in the building, the guests grumbling and Claudine reassuring them, in a voice that betrayed none of her former misery, that they would receive a free meal in the restaurant this evening to make up for the inconvenience. Other guests, who'd been out for the afternoon, began returning, confused to see the *pompiers* driving away, the muddy footprints in reception where they'd rushed through in haste – unnecessarily as it turned out.

Upstairs, Bella stood by the entrance of one of the Superior rooms, hardly moving. Her face was fixed on the decor inside, her heart sinking anew every time she glanced at something she hadn't noticed before.

The paintwork was streaked, the bedding saturated and covered in foam. The rugs that she'd painstakingly sourced were sodden. The antique-looking chest of drawers had a black, burnt area, and the beautiful, expensive art that she'd carefully chosen had been soaked by the sprinkler, the canvas sodden, foamy, its paint bleeding onto the wall. The curtains, so carefully made to measure, were half eaten by fire, the shreds remaining blackened.

If someone had planned to destroy every item in the room, render each thing unusable, they could hardly have done a better job. Yves had clearly panicked and foamed nearly everything in the room. The sprinklers had finished the job. The fire itself had hardly damaged anything.

Any thoughts she'd had, any hopes that things might have been rescuable were scuppered. Nobody could turn this around in time, not even Laurence Llewelyn-Bowen himself. Not even the House Doctor, or Kim and Aggie, or the entire team on *Changing Rooms*.

It was over.

* * *

She knocked, tentatively, on Claudine's closed office door.

'*Oui*?' said a weary voice.

She opened it. 'Claudine, I'm so sorry.'

Claudine regarded her, her mouth a miserable fixed line. 'Yes, I am sure.'

'I can— we can—' her voice trailed off.

'You should go,' Claudine said. 'I will cancel the visit. We don't have the budget to re-do those rooms – you know that. The decor you chose was not cheap. And there is really no need for you to be here now. I am sorry, I will not be able to extend your contract further. I am sure you understand.'

Was this financial or was she being punished for her negligence? Either way, Bella didn't blame her.

She opened her mouth to argue, but then realised that there wasn't really any point. What else could Claudine do? Even if it hadn't been her who'd caused the fire, she'd have had to let Bella go anyway. If the hotel was in trouble and this might have been its final chance at solvency, then pretty soon – barring a miracle – there wouldn't be a hotel to work at. And there certainly wasn't space for a project manager who'd managed to spend thousands of euros making things better before tearing the whole thing down.

'I'm so, so sorry...' she began. 'I—' But she found she had run out of words. She looked at the woman who'd been her boss, who'd started to become her friend.

Claudine leapt to her feet so suddenly that Bella stepped back in shock.

'Ah, yes,' she hissed, leaning forward over her desk. 'You are often sorry! But this is not something that a "sorry" can fix! You are incompetent, careless. Foolish! I should never have taken you on – and now you have ruined everything!' Claudine's eyes flashed and Bella took another step back. 'I want you out of my hotel. And if I have anything to do with it, you will never work in the French hospitality business again.'

'But Claudine... I—'

Claudine's expression was so thunderous, Bella's words fell away. 'Just go,' she said. 'Go back to your beautiful home. Or, better, back to England. I never want to see you again.'

Filled with sudden, nervous energy, Bella rushed to her office, gathered her things and made her way to the lift. The doors opened to reveal Madame Roux with her dog and some sort of wheeled basket at her feet. She regarded Bella's tear-stained face as she entered the lift.

'Ground floor?' she said, raising a well made-up eyebrow.

Bella nodded, miserably.

'So you are leaving?'

She nodded again, not trusting herself to speak.

'Claudine asked you to go?'

'Yes,' she managed. 'The fire. It was my fault, you see. I— And now everything is ruined and... well, you know the rest.'

Madame Roux shook her head. 'I have already told you. When you are old, nobody tells you anything. Certainly not Claudine. What's the rest?'

Bella looked at the old lady. It couldn't hurt to tell her; after all, everything was already as bad as it could get. 'Claudine's in financial trouble,' she said. 'She's struggling with the hotel, and hoped she'd be able improve things if the presentation went well. But now—'

Madame Roux frowned. 'Silly girl.'

'We all get ourselves in difficulties sometimes.'

'Perhaps.' The old lady looked thoughtful. 'But now you are going too, just when Claudine needs you most.'

'Claudine made it quite clear I'm not welcome.' Bella fought to keep her voice under control. 'She never wants to see me again.'

'Pah!' The word was loud and made Bella jump. 'Of course

she says things, but she doesn't mean them. Claudine is proud; she won't be able to ask you for what she really needs.'

'Which is...?'

'Comfort. A friend.'

Bella sighed. 'If you'd seen her...'

'Oh, I can imagine. But that is just her exterior. Surely you are old enough to understand now that nobody is the person they present to the world. It's just a version of themselves they think is palatable enough for others to like. We are all secretive. We all have our worries, our pain. Claudine needs you.'

The lift reached the ground floor, giving its habitual lurch. The doors slid open, revealing a reception covered in footprints, one of the large plants turned on its side. Bella held her finger on the 'door open' button to prevent them closing and turned to Madame Roux.

'I just can't. I— I should never have taken this job in the first place. And I'm definitely not the right person to help Claudine now. She's much better off without me. I can't go back there. I just can't.'

Madame Roux regarded her steadily. 'We do not know what is possible until we test it.'

'I'm sorry,' she said, more hotly. 'But I do. And I just know that I'm not up to the job. I never should have come here.'

And with that, she turned and walked past Mélodie, face fixed forward to avoid eye contact. She made her way through the glass doors and, without glancing back, began to run.

40

2021, FRANCE

They looked at each other over the kitchen table. Accounting books were spread across its worn, wooden surface.

Tentatively, guests were starting to return post-lockdown. And they'd had financial support to keep going. Still, the margins were tighter than either of them would like.

'Well, we should be OK, as long as the summer's good,' she said at last. 'Maybe even get back in the black by autumn?'

Pete was leaning on his hands as if holding his head up was too much for his neck to bear. 'I don't know, Bella. I really don't.'

'We've done the maths! It will be OK,' she repeated.

'But is it worth it? I mean, seriously?'

His words felt like daggers.

'What do you mean?'

'I dunno,' he looked away, out over their land, drenched in early spring sunshine. In contrast, the kitchen felt gloomy and dull. 'We barely make a living, Bella. Back on the site, I was making three times as much and that was five years ago... and I dunno. I guess I felt better about what I was doing.'

'But we get to live here! We own our own house! We could never afford anything like this back home.'

'Home?' He raised an eyebrow, seizing on the word. 'See, you don't like to admit it, but you do still consider England as home. It does still feel... foreign to you here.'

She flushed. 'France is my home. It was a slip of the tongue. Come on, Pete. It's been a shit time for everyone with the pandemic and all. It'll get better.'

'I just—' He paused. 'I suppose the French thing. I thought it would be easier. I thought I'd be— I'd have some free time, you know? Not spend it all fixing things and doing the garden.'

'I know. It'll get easier,' she said, reaching out a hand towards him.

'Yeah. I guess.' He placed a hand over hers, seemed to be wrestling with something. 'But if it doesn't...'

'It will.'

'But if it doesn't... Would you think about trying something else? For me?'

'Another business? Actually, I've been thinking of learning how to make chocolate... maybe we could do something with that on the side? Boost our income?'

'No, I mean another place. Maybe back home? England. If I did want to go, you'd come with me...'

She looked at him.

'Right?'

'I can't, Pete, you know that. And look, it's not something we have to worry about. Because things will get better.'

41

NOW

'Right.' Brad seemed to have taken up the position as chair of the impromptu meeting they seemed to be having at the kitchen table. They were seated around, each with a steaming mug in front of them, Odette and Brad on one side, Henri and Bella on the other. 'What do we need to do to make this right?'

When Bella had arrived home an hour ago, breathless and tearful, she'd wanted to dash straight to her room. But Brad had been in the hallway, guitar-case in hand, and seen her face straightaway.

'What's wrong?'

'Nothing, just—' But she hadn't been able to hold it together. The minute she'd started sobbing, he'd stepped forward, wrapped his arms around her. Let her cry messily into his white shirt.

Now, he'd taken charge, was heading some sort of meeting. So sure, so confident that he could fix things.

Bella shook her head. 'We can't.'

'We could try?'

'The paintwork is ruined, the curtains are burnt. The

artwork – God, expensive original artwork – is totally destroyed. The furniture is soaked, or singed, or covered in foam.' Bella's voice started to break. 'There's no money and no time.'

'But we can try?' Brad said simply. 'You can't let being afraid get in the way. You know. If we fix it, you could stay. Things could— it could be cool.'

Bella felt her hands ball into fists. 'First of all, nobody says *cool* any more!' she said, wondering why she'd started with that. 'And you can talk! About being afraid!' She turned to Odette. 'Did you know that he's been scared to play guitar in public, or even in front of friends, for twenty years? And he's brilliant. I heard him a couple of times when he thought I was out.'

Brad's cheeks flushed and she felt a tiny niggle of guilt. But not enough to stop.

She turned back to Odette. 'And Odette, you are a brilliant artist. I mean life-changingly, staggeringly brilliant. And you're keeping all your paintings – which you could probably sell for hundreds or thousands even – in your room because you're too afraid to make a phone call and face the possibility of being rejected.'

Odette's face fell, crumpled.

Bella paused for breath, her heart thundering, then her eyes fell on Henri, who was clutching his coffee with both hands. 'And YOU—' she said.

'Me?' Henri looked affronted.

'Not telling your dad you don't want in on his business! He's setting all his hopes on you and yes, maybe he's a bit pushy. But he has the right to know the truth. At least you have a father who wants to be in your life.' She stood up abruptly, her heart hammering. 'So don't accuse me of being scared,' she finished, her voice a little wobbly now. 'Because we're all scared. All of us. And sometimes,' she looked at Brad, his pen still hovering over the notebook, 'we can't fix things. For God's sake. I don't know why I even sat down with all of you. You're the last people I should be taking advice from.'

Seeing them all look at her, affronted, hurt, annoyed, upset, was too much. She turned and ran from the room to her bedroom and slammed the door, leaning against it as the tears came.

42

NOW

The knock on the door was hesitant. Then came the voice: 'Bella?'

Odette.

'Hey,' she managed.

'Open the door?'

Bella looked around her room at the strewn clothing, the abandoned plates. 'I can't. I'm OK, I promise.'

For the past twenty-four hours, she'd stayed in her room, only sneaking out when she was sure they were all asleep to grab food, use the bathroom quickly, before rushing back. After her outburst, the house had been strangely silent, and as she'd gradually calmed down, she'd felt sick with herself. She'd burned down the hotel rooms, and now it seemed she'd set fire to her entire life.

Tomorrow she would get up properly and start to pack. Book a ticket and get out of here.

Bella felt an almost painful wash of emotion, her eyes stung from suppressing tears. She just couldn't afford to break down any more. It was lovely – sweet – that Odette wanted to help. Especially as they hadn't been on great terms recently. But it was hopeless; just hopeless.

'Please.' Odette's voice was hesitant, nervous. 'It's OK. What you said. It was the truth, at least.'

'Oh, Odette. It wasn't. Not really. Not the way I said it. I was — It was—'

'But it's OK.'

There was a silence.

Bella could sense Odette still outside the door, probably wondering what to do next. But then heard her footsteps retreating across the creaky landing floor and let herself relax back onto the bed. 'Sorry,' she whispered, to no one.

Brad tried a little later. 'I've made you a cup of tea,' he wheedled. 'It's a good one. Strong, the way you like it?'

'Thank you; I'm sorry. I just— I can't,' she managed.

He sighed. 'Bella, come on. I still think we could sort this. We could at least try to salvage things. Talk to Claudine – she was upset when she fired you. She probably didn't mean it. And the rooms... you never know, we could make them look better. Explain. You can't be the only enterprise in Hotel Club that's suffered some sort of setback.'

The word 'setback' almost made her anger flare again, but she swallowed it down as best she could, ashamed of the damage she'd already inflicted.

'I know. But she can't afford— I used the entire budget. Insurance probably won't pay out, and even if they do it'll be too late. It was a now or never thing.'

'Then why not try now? What have you got to lose?'

He was right, in that way. She hadn't really got anything to lose. But she also didn't have the energy or impetus to try. What she wanted to do was abandon the whole thing. Get on a plane, forget about this chapter of her life. Sort out her divorce, take the equity she'd get from the sale and reconvene. Maybe in France. Just not in Versailles and nowhere near Hôtel Benjamin.

She didn't reply.

Eventually he set the cup down outside and, once checking the coast was clear, she collected it gratefully. It was lukewarm, but still more than welcome.

She was embarrassed in many ways; acting like a child and she knew it. But it was as if she had no fight left.

Better just to go. To get away.

* * *

She must have fallen asleep. When she woke, the sun was still streaming through the gap between the half-closed curtains, but had the golden quality it seemed to acquire in the early evening. Footsteps sounded on the stairs; probably what had woken her. She hoped it was Brad or Henri going to their rooms rather than anyone else trying to speak with her.

She'd promised she'd go downstairs, but in truth she was hoping to pack her things, disappear in the morning for her plane. She'd write a note, maybe call them from England.

She knew that running away was immature, wrong. That she was, after all, her father's daughter. But that was something she'd have to unpick later. Because she simply wasn't capable of more. She never should have thought of aiming higher.

There was a knock on the door. Not the hesitant knocks of earlier, but something more urgent: a rapping. She froze and willed the person to go away.

But they clearly had no intention to.

'Bella!' they called. 'Open up now!'

She stiffened, her eyes widening with recognition.

'Bella...' The voice had a warning tone which snapped her into action.

She found her body obeying before her brain had a chance to catch up. Getting to her feet, she walked to the door and opened it.

Kitty was leaning against the door-frame, foot tapping with impatience. 'For goodness' sake, woman, I've been travelling most of the day. The least you could do is give me a proper welcome.'

'Oh my God, Kitty!' Something inside Bella crumpled and she flung herself at her sister. They embraced, holding each other tightly. 'What are you doing here?' she asked.

'What do you think?' Kitty replied dryly. She pushed past her sister into the room, inspecting it. Instinctively, she went to the window and opened the curtains fully. Sunlight flooded in, revealing dancing dust particles, a half-packed case. 'Nice place,' she said.

'Very funny.'

Kitty shook her head, hands on hips. 'We'd better get this lot cleaned up.'

'Who are you? My mother?'

'No,' Kitty said. 'But I suppose I'm the closest you have. And anyway, if you're going to behave like a petulant teenager, how do you expect me to act?'

It was probably meant to be a joke, but something about it made Bella stiffen. 'I'm not being a teenager, Kitty. Maybe you don't know, but everything is ruined. I've been fired, I've ruined Claudine's future, I've— I hurt my friends. I said some awful things.'

Kitty shook her head. 'I know about the hotel. Why do you think I'm here?'

'But who—?'

'Your landlord guy. He got my number from the contract. Remember? I'm your guarantor. And from what he said, your friends are just fine. Worried about you, if anything.'

'Oh. Well, he shouldn't have. I'm sorting things.'

'Yes, it really seems like it.'

They both looked at the tangled mess of food and clothing, toiletries and packing that littered the room. Then at each other. Then, as if some invisible agreement had passed between them, both began to laugh.

'The state of this place!'

'Looks better than the state of my life!' Bella's own remark dampened her laughter.

'Talking of being someone's mum, where's Ty? Who's looking after him?' she said suddenly.

Kitty tilted her head. 'I do have a husband, remember?'

'He's babysitting?'

'He's *parenting*. It's not like—' Kitty sighed, sat down on the bed as if devoid of energy. 'Not all dads are like— well, like ours. Stu does his bit.'

'I know.'

'Dad was always a bit... hands off, even before Mum. But I mean Stu isn't— He's not reluctant about it, not resentful. Doesn't have to be told what to do. He's a father. It makes me think about Dad. How little he gave us. Not money, I mean – we're quite lucky in that way... but of himself. I don't feel that we ever really knew him, not properly.'

Bella was silent. Then, 'You're right,' she said.

'Not all families are like that. I've realised that now even more.'

Bella nodded.

'It affects me too, you know,' Kitty said. 'The Dad stuff. I know he came to my wedding, but it was only down the road from him. There was no... effort. But he never remembers Ty's birthday, forgets him at Christmas. Sends money when he remembers... but—'

'That's awful.'

'I know. I don't mind so much when it's me. But... I mean, it's Ty!'

'Poor kid.'

'Yeah.' Kitty shook her head. 'Look, I didn't come to talk about Dad, obviously. But I do think maybe having the father we had— it makes it hard to rely on anyone, doesn't it? But I think your friends here, they can help. Brad, especially. He seems desperate to try.'

It was hard not to smile a little. 'I know.' Bella said. She shook her head. 'Just— I can't. I'm just going to go home. If you'll let me.'

'Of course,' Kitty nodded. 'You're always welcome. But come because you want to. Not because you're running away. Not because you're afraid.'

'Afraid?'

Kitty turned slightly so they were facing each other properly, still sitting on the soft duvet. 'Bella, I know you. If you run away from this now, you won't ever feel OK about it. Remember what we said? After Dad?'

'I knew you were going to say that.'

'Remember?'

Bella sighed; a schoolgirl caught out and forced to toe the party line. 'We'd never abandon our responsibilities like he did.'

Kitty nodded.

'But this isn't the same! I've been asked to leave. Claudine told me it was over.'

'Well, convince her it's not.'

'I just—' Bella's body slumped. 'I can't. I'm so tired, Kitty. I don't even know where to start. You should have seen the rooms. They were—' She felt a new wash of tears as she heard the truth in her own words. It was pointless. What could be done in just five days? 'I can't— it's all such a mess.'

'I *know* you, Bella. If you walk away from this, you'll regret it.'

Kitty was gazing at her intently, as if she could see right through anything Bella was putting in their way. 'Bella,' she said. 'Look at me.'

Bella raised her eyes.

'You need this. You're not incapable. You're just afraid.'

She nodded miserably. 'Maybe I do need this,' she said. 'But you're right. I *am* afraid. It's human to be scared. Human to avoid things because of it.'

Kitty was looking at her, face impassive.

'We can't all be like you, Kitty. We can't all be perfect, with a perfect life.'

Kitty's eyes widened. 'Is that what you think of me?' she said, her voice growing louder. 'You think I live this perfect, stress-free, *fear*-free life?' She stood up, faced Bella. 'I'm terrified, OK? I've been terrified ever since Mum died – because I knew you needed me to be a grown-up, and I felt like a kid. And even more terrified since Ty was born. And maybe I should have shared that with you, but you— I just didn't want to worry you.'

'Terrified?'

'Yes. Terrified. Terrified something's going to happen to you or to him, or that I won't be enough for you. Terrified that I'm losing myself. Terrified of going back to work, but terrified of what will happen to me if I don't. Me. Kitty. Not Ty's mum. Not your sister. Me.' Hot, fat tears began to roll down her cheeks. 'Oh, I know you think I have it all together. And maybe that's an image I wanted you to see. I thought you needed someone to depend on after Mum... after Dad... But there. It's not the truth. I'm scared too. All the time.'

43

NOW

'Here you go.' Bella put the mug of tea down in front of Kitty who held it in cupped hands as if needing its warmth as well as its restorative powers.

Bella sat down next to her sister, put an arm around her. At first Kitty remained upright, but then something inside her seemed to break, and she slumped into Bella's shoulder. 'I'm sorry,' she said. 'What an outburst. Your housemates must think I'm a nightmare.'

Odette and Brad had quietly slipped out of the room when they'd come to the kitchen, Kitty still red-faced from crying. Bella was grateful for that. Clearly, they needed time on their own.

'Don't worry about them,' she said. 'They have their own stuff going on. And it doesn't matter. What does matter is why didn't you tell me?'

'You were so young when Mum died. I just sort of... picked up the reins, or as much of them as I could.'

'Yes, but Kitty, I'm thirty-four now. I can cope. I'm an adult.'

Kitty looked at her. 'I know.' She sipped her tea. 'I just— I can't seem to see you any other way than that sixteen-year-old girl who'd lost her mum too soon. Whose dad just wasn't prepared to stick around, but ran away instead.'

Bella gripped her hand. 'I guess I'm guilty too. Of not realising how much you were doing. Of taking you for granted. Your... steadiness. I just— I always believed that you had it all figured out and that I was the one in a mess. Your wedding, your job, Ty. You seemed to have more purpose and direction in life, and I was the one bumbling along.'

Kitty smiled. 'How do you think it feels to live in the same town where you grew up, to marry a guy who went to your school, get a predictable job in the city and tell everyone your sister lives in a beautiful farmhouse in France and is having an adventure? I always felt people must label *me* the boring one.'

'Well, if they did, they know nothing of what it's actually like to run a B & B. Because it's hardly a glamorous dream life.'

'But you love France!'

Bella looked at her. 'I do. But just— When I was on that trip from school it was probably the best week of my life. At least, it felt like that at the time. Then I came home and Mum—' She paused, couldn't find the words. 'The crash. You know. And things were never the same. I sometimes wonder if I fell in love with France or just wanted to... go back in time, you know? To how things were when I was here.'

'But it doesn't mean that what you've done, what you've created, isn't special.'

Bella nodded. 'Sometimes I wish that I'd known, back then, what would happen to Mum. Because the day before she— before the crash, I was being so bloody petulant. I was fed up being back in boring England after France and moaning about everything.'

'Bella, you were sixteen.'

'But I—'

'You were sixteen. Mum had been through it all with me. She knew how it was with teens and hormones. She knew you loved her. It wouldn't have— Honestly, you didn't do anything wrong.'

Bella felt hot tears well in her eyes. 'What really gets me is Mum died so young. I mean, forty is nothing, is it? When I was sixteen, it seemed like she was pretty old, that at least she'd had a good life. That kind of thing. But the more I grow up... I'm in my thirties and I still feel like a kid.' She laughed softly. 'Mum lost so many years. We lost so many years with her. She should still be here.'

'I know.'

'It doesn't seem fair that I've had this time, and she hasn't, and I've wasted it!'

'No, you haven't, Bella. How can you say that?'

'Well, what have I got to show for those years then?' Bella challenged. 'A divorce, a failed business and a CV so empty I had to lie to get a job. And after what Claudine said, I'll never work in France again.'

'Bella, you lived them.'

'But I—'

'You *lived* them,' Kitty said firmly. 'Not everything has to work out. But you had some wonderful times. And you're still young. You have time to build something brand new, whatever you want!'

'I just feel—' Bella picked at a bit of uneven wood on the table's surface. 'I feel as if I'm running out of time. I mean, Mum only had six years left when she was my age. What if something like that happens to me?'

'It won't.'

'I keep thinking I wish I could go back, do it better.'

'Which is why you let Henri and Odette think you were in your twenties?'

'Maybe on some level. But it was mostly a way of getting them to like me, I think.'

'Oh, Bella. Well, it clearly worked. They seem to love you.'

'You think?'

'Look at the way Odette and Brad are falling over themselves to help you!'

Bella shrugged.

'And Henri dated you – he must have seen something in you!'

Bella felt a little flushed, took a sip of her own tea. Then, 'It's just— well, if I die at forty, what will I really have done with my life?'

'Bella. You are not going to die at forty.'

'You can't know…'

'OK, well, you have maybe a 1 per cent chance. There's a 1 per cent chance of tons of things happening, good and bad. You can't waste time worrying about that. Which means, based on Gran's age when she died, you probably have at least six decades left. You have all the time in the world.'

'But Mum—'

'Mum,' Kitty said firmly, putting her arm around her sister, 'would not want you to let what happened to her colour your life for the worse. She would want you to live. And you are! You have! It's amazing what you've done.'

Bella felt a flush of warmth. 'You really think so?'

'I know so.'

'You too, you know. I'm in awe of you most of the time.'

Kitty smiled. 'Look at us.'

'What a mess we've made.'

'Well,' her sister said, straightening and sounding more like herself. 'What do we do when there's a mess?'

'Run away?' Bella said hopefully.

'We clean it up. We make order out of chaos. We make things right.'

'I was worried you were going to say that.'

44

2023, FRANCE

'Bye!' Bella waved the guests off. The minute they'd finished, both she and Pete flung themselves down into their newly reupholstered chesterfield.

'Thank God for that,' Pete said.

'Yeah.' She blew air from her mouth, making her fringe dance. 'Hard work.'

'You can say that again.'

The visitors had stayed two weeks, for which they were grateful. But their exacting demands, teamed with the fact they were both late to bed and early risers, meant their visit had taken its toll.

It was the first week of September, and she and Pete had purposefully blocked out the next seven days for a rest before the weather began to turn.

'Freedom at last,' Pete quipped.

'Yeah,' she smiled.

'We could go out somewhere, maybe?'

'Yeah. Tomorrow?'

'Sure.'

Silence settled over them. For the past fortnight she'd longed for the relief of silence; but this was a different kind. A kind that demanded to be broken.

'So, any plans for today?'

'No. Might get into the garden. You?'

'Not sure.'

The silence returned.

Ordinarily they'd be talking about plans for the house or preparations for guests. They'd be compiling to do lists or nipping to the shops. But now that a week free of those responsibilities yawned in front of them, those things had become obsolete.

What did ordinary couples fill those gaps with?

She smiled at him. 'Garden sounds good.'

'Yep.' He got up and stretched. 'OK, well, best get on.'

'OK.'

And he walked out of the door into their sun-drenched land, shutting it gently behind him.

45

NOW

The side door opened, and Yves beckoned them inside, his eyes darting as if he were granting them access to a secret criminal lair rather than the hotel kitchen. They walked through, ignoring the curious stares from the kitchen assistants, and made their way through the dining area to the main corridor.

'And you're sure Claudine isn't here?'

Yves nodded. 'She's off sick. If anything changes, I'll call.' He looked at her. 'I'm sorry for what I did with the fire extinguishers.'

'Don't be. You did the right thing. It could have been much worse than some ruined decor.' She tried to smile.

'And you think you might be able to... improve things?' He glanced around him, as if still worried about being caught.

She shrugged. 'I hope so? But you know, either way, if Claudine does find out, I won't mention you... helped.'

Yves's face relaxed. 'Thank you.'

Feeling sick, Bella walked towards the Superior rooms, Brad, Odette and Kitty trailing in her wake. Henri had had something he had to do, so hadn't been able to come with them, but in a way she was relieved. The fewer people, the less chance they'd be discovered.

When she opened the door to the first, then the second room, they all fell silent. The smell was the first thing to hit them – a singed, revolting stench, overwritten with something chemical. Then, once they adjusted enough to focus on other things, it was impossible to miss the streaked walls, the ruined artwork, the curtains, the mess.

'*Oh là là,*' Odette whispered to herself.

Brad gave a low whistle.

'See!' Bella said. 'I told you it would be impossible.'

'No,' Brad said.

She turned to look at him.

'It's not impossible,' he said. 'Difficult, sure. But doable.'

'You aren't serious?' She wasn't sure whether to laugh or finally allow herself to hope a little. 'You really think we can mend this?'

'Well, maybe not make it exactly as it was,' he said. 'But yeah. I've got a painter contact who owes me a favour.'

'Is there anyone in Paris who doesn't owe you a favour?'

'Probably not.' He grinned.

'And...' Odette's voice was quiet, she cleared her throat. 'And if you want, I can— well. You can have a painting, if you want.' She spoke in English for Kitty's benefit, her accent making the language sound prettier than its reality.

'Really? You'd do that?'

Odette nodded, her cheeks flushed.

'Oh, my God! Thank you!' Bella grabbed Odette and squeezed her in an enormous hug.

Odette was seemingly surprised either by her own offer or the tightness of Bella's squeeze.

'See!' said Kitty. 'And I'm sure we can clean up the worst of the mess. The carpet's still OK, thank God.'

'Yes, but that's still not all of it! What about the curtains. They were beautiful! Hand-stitched. And what about the furniture?'

Kitty looked at her. 'It hasn't occurred to you?'

'What? What hasn't occurred to me?'

'Well... if only you had a house full of beautiful furniture sitting somewhere, say, in the countryside, that you could borrow from.'

Bella's mouth fell open. 'The Peyrat house!'

'Well, yeah. I'm surprised you didn't—'

It hadn't crossed her mind. But then Peyrat seemed so many miles away, a different life. She couldn't imagine that she could actually travel from this world to that. But she could... just.

'*Je peux vous aider*?' said another voice.

They all jolted with surprise. Turning, Bella's eyes travelled down to meet those of an old lady, whose dog sat patiently at her feet. 'Madame Roux!' she said, slipping into French. 'Oh, it's nice to see you. I— We were just looking... We—'

Madame Roux laughed. 'You think I am stupid? I know what you are doing.'

'Oh. Please don't tell Claudine.'

'You must think me mad also? Claudine would ask you to leave immediately.'

'But you don't want us to?' Bella tried.

'Claudine is a silly girl. Proud. She has decided that it is all over. But if you can give her some hope,' Madame Roux shrugged, 'then I am happy to help you.'

'Thank you. For not telling her.'

Madame Roux laughed. 'I offered to help, not keep secrets.

You think the only thing an old lady can do to help is to keep quiet? *Non*; do you not remember that I am a seamstress?'

'Oh yes!' Bella couldn't help but glance at Madame Roux's rather gnarled fingers. 'But—'

Madame Roux followed her eyes. 'Ah, they are old, my hands, but they work!' she said. 'In any case, I have curtains at my shop.'

'Your shop?'

'*Oui*. It is small. It is closed for many years. But I have my materials, some curtains. My machine for alterations.'

'You really think you could make... something beautiful?'

'As if I would make anything other!' Madame Roux tsked. 'I am sure if Jean-Paul Gaultier trusted me, then you can too.'

Brad grinned. 'Jean-Paul Gaultier?' he said quietly to Bella.

'I'll tell you later.' Then, 'Well, thank you. I don't know what to say.'

'It's OK.' Madame Roux's face fell a little. 'It is nice, to be able to help. Claudine is too proud to ask, thinks too little of me, in any case. But perhaps this will show her that I can be an asset, not just an inconvenience.'

They all stood looking at one another, stunned for a minute that they had, somehow, put a plan together. Then, 'I'd better call my buddy,' Brad said, pulling his phone from his pocket.

'I'll go and select some art for you to choose from,' said Odette.

'I will get a taxi to my shop,' Madame Roux said. 'Yves can help me.'

'And I guess,' Bella said, looking at her sister, 'I'm going to Peyrat.'

'Looks like it.' Kitty smiled. 'Although I hope you'll still have time to come with me to the airport later? And on the way you can tell me all the other plans. My French is pretty basic, so unless you were just telling them that Jean-Paul Gaultier is coming to help, I haven't got a clue what's going on.'

At 6 a.m. the following morning, Bella was standing by the kerb waiting for Brad to bring his car around from wherever he kept it. At her feet was a small overnight bag – they hoped to do everything in a day, but had both decided to bring some basics just in case. Yesterday, she'd seen Kitty off at the airport as promised, and although she was used to not having her sister around, life felt emptier now she'd left.

Brad had been waiting for her when she'd returned yesterday evening, glass of wine ready-poured at the table. 'Drink?'

She'd sighed and sunk into a chair. 'How did you know?'

'Must be difficult living so far from her.'

'Yeah,' she'd said, taking a sip. 'I mean, sometimes.'

'Look, I've sorted my painting guy, and Yves is going to let him in. So I'm kind of at a loose end tomorrow. Thought you might like a bit of company on your trip?'

She really would. But 'No, I'll be fine,' she'd said. 'I'm going to hire a van. They've got some at Super U.'

'Oh, come on. It'll give me a chance to run the car. It'll seize up soon. Don't waste your money.'

'You have a car?'

'Sure.'

'That's so nice of you, but we're hardly going to fit a couple of chests of drawers or bedside tables into a car.'

'Ah, but I know a dude with a trailer,' he said, as if he'd already thought it all out. 'He owes me a favour.'

'Brad?'

'Yeah?'

'Seriously? Another IOU?' That said, it would be lovely not to have to hire a van. And the idea of company – especially company with strong arms – was more than welcome. But 'No, honestly, I don't want to put you to any trouble.'

'Bella?'

'Yeah?'

'Are you giving me the brush-off, or are you just being British and awkward and saying no because it feels impolite to impose?'

She'd flushed, looked at the table. 'I guess, being British?'

'Well, I'm an American,' he'd said. 'So I'm not buying it. Accept the help.'

She'd taken a sip of wine. 'OK,' she'd said, meeting his eye. 'If you insist.'

Later, she'd emailed the *notaire* saying that she was driving down and that she'd pop into the Aubusson office to sign the papers at the end of the afternoon, after visiting the house.

Then she'd braced herself and written to Pete.

Hi Pete,

I'm popping over to the Peyrat house tomorrow. I need to pick up a couple of things. I hope that's OK? Not sure if

you're still around, but thought I'd warn you so we can avoid
any awkwardness. Talk soon.
    Bella

She'd dug out her keys, feeling rather nostalgic at the sight
of the enormous, old-fashioned set – so different from her
current single house key. Her small handbag felt heavy with the
weight of them, and she hoped she'd be able to remember
which of them actually opened the front door of the main
building.

It had felt almost impossible to drag herself from bed at five
o'clock that morning – only an hour earlier than her usual time,
but far too early after a late and restless night. To make sure she
was alert enough for the drive, she'd downed two espressos in
quick succession and while she now felt awake, she also felt
vaguely sick.

The only advantage so far of her early start was the fact that
she'd seen the sun rise over Versailles for the first time. It had
been dark when she'd woken, the first slivers of light breaking
through the gloom just after five thirty. The day had gradually
come into itself as she'd dressed and readied herself. Now, the
street was in a rosy half-light, promising sunshine.

The early morning air had a fresh, crisp undertone and
there was something energising about breathing in great gulps
of it, despite the fact it still had the underlying scent of the city
– the smell of car exhaust fumes, people, cigarettes, coffee, and
the multiple lives that flowed together around its streets during
daylight hours.

She watched one or two people make their way along the
road – a jogger in professional-looking running gear; a woman
dressed in a coat that looked far too thick for this time of year
walking a reluctant-looking dog on a lead.

Then, before she could take in any more, she heard a throaty roar, and there was Brad behind the wheel of a rather rusty 4x4 in a muted green. Attached to the back was a trailer with a handwritten number plate and rather dodgy-looking tyres. He parked, bumping the kerb a little, and climbed out of the slightly sunken driver's seat with some difficulty. 'Voilà!' he said and gave a little bow. Despite the stress of thinking about the hotel rooms and whether Claudine was going to return to work and discover their secret, it was hard not to laugh.

Then he held out the keys. 'Your chariot awaits!'

'And you're sure the insurance is OK?'

'All sorted.'

'And you're OK if I, like, bash it up or ruin the gears or something?'

He laughed. 'That won't happen.'

She looked at him.

'But yes, if it does, I will forgive you,' he added, smiling and shaking his head as if she were being ridiculous.

It was pretty clear he'd never seen her drive before.

'OK.' She took a breath and climbed into the worn, leather driver's seat. Brad walked around the car and climbed in beside her.

Inside, the car smelled of oil and some sort of pine air freshener. The plastic dashboard was sun-bleached and scratched. This was probably the perfect car for driving garden waste to the déchetterie or bumping down muddy tracks. But for someone wanting a reliable car for eight hours of driving in a day? She hoped it would be up to the job.

'Fully serviced and checked a couple of months ago,' Brad said, as if reading her mind.

She nodded and started the engine, pleased that it caught and roared into life first time.

'See,' he said confidently, as if starting was all the car needed to do to prove its worth.

It's got 400 kilometres to go yet, she wanted to say – but didn't.

She tried to think about the €200 of hire fees she'd saved by accepting his offer and put her foot on the accelerator. And they were off.

Navigating the city streets was unnerving – driving on the right side of the road had seemed difficult even when she'd lived in the quiet Creuse *département*. But here with traffic lights, one-way systems and people who strolled casually in front of them deep in conversation, the stakes felt frighteningly high.

Bella found that she was gripping the wheel tightly, her leg hovering constantly over the brake, ready to slam it down if necessary. Her slow, careful driving earned a couple of angry beeps from other drivers. 'I thought the French were meant to be laid back!' she found herself saying to Brad.

'You think this is bad? You should try driving in Chicago,' he told her cheerfully. 'If you don't get blasted by someone's horn on every trip, you wonder if you're invisible.'

'But still—'

'Ah, you'll be OK once we're on the main road,' he said, leaning back as if he weren't in almost constant mortal danger.

The roads leading out of the city were busy, despite the early hour, and she made a couple of wrong turns, forced to travel miles out of their way in order to turn round. Once or twice Brad looked at her, and she sensed he was thinking about offering to take over. But he said nothing.

In reality she'd have loved someone to step in – just for this bit, the busy bit. But the last thing she wanted to do was surrender and ask.

Almost an hour later they were finally on the autoroute and

things had started to feel more civilised. The road was long, straight, two-lane and virtually empty. As they headed towards Orléans, she began to feel her shoulders and stomach relax a little.

'You OK?' Brad asked after they'd been driving smoothly for a while.

'Yeah,' she said. 'I'm fine.'

'You're driving pretty good.'

'What? Now? Yeah, it's pretty easy now.'

'Don't beat yourself up. I thought you handled Versailles pretty well too. It's a nightmare getting around that one-way system – and those idiots on their phones who step into the road. Terrifying.'

'Are you saying that just to make me feel better?' she said.

He grinned. 'Maybe. But I mean it too. You handled it well. And I'm pretty sure Maureen approves.'

'I'm sorry – Maureen?'

'Yeah,' he slapped the dashboard. 'She'd an old bird, but she's a fighter.'

'You named your car?'

'Sure, why not?'

'Because it's weird!'

'How so? She's got a character. The least she deserves is a name!'

'Fair, I suppose.'

They lapsed into silence for a while, but it was comfortable, companionable. The roads were empty, the sun now fully risen, and driving had almost become a pleasure. She changed gear, leaving her hand on the gear stick and settling back into a more comfortable position now that she could relax.

Unexpectedly, Brad's hand covered hers, squeezed gently, affectionately. Then, just as quickly, retreated.

'Sorry,' he said. 'Wasn't thinking.'

She gave him a sideways glance.

'Just,' he said, 'I guess I'm proud of you.'

'What are you, my dad?' she joked, instantly regretting it.

'No, I— I mean, you had this setback, but you picked your-self up. Not many people can do that.'

'I had quite a bit of encouragement,' she said, glancing at him again.

He was looking at her with his clear, honest eyes. 'Sure. But still.'

'I appreciate it, you know.'

'What?'

'The encouragement.' She sighed, shifted gears into fourth as they neared a bend. 'I'm sorry that I find it so difficult to... respond to it.'

'Britishness?'

'Yeah, a bit. But also... well, shit childhood.'

'I get it. More than you know, probably.' He fell silent.

'Sorry to hear that,' she said into the empty air.

'Yeah. Anyway, though, I— I'm getting it all wrong. I'm trying to say I'm impressed, I guess.'

'Impressed?' There it was again, the incredulity, knocking back his compliment.

'Yeah. And... I guess in more than just a business sense.'

Another glance and she was surprised to see Brad looking flushed. Was he actually embarrassed?

'I guess—' he continued. 'I mean, what I want to say is that I like you. You know?'

'Oh.'

'I know. Stupid, right?'

'Not at all!' Something fluttered inside, as if a bird were

beating its wings in her chest. As if something dormant had woken at his words. 'I mean, it's good. It's fine.'

'"It's good, it's fine"?'

'Sorry. I'm crap at this stuff.'

'You're not the only one. Used to be quite the charmer back in the day. Before Naomi, my ex, and the money stuff. I guess I thought I had something to offer.'

'You still do. Seriously.'

'Thanks.'

'I mean,' she said, hardly knowing the words that were going to come. 'I like you too. A lot, actually.' Where had that come from? Not from her conscious mind. But it was right, wasn't it. She did, didn't she?

'But?' he said into the silence, sensing her hesitation.

'But,' she echoed, 'I've been on a roller coaster. You know, with Pete. Then Henri. And all this stuff with work and Kitty and... my head is all over the place.'

'OK.'

'I'm just not—'

'It's OK. I get it.'

'I need to sort myself out. I need to work out what I'm doing. And I just don't think—'

'I get it.' His tone was slightly sharper. 'Shall we just drop it?'

'But you understand. It's not a... it's not a no. It's a not now.'

There was a silence. Then he gave a deep sigh. 'I get that,' he said. 'I do. And you know what, I'm good with being friends. Life can get crazy sometimes.'

'I know, right?'

'You know, that seems kind of a mature attitude for a kid in their twenties,' he said, winking.

She looked at him wryly. 'I'm the oldest twenty-year-old in the world.'

47

NOW

It was a strange feeling navigating the roads close to where she'd lived for so many years. Gradually, the style of the buildings then the buildings themselves became familiar, and she found herself driving through the series of small villages and hamlets that surrounded Aubusson. On the other side of the historic town, the stone house she fell in love with nine years ago was sitting waiting for her.

It was almost lunchtime and they'd been travelling for five and a half hours – two stops on the way and a hold-up close to Bourges had added an hour or more to their total trip time. After the awkward conversation was out of the way, the air had felt cleared and she and Brad had been able to chat about ordinary things – she'd told him about growing up in Hertfordshire, about meeting Pete, their wedding and the French B & B plan.

'Looking back, I was so naïve,' she'd said.

But Brad had shaken his head. 'Brave, more like. I mean, taking all that on at a young age? It was a lot. And you did it!'

'This journey kind of proves that I didn't. Not really.'

'You kept that place going for eight years. And sure, you weren't making as much as you'd hoped, but you were doing it!'

He'd told her about Chicago, about coming to France and staying with his grandmother for holidays. 'She was from New York originally but married a French guy in the forties, some guy her brother met during the war, I think. I had a lot of holidays in Versailles growing up. Some of my friends were super jealous but actually it was a pretty boring place when you're thirteen and your French is kinda basic.'

'I can imagine.'

'There are only so many times you can be dragged round the Palace, or go sightseeing in Paris. I appreciate it now, but then...' He shook his head. 'Man, those days were long! Then I met Naomi when I was about twenty and things got a bit more interesting.'

'When did you inherit the house?'

'About five years ago.' He'd looked sad. 'If I'm honest, things were already going a bit wrong with Naomi by then. I used to come for a couple of months from home to give us both a break sometimes, although it was always about business on the surface.'

'Are you OK?' he asked her now. 'You've gone quiet.'

'Yeah. It's just weird,' she said. 'Knowing I'm going to see Peyrat again; the house. It hasn't been that long, not really, but it feels like so much has happened since I left.'

'Yeah, I get that. Do you ever miss it?'

She thought about Versailles, her new job. How exciting but terrifying everything seemed now. Her new look and energy for life, but the unsustainability of everything – the feeling that it was all going to crumble away from her at any moment. 'I miss the peacefulness of it,' she said. 'People. Obviously, I stay in touch with friends. But I miss the community – those I used to bump into locally and have a chat with.'

He nodded. 'Makes sense.'

'And the quiet, sometimes,' she admitted. 'You know, there were nights when I'd go outside after dark – just out on the front steps – and I used to feel astonished at how close the stars seemed. The street lights in the village would go out about 10 p.m. and there were only about five of them to start with. But the sky was brilliant – like nothing I'd ever seen.'

'Sounds cool. Maybe I'll get to see them.'

'I hope not,' she said drily.

'How come?'

'Because it only gets dark about eleven, twelve maybe, at this time of year. And I hope we'll be back in Versailles by then.'

'Good point. Still, it sounds beautiful.'

'It really is.'

The silence settled on them again. Then: 'What's the house like?' Brad asked.

'You'll see it soon,' she said, feeling something well up inside her as they drew ever closer to the place she'd used to call home.

'Humour me.'

'OK, well, it was made of stone – surprisingly. An old farmhouse and a couple of small, converted barns. Old world on the outside, bit more modern inside. Garden large, but workable. Great views.'

'Cool. How many people did you do B & B for?'

'We had about six rooms in the house, then the two outhouses where families could stay. I think the most we had at one time was twenty-two people.'

'Hang on, twenty-two people?'

'Yeah. Some of them were self-catering, so...'

'Man! The way you spoke about it before, I was thinking you had maybe four rooms tops,' he said. 'That's a proper hotel, almost. I mean, that's a serious business.'

She smiled. It felt nice to hear him say that. 'I suppose it was.'

She'd got used to the car on the drive down, although the rather meagre padding in the driver's seat had left her feeling a bit bruised. As the roads narrowed, she passed the first sign for Peyrat and felt a strange shiver of recognition. 'Almost there,' she said, trying to sound upbeat, but wondered whether Brad could detect the tremor in her voice.

Then suddenly, they passed the sign, and she found herself driving past the fields and gardens, the scattered stone houses. In one garden, an enormous parasol under which there was a table covered in plates and glasses. Another had a pool, its still surface glistening blue and white in the sunshine. All was peaceful and drenched in light.

'This is really cool,' said Brad, his tone almost reverent.

'Yeah?' She felt a kind of uplift, as if he'd told her *she* was cool. 'I guess it is, kind of. Gets a bit quiet in the winter, mind.'

'I can see it,' he said. 'Snow, and dark skies and roaring fires inside.'

'And ice on the roads and gritters and having to stock up on horrible UHT milk just in case you can't get out for a few days.' She glanced at him and grinned. 'But you're right, beautiful too. I did love it here.' She was surprised at her own words for a second. Things had deteriorated with Pete and had been so stressful with the B & B she'd almost forgotten why she'd chosen to move to Peyrat in the first place. It had been the beauty of it, its unspoilt nature. The air so fresh it almost made her feel drunk.

Those first evenings, sitting in the garden with Pete,

laughing at how ridiculous it was that they could afford a house like this in rural France when their friends were trying to save up deposits for bedsits priced twice what they'd paid. They'd felt so very clever and on top of the world.

When the stars had come out and she'd seen them for the first time – enormous, fat and glowing in the navy sky – she'd vowed to herself that she'd never take it for granted. The view over the countryside, the freshness, the simpler way of life and the space.

But life had taken over. Stress over bills. Pete's lack of practical support, his boredom. Their arguments. Preparing things for customers, having to tiptoe around the place when visitors were *in situ*. She'd started looking only at the tedious minutia of daily life when she should have been gazing upwards.

And there it was, the house they'd fallen for when they were deeply in love. The grey stone walls, with climbing roses. The iron and glass canopy set over the front door, the one she'd painted a deep blue. The windows where some of her curtains still hung. The drive that sloped slightly, welcoming you in somehow. The garden stretching forth and crying out for an allotment and chickens and maybe even a goat or two – the whole French dream that she'd never gotten around to fulfilling.

'*This* is your place?'

'Well, *was*, I guess.'

'Man, it's really something.' Brad was shaking his head.

'Yeah,' she said, parking up. 'Yeah, it is.'

It wouldn't help to start crying. And if she let her tears fall, she wouldn't be sure whether they were for the younger version of herself with the dreams she was so convinced would come true, the marriage to Pete that she'd thought would be forever, or nostalgia for the place she'd called home for almost a decade.

Brad was still looking at the house in awe. 'I can see why you loved it,' he said.

'Bit different from Versailles?'

'Just a bit.'

She loved the house in Versailles, her work at the hotel. Loved the feeling of momentum, something she'd lost in Peyrat with its sleepy way of life. People were content here, and she'd been happy for a time, but she'd never quite lost the sense that somewhere, life was going on without her, and she ought to be part of it. 'It was lovely for so many years,' she told him. 'But I think after a while I started to get restless.'

'I get that.'

'But then, sometimes Versailles seems so busy, I sometimes long for a little peace and quiet! It's hard to know which I'd love more, long term.'

'I get that too.' He smiled. 'I think when you uproot your whole life to a new place, it opens up the world. But that's not always a good thing.'

'Really?'

'I mean,' he shrugged. 'It's 90 per cent a good thing. But it changes you. Because you realise that if you're not sticking to the neighbourhood you grew up in, or even the country where you started out, that you could actually live anywhere. And that's quite—it messes with your head sometimes. Harder to settle, or believe you're in the right place.'

'Yeah,' she said. 'I never thought of it like that. I suppose we're spoiled.'

'We certainly are.'

'Although I don't feel particularly spoiled,' she said, as she rummaged in her bag for the keys.

'Nope.' He laughed.

And there it was again. That feeling of nostalgia, sadness for what she'd lost, for how things had turned out. When she and Pete had fallen out of love with each other she'd lost her anchor, the thing that kept her in one place. And now she was being tossed around on an ocean that looked beautiful but also felt unpredictable, dangerous.

She inserted the key in the lock, wiggled it expertly into place then turned to Brad. 'Sometimes,' she said, 'do you wish you and your wife had found a way to make it work? That you still had that old life?'

'I guess,' he said. 'Or at least, I wonder what life might have turned out like.'

Clicking the lock, she turned the handle and pushed the door open. 'Right,' she said. 'Let's see if we can make any of this furniture work.'

Then she stopped, frozen. Brad narrowly avoided bumping into her as he made to follow her into the large entrance just inside the front door. Because standing there was a man with short brown hair, a smattering of stubble. He was wearing a white T-shirt, a pair of army green chinos teamed with trainers. In his hand he was holding a rather wilted flower clearly plucked from the garden outside.

He cleared his throat. 'I was leaving. But I got your email,' he said. 'And the thing you're coming for... I suppose I was hoping that might be me.'

Bella's eyes widened and she leant a hand against the door-frame for support. 'Pete!'

48

NOW

Pete noticed Brad, standing behind Bella, his brow furrowed. 'Who's this?'

'Brad. Good to meet ya.' Brad stepped forward, hand outstretched. Pete shook it.

It was, thought Bella, one of the more surreal moments of her life. 'Pete,' she said again. 'What are you doing here?'

'Isn't it obvious?' He looked at her, his eyes pleading. 'Bella, I thought I'd had enough of us. But after being in England, then coming back over here to sign the contract, seeing everything with new eyes... I was an idiot.'

'I'm just going to check out your garden,' Brad interjected. 'Give you a bit of space.'

Neither of them replied. He walked off, hands in pockets, whistling nonchalantly as if this were a completely normal situation.

'Pete,' Bella said, putting a hand on her forehead as if checking her own temperature. 'I— You realise that this is insane, don't you?'

The hand with the flower dropped to his side. 'Why? Lots of

people get back together after a separation. Lots of people struggle in a marriage.'

'I know. And maybe a few weeks ago I'd have felt differently. But I've realised a lot of things... about us, about myself. I know it sounds weird, but I've changed.'

'You mean you're with the American guy,' he said pointedly.

'No! Actually, I'm not! I'm not with anyone.' She opted not to mention the French bloke she'd had a fling with.

'So why not try?' he wheedled.

'Pete! You literally abandoned me out of the blue. You left me in a terrible situation, with no notice. And disappeared!'

'Yeah, but I said sorry.'

'Sorry isn't a magic word, Pete! It doesn't undo damage that you've done.'

'Look,' he said, more softly, reaching out a hand. 'I know that you've got abandonment issues, after your mum then your dad, but...'

'Seriously? You're blaming this on me? Because even if I didn't have abandonment issues, I'd still have objected to literally being abandoned, Pete.'

'OK. OK. I'm sorry.' His shoulders slumped. 'Look, I can make it up to you. I want to. We were good together. Eight years of marriage, Bella. You surely don't want to throw all that away.'

He looked crestfallen and somewhere under the shock and anger, she felt a pang of sympathy. 'Look, Pete,' she said, 'I know when you told me about wanting to split up, I was upset. But the more distance I got from it all, the more I realised that you were right. We were kids when we got together. We tried to do something— well, amazing. And we did it! We really made it work. But things between us hadn't been good for a while.'

'Yes, but a lot of that was the stress of running the business and—'

'*Running the business*?' She felt a familiar prickle on her skin. How did he manage to do this every time. '*I* was running the business. You were... you were just *there*, Pete. Yes, you did some great work in the garden, and you were chatty at breakfast with the guests. I'm not saying you did nothing, but it wasn't the business that broke us. It was the fact you left me to struggle. We weren't a team. You didn't *listen!*'

'You just got so stressed and—'

'*Why do you think that was*?' she almost screeched. She was reminded now of some of the arguments they'd have time and time again. They would start with an accusation from her, a request for help or support, a plea for him to take over some of the mental load that came with running a B & B. And would end with them hurling insults at each other.

Later, they'd make up and life would resume. A couple of weeks on, she'd realise that nothing had changed and they'd fall back into arguing again.

Over in the garden, Brad glanced towards them, and she felt ashamed that he'd heard her.

'Look,' she said, more quietly, stepping properly into the entrance hall. A set of steps led from there to the upstairs rooms and she sat on one, patting the space next to her. Pete obediently dropped into it. He was close and the scent of him – fresh with the slight spice of his aftershave – filled her with nostalgia. It would be easy to fall for this, to step away from the complications she'd created for herself in Versailles and resume her life here. But she wasn't the same Bella who had left this place three months ago. 'Look, Pete. I get it. This wasn't your dream, it was mine.'

'It was my—'

'Just listen for a sec.' She put her hand on his arm and he stopped, his eyes looking at her hand where it lay on his skin.

'You bought into my dream. And I'm grateful. But I suppose I understand more, with a bit of distance, time, that the reason you never felt fully *in* it with me was because you weren't. Not really. You wanted to learn to build, and you certainly got some experience here. But when we were done with the renovations, there wasn't the same buzz for you any more.'

'Yes, but that's not a reason to run away,' he said. 'I should have looked for different work... maybe set up my own business. I still could. I blamed the marriage for my unhappiness.' He looked down at his hands, now knitted together. 'But it was me. I was just unhappy; stuck.'

'I wish I'd known.'

'I should have said. But you know, it isn't too late, Bella. We're still married, legally. And we could try again. You could run a business. Maybe hire some help. I could find something that would make me happy?'

'Yes,' she said. 'You could, Pete. But not with me.'

'Why not?' His tone was sharper now. 'Because of this American bloke?'

'Brad? No. Not because of Brad.'

'You looked pretty cosy with him a second ago.'

'He was standing behind me. We weren't exactly locked in a passionate kiss.'

Pete shrugged. Not the nonchalant Gallic shrug of Yves or Henri, but a petulant, childish one. 'Still.'

Bella looked at Pete. The man whom she'd spent nearly a third of her life with. It was impossible not to feel something for him. Because their split hadn't been bitter and acrimonious. Just a gentle pulling away, a loosening of ties. 'Anyway, we couldn't go back, Pete. We're signing the house over in, like, a week.'

'Not back to the house. Go back to us.' He touched her hand

where it was still resting on his arm. 'Think about it. We'll have a little bit of money to tide us over. We could find somewhere to live. Maybe near your new job if you like it there? I could set up as an artisan – use some of my new skills. And we'd be us again! Pete and Bella, Bella and Pete.'

'I just don't know, Pete,' she said at last. 'It's too late. I just can't go back. Don't know if I want to.'

'Think about it,' he said. 'Just think about it.'

She shook her head. 'Pete, I—'

'Don't say anything,' he said, putting a finger on her lips as if he thought they were in some sort of romantic movie. 'Just give me twenty-four hours. Think about it for one day. Don't say anything until then. That's all I'm asking.'

It didn't seem unreasonable. She nodded. 'OK.'

There was an uneasy silence. Then Pete suddenly stood up, his smile as wide as if she'd told him 'I do' and they were about to head off into the sunset. 'I'll leave you to sort your bits,' he said. 'And there are a couple of boxes of stuff in the kitchen you're welcome to.'

'Where are you going?'

'I'll give you some headspace,' he said. 'I'm around for another couple of nights. Staying in Hôtel France in the centre.'

'Aubusson?'

He nodded. 'So, I'll see you?'

'But Pete—'

'Twenty-four hours, remember.'

'OK.'

He walked out through the front door, down the steps and disappeared. Shortly afterwards, she heard a car engine purr into life and he passed on the front drive in a small Nissan – a hire car that he must have tucked around the back.

She wondered how long he'd waited at the house for her,

clutching that poor wilted flower. Then she got to her feet and stood brushing dust from her bottom. Brad appeared at the doorway, his smile almost a grimace. 'You good?'

'Um, not sure,' she said, making a face. She told him about Pete, his sudden desire to reunite, to try again.

'Oh wow,' Brad raised his eyebrows. 'That's a brave move, my man.'

'Just a bit.'

'I mean you were saying that he hadn't even sent you a text message for months?'

'Not a single GIF.'

'Phew! And I thought Naomi was difficult!' He grinned. 'I take it by his sudden exit that you told him exactly where he stands.'

She was silent now, and as he looked at her his expression changed. 'I mean, you told him *no,* right?'

'Not exactly.'

'Oh.'

'It *is* a no. It will be,' she said quickly. 'But he asked me – begged really – to think about it for twenty-four hours, so I said I would.'

Brad's cheeks were flushed. 'OK.'

'I didn't feel I could tell him no, after he asked that. He's a good guy, you know?'

'So you might get back with him?'

'No! Of course not! It's the last thing I want.' She heard the frustration in her own tone. 'He just told me not to give him an answer for twenty-four hours, and I agreed. But...'

'Right. I see.' But Brad's tone suggested otherwise. He cleared his throat as if trying to reset himself. 'Anyway,' he smiled, but there was something slightly off. As if his eyes hadn't received the memo. 'Are you going to give me a tour of this beautiful house?'

'Sure, of course.' She gestured him towards the door that led off the tiled hallway to the kitchen.

'Thank you,' he said, his smile still fixed.

'Brad,' she said as they walked through into the large open plan kitchen, each cupboard painstakingly chalk-painted by Pete three years ago. 'You do know that I have no intention of getting back with Pete, don't you?'

'It's fine if you do.'

'Right. OK. But I wouldn't—'

'I mean, we're not— it's not like there's anything between us,' he said with an exaggerated shrug.

Her heart sank. 'Oh. But didn't you—'

'Great kitchen! Hey, is that an Aga?' His voice upbeat but artificially loud, Brad shut down the conversation, firmly changing the subject.

She found herself momentarily lost for words. He slapped the top of the cream-coloured double oven with its multiple doors.

'Um. Well, yes, it is.'

'Man, I love these things!' he said, bending down to inspect it.

'Me too.' She opened her mouth to say something else but found herself shutting it. For now, there was nothing more she could say.

'*Bon Dieu*, I hope this works,' Yves said as he opened the side door once again and saw the four pieces of solid-wood furniture they'd carted back from Peyrat. He put his hands to his cheeks.

'What's the matter, buddy. Don't like the furniture?' Brad asked.

'No, it looks—' Yves peered into the darkness, 'it's fine. Beautiful, actually. But there are so many lies! I am beginning to fear for my job.'

Bella gave a half-smile. 'Sorry, Yves. You know this couldn't work without you.'

'I know. That is what I'm afraid of.'

Claudine was back, and Yves had spent his day making sure she didn't venture to the rooms, and helping them keep out of sight. He had been their man on the inside, and it was clearly wearing on him.

'It'll be great!' Brad said. 'You'll be the hero of the hour. Now can you help me with this chest of drawers?'

When it had been clear that they'd reach Versailles by 9 p.m., Brad had encouraged Bella – who'd wanted nothing more than to go straight home and collapse – to call Yves. 'We can't deliver the furniture in broad daylight,' he'd reasoned. 'And we don't have another day to lose!'

Yves had agreed to stay back until 11 p.m., when most of the guests would be in their rooms and reception would be closed for the night. Claudine was back at work, but had sloped off about five hours previously, so the coast was clear. But the subterfuge looked as if it might be too much for Yves; his eyes were ringed with grey.

'We really do appreciate it,' Bella said again.

'Ah, it is not completely altruistic,' he admitted. 'I don't want to lose my job if Claudine has to close.'

As the two men took each end of a chest of drawers, Bella picked up a small bedside cabinet and followed, setting it down every few metres for a rest. When they reached the corridor, she could smell fresh paint; she momentarily closed her eyes, praying to the god of interior design – if such a being existed – that they'd be pleased with the job that Brad's friend had done.

The automatic light illuminated the corridor as they manoeuvred along in virtual silence, and for a moment it was as if the whole hotel were holding its breath. They were all so focused on reaching the room and getting the furniture inside that when the door at the opposite end of the corridor clicked open, they all jumped.

A figure approached, most of its body hidden behind an enormous rectangle. Bella glanced at Yves and saw the horror on his face. Was it Claudine back for an impromptu visit to the scene of the crime?

'Oh!' the rectangle said.

The light at their end of the corridor flicked on as they passed, and Bella gave a sigh of relief. It was Odette, carrying a new seascape Bella had never seen before. As her friend set it down with a groan, she put down the bedside cabinet she was carrying and rushed forward, arms outstretched. 'It's so good to see you!'

'It has only been a day!' Odette looked amused. 'I am sorry if I shocked you, but I wanted to get this in the room before the manager returned. I came earlier and she was back. I had to pretend I was from the original gallery.' Her cheeks pinked.

'I'm sorry,' Bella found herself saying.

'It's OK. She believed me. So that was good. Perhaps brilliant – after all, she thought my painting was from the gallery. But she told me to go, that they couldn't afford any more art.'

'Odette, you must know your work is good enough for any gallery.'

Setting down his end of the chest of drawers, Yves flicked the key card against the sensor and the door opened.

'Oh my God,' Bella breathed. The walls were immaculate, the bedding replaced. Odette's paintings hung on two of the walls, clearly original and high-end. The tray of delicacies had been replaced, and the candles removed. And a curtain hung at the window, resplendent in light green silk, embroidered with gold thread. Then, 'Oh my God!' she said again when she realised that at the other end of the curtain pole was a diminutive old woman, standing on a stool, balancing on one leg as she threaded the curtains back where they belonged. 'Madame Roux!' she said, rushing to steady her. 'You should have waited.'

Madame Roux looked down, her eyes glittering. 'But I could not,' she said, threading the last ring and allowing Bella to help her down. She dusted her hands together with satisfaction. 'I cannot tell you how satisfying it has been to be working again. To feel useful.'

'And you really have been,' Bella said, taking in the transformation to the window as if for the first time. With Madame

Roux's embroidery and Odette's original artwork, the room was more impressive than it had been the first time.

Yves and Brad heaved the chest of drawers into place, and they all stood back and looked at the result.

'Well, one thing's for sure,' Brad said confidently. 'If the guys from Hotel Club don't like it, there's something wrong with them.'

Bella looked at his face, which seemed to be almost glowing with satisfaction, and had three thoughts. The first was that he was right – they'd be fools not to love the new rooms. The second was that it was amazing that someone who didn't really have a vested interest in their success seemed so pleased on their behalf. And the third was accompanied by a pang of regret. She'd had the chance in the car to tell him how she felt, how she was beginning to feel. But she'd brushed him off. Because somehow, this man, who'd come into in her life in the most unexpected way – appearing in her bedroom in the middle of the night, and making her angrier than she'd been in months – had made her feel something she hadn't experienced properly since her mother had died. Hope. Excitement. And a sense that, after all, her story might even have a happy ending.

'You know, I should really have you arrested,' Claudine said the next morning when Bella nervously entered the office and confessed to what they'd done.

She looked tired, her eyes edged in grey.

'Seriously?'

'Why not? You are telling me that you broke into my hotel, made material changes without consent?'

'But criminals don't usually—' Bella's words faded under Claudine's severe gaze.

'What? Gain entry without permission?'

'Paint,' she finished lamely. 'Sort out the decor.'

Claudine snorted. 'Perhaps not, but what you did was still wrong.'

Bella maintained eye contact, hoping to see her friend's eyes soften. 'Claudine, it was the only way we could help. And I honestly think— Look, just come and see.'

With a world-weary sigh, Claudine stood and made her way to the door, passing through it so quickly Bella had to rush to keep up.

As they approached the rooms, Bella began to be plagued with doubts. Had the rooms really looked *that* good? Would it really be enough to sway Claudine into at least trying to move forward?

They opened the door and the pair of them stood, peering in.

'So, what do you think?' Bella asked after a painful moment of silence.

Claudine walked into the room which still smelled of fresh paint and fabric, of polish and cleaning products. And as she watched, trying to see it through Claudine's eyes, Bella felt her heart soar again – had this really been the burnt, foam-soaked shell she'd despaired over just a few days ago?

'It's— you have worked so hard,' Claudine said, her voice catching.

'So... you think we can go ahead with Hotel Club?' she asked timidly.

'*Non.*' Claudine shook her head sadly, defeated.

Something inside Bella plummeted. 'But... I mean, it's great. And we still have the presentation. Everything could—'

'*Non,*' Claudine said firmly. 'It is too late. I have cancelled the Hotel Club representatives. Nobody is coming, the caterers, the string quartet. It is all cancelled.' She turned to Bella. 'Bella, what you have done is beautiful and I should have had more faith in you. But we cannot proceed with Hotel Club. I will have to sell the hotel.'

'Oh, but... Claudine!'

'There is nothing to be done.'

'But that's just it, Claudine. It's not cancelled.'

'What do you mean? We sent emails to everyone, Yves called... I—'

'Nothing was sent. Yves— he kept everything back.'

Claudine's eyes widened. 'Yves knew about this?'

'Yes, but don't be angry. He— I mean we very much coerced him, and he was worried.'

'Angry? I am not angry! I am amazed. You did all this, took this enormous risk. For me?'

Bella shook her head. 'Not entirely. It was for me too.'

'Of course. Your job.' Claudine nodded.

Bella shook her head again. 'Not really. I mean, I love my job. And I hope it goes well and things can... carry on. But I did it because I— well, I know what it is to be abandoned. I know what it is when people walk away. And I didn't know if I'd be able to fix it, but I wanted to at least try.'

Claudine walked forward, her eyes shining, and placed a hand on each of Bella's shoulders... 'Then you are truly admirable.'

'It's not just me,' Bella said hastily. 'Brad, Henri, Odette – I had so much help. Oh, and Madame Roux!'

'I'm sorry?' Claudine said, shaking her head a little as if doubting what she'd heard. 'You had help from Madame Roux?'

'Yes, Claudine. Perhaps I am not so very useless, so very old after all,' said a sharp voice.

It was as if the very mention of her name had summoned her. They both turned to see the diminutive woman, this time dressed in turquoise, her make-up perfectly done, hair coiffed, Coco on a lead. 'I do have some skills; perhaps I am not yet ready to be consigned to a home after all.'

Claudine flushed. 'Oh. I'm— I know you have skills. Of course.'

'Then why do you never ask me for help? For anything?' Madame Roux's voice shook slightly with emotion.

'I—' Claudine looked down. 'I suppose I didn't realise you'd want to.'

'Nonsense! You thought I was past it! Just a silly old woman who needs to be consigned to an old people's facility.'

'No. You have to believe that I thought the home was a good thing! I wasn't trying to—'

'Ah, it is not just your fault,' Madame Roux said, her eyes suddenly downcast. 'After George died, I was not myself, when I first came here.' She waved her hand as if filling in the blank in her sentence. 'But time passed, and I became myself again. Only nobody realised, and I had forgotten how to show them.'

'If you didn't want to go to a home—'

'I know. Perhaps I accepted my lot too much,' the old woman continued. 'People forgot to listen to me, but I also forgot to speak. It was only Bella… When I saw that she took my advice, I began to wonder whether I was complicit in my own downfall because I had not raised an objection.'

Claudine nodded. 'Well, nothing is fixed,' she said.

'And Bella, she gave me a chance to show what I could do. When I had forgotten myself. And I had forgotten what a joy it is to create something from nothing.'

Bella found herself welling up.

'Of course she has not taken my fashion advice today,' Madame Roux said, her eyes darting up and down Bella's skinny jeans and loose blouse. 'She looks as if she is here to collect the trash. So I suppose I still have a lot of work to do.'

Claudine and Bella looked at each other momentarily before both started to smile. 'Well, thanks, Madame Roux, I think…' Bella said.

'*Non*. Thank *you*.'

51

NOW

Time passed in a flash. The next day was spent rehearsing, standing on the podium that had been erected in the event room, in front of the screen which scrolled through images of the hotel, the biographies of key players, the wider Parisian setting.

At five o'clock she finally made her way to the door; there was just enough time to go home, shower and change, then return. Bella had bought a black, elegant dress especially for the evening and she was quite excited about getting dressed up, about everything she'd worked for over the past few weeks coming to fruition.

She was exhausted, spent from cleaning, from worrying, from rehearsing so much her throat felt a little sore. But the exhilaration and adrenaline she felt raised her above this, and she was almost buzzing as she walked along the road to the house she'd begun to think of as home.

It was only when she rounded the final corner and the house came fully into view that she realised something was

different. At the bottom of the steps leading to the front door
was a woman wearing a long white dress, enormous boots, a
light jacket. Her hair was loose and glistened in the sunshine.
And as she looked towards Bella her face split in a wide smile.

It couldn't be.

'Juliette!' she called, running towards her.

'*Ma chérie!*' her friend replied, laughing and opening her
arms.

Bella flung herself at her old friend and, once she was
wrapped in her embrace, felt a weight she didn't know she was
carrying slip from her shoulders. 'With everything going on, I
forgot you'd said you'd come!' she said.

'This is the welcome I get, after travelling for almost four
hours?' her friend replied with an arch look.

'I'm sorry.' Bella stepped back and looked at Juliette as if to
check whether she was really there. 'It's wonderful, it really is.
Only it nearly didn't happen, the presentation. I was sort of
fired. And there was a fire. And... but it's all fine. Don't worry.
Honestly. And you're here.'

'Yes,' Juliette said drily. 'I am here. And I've brought you
something for tonight.' She stood and for a moment Bella
thought her friend was reaching forward to hug her. Instead,
she fastened something around the back of Bella's neck. Bella's
fingers flew to her throat. 'Oh, your lucky pendant! I can't.'

'No,' Juliette said, showing Bella the pendant she still wore
at her own neck. 'This one is yours.'

Bella's fingers touched the tiny four-leaf clover. 'I don't know
what to say.'

'Say thank you. And go and show those delegates what
you're made of. Then come and tell me all about it.'

* * *

An hour later she was ready. Odette had helped her to create a half-up, half-down do with her hair, which was now past her shoulders. Juliette made her up, using some of the posh cosmetics she swore by. And it had been hard not to notice Brad's eyes widen when she'd stepped into the kitchen earlier for a quick drink of water before setting off.

It was still light, the June evenings were stretching towards the longest day, but cloud cover had given the light a muted tone. It seemed to Bella as if she were looking at the sky through a pair of thin sunglasses, a faded vignette at the edges of her vision. She was suddenly aware of time passing, slipping through her fingers like sand.

She'd been in Versailles for almost three months, but it almost felt like a lifetime. And everything she'd done had been building up to this, this special night. Once she'd stepped out of the taxi a couple of streets away from the hotel, she stood for a moment, looking up at the sky, beyond the buildings and the lamp posts and the visible signs of the city. She focused on the golden sheen of evening on the edges of the clouds, the still deep blue of the sky beyond. Closing her eyes momentarily, she tried to steady herself before everything started to move in fast forward again.

When she opened her eyes, as if she'd conjured it, she noticed a small, white feather a few paces in front of her, moving slightly along in the evening air.

She picked it up, swallowing back the tears that threatened almost every time she thought about her mother. The only person in her life who'd been able to quiet her just by being there, at whose side she'd felt completely protected. She knew it was an illusion; something from childhood. That her mother had just been a woman, not a superhero. But she still craved that sense of sanctuary.

So much was riding on tonight, not for her as much as for Claudine. She knew how much her boss, her friend, needed this to work. Claudine would be doing the lion's share of the presenting, but Bella had her part to play too. And the rooms, the brochures, the slides that would appear on the PowerPoint were all hers.

'Here we are,' she said to herself as she started down rue des Arbres. Hôtel Benjamin was visible, halfway down. The flowers Bella had asked staff to place outside the entrance were there, gorgeous greens and whites in ceramic pots. The door was open, throwing a little yellow light out into the early evening air. As she neared, she could hear music – the string quartet had already arrived. She picked up the pace.

Inside, everything looked perfect. Wait staff moved silently among the guests with silver trays laden with champagne or elderflower fizz; delicious-looking finger food was arranged on small tables scattered through the room. At the front, there was the stage and behind it, a screen where the presentation would take place.

Claudine was at her side immediately. 'Bella!' she said. 'You look amazing.'

'Thank you. You too.'

Her friend looked at her for a moment, her eyes full of something Bella couldn't read. 'We will speak more tomorrow,' she said. 'But I wanted to say that I'm sorry. For doubting you.'

'Claudine, I burned down your Superior rooms.'

'Yes, but look what you were able to achieve in such a short time. I should have always given you that chance.' Claudine flicked at the corner of her eye, swiping away a threatening tear. 'But I must stop. I will cry. And it will not be good for business.' She took a deep breath, then smiled. 'Ready?'

'Ready as I'll ever be.'

There were around thirty people in the room – alongside the Hotel Club representatives, there were friends of the Hôtel Benjamin, local business delegates, some representatives from the *mairie*. The men wore muted, corporate suits, but the women in dresses or wide-legged trousers were a riot of colour. The sound of laughter and chatter filled the air.

They made their way up to the back of the stage and began running through their lines one last time. Then Claudine gripped Bella's arm. 'This is it,' she said.

Bella felt her stomach constrict. 'Yes,' she said. 'This is it.'

Ten minutes later, she was seated on stage, watching Claudine deliver the presentation seamlessly. Her own introduction had been fine – she'd stumbled a little over her words but overall felt pretty pleased with what she'd achieved. Not bad for a dropout.

With no more lines on the script for her and the audience watching Claudine, seemingly rapt, she allowed herself to relax a little. After they got off this stage, she'd reward herself with the first glass of fizz she'd had all evening, try to enjoy the party a little more in the knowledge that whatever was decided, she'd done the very best she could.

And then her eyes caught his.

It was surreal seeing him in this context and so unexpected that she was momentarily dazed. What was he doing here? Why was he dressed like this?

Why hadn't he said anything?

She almost didn't recognise him in a neat corporate suit, buttoned waistcoat, white shirt. His hair had been professionally styled, combed back with some sort of product making him look a little as if he'd stepped out of a Brylcreem advert from the fifties.

He was sitting with a group of much older men, holding a

leaflet on his lap. But while everyone else's eyes were fixed on Claudine, his were focused on her. Henri. Was it her imagination, or did he, briefly, give her a wink?

She thought about when he'd met her for lunch at the hotel, about how he'd told her about his father's wealth and position, but never details of his business. She remembered now how he'd told her he'd promised his father he'd attend an event. She remembered the moments when he'd hesitated, shaken his head, decided not to speak.

An older gentleman whispered something in Henri's ear and Henri nodded. And as the realisation dawned, she didn't know whether this was terrible or the best possible news: Henri's father was Michel Martin, the head of Hotel Club.

Her hands had begun to sweat, and she shifted in her seat. She tried to take in what Claudine was saying, to fix a smile on and pretend to be as impressed and rapt as everyone seemed. But she had a horrible feeling that with Henri involved, things might be about to get personal.

* * *

The moment the applause died down, the delegates began to stand and mingle, and Bella flew to Henri. 'Henri!' she said. 'I—'

He gripped her arm and shook his head, a warning look in his eyes. 'No,' he said, 'not here.'

He led her by the elbow out of the room into the corridor carpeted in reds and browns.

'Why didn't you tell me?' she whispered, not wanting to be overheard.

'Why do you think?'

'Your dad is Michel Martin.'

'The very same.' He smiled. 'The worst of the corporate monsters. Swallowing up little hotels into his great conglomerate. Like... like the old lady with her fly.'

'What?'

'You know, like in the story. She swallows a fly, then a rat, then a hare... she cannot stop the greed.'

'I don't think that's what that poem is about. Anyway, aren't you a literary scholar? Is that the best reference you can think of?' she grinned.

'OK, my father is Ebenezer Scrooge.'

'Before or after the haunting?'

'What?'

'Well, are you saying he's mean? Or just a rich businessman?'

'I feel as if we're going off track.'

'Maybe a little.'

Henri gave a self-conscious smile. 'After the haunting. My father is not a monster. But still, he is very rich and successful and seems never to want to just stop and enjoy what he has built.'

'That's so sad.'

A few people left the room, laughing, walking in the direction of the loos. Henri pulled Bella into a locked doorway, out of sight. 'For what it's worth, I tried to tell you, once I realised the connection. I was worried when I thought you were an intern at the hotel. Because it might look... underhand to have a girlfriend in the business. But then you were no longer my girlfriend.'

She nodded, feeling slightly awkward.

'Then there was the disaster with the fire, and I found out

the truth of what you were doing.' He shook his head. 'And I didn't know what to do. That's why I couldn't help with the rooms. Because my father, he wants me to make this decision. It is his way of forcing me to participate. And I cannot tell him about you because he might feel he has to withdraw altogether.'

'Oh! Don't do that. I can quit! This is Claudine—'

He put a finger on her lips. 'Shh. I know. I will not. And from what I have seen – when I try to look without prejudice – I think this is a good hotel, that it would be a good addition to the group. But... I have to know, Bella. Do you really think this is a good place? Because so much is based on how things appear. It looks good, but behind the scenes...' He ran a hand through his hair. 'I love my father. I do not wish to steer him wrong.'

Bella opened her mouth to say yes. Then paused. Thought. Finally, she nodded. 'Henri, I really think this is a great place,' she said. 'Claudine is very passionate about it, and I know that she wants to work very hard to build things... I don't think you'd be making a mistake.'

He nodded. 'Thank you. And don't worry, your secret is safe with me.'

She laughed. 'And yours is safe with me!'

'My secret?' He looked confused.

'You know, the fact your father doesn't know that you don't want to go into business with him anyway!'

He put a finger to his lips. 'It is between us.'

She smiled.

'And thank you.' He looked at her, his expression softening. 'I know that I paint my father in a bad light, but I love him. I need to know that the organisation, the people he will be investing in won't let him down.'

'I understand. And I'm sorry,' she added. 'I'm sorry that I lied, that I hurt you. I never meant to...'

'*Oui*, it is OK.' Henri gave her one, brief nod and turned back into the party. Moments later, Bella followed.

Neither saw the silver-haired man standing in the shadows a little farther along the corridor.

52

NOW

She was almost euphoric when she left work two hours later. She and Claudine had stayed behind, ushering the other guests to their rooms, making sure the cleaning staff had started work before they departed. They'd sat down afterwards and drunk coffee, something to take the edge off the fizz of the wine and the fizz of excitement they both felt.

'It went well, I think?' Claudine kept saying.

'Yes. I think it did.'

Bella wasn't sure whether Henri had taken her words on board, she wasn't sure what he'd say to his father. But he'd said enough to give her hope.

And whatever happened next, it was over. There was nothing more they could do. There was a kind of relief at being briefly powerless, the sort of feeling she remembered from exiting her A levels, knowing she'd possibly not done as well as she could have, but also knowing that she had a few weeks to at least live in a limbo in which she could hope. And in which revision was useless.

Claudine had elected to stay at the hotel, to see the delegates off in the morning for their early flight. But although Bella had offered to stay too, she had been relieved when her boss had told her she needn't. 'It's fine,' she said. 'You go home. You've earned a rest.'

It was the time of night where the sky was at its darkest – evening had faded to black, and the first tendrils of morning light had yet to touch the sky and give a sense of approaching light. But it was Paris, the city was very much still alive – lights emanated from the windows of closed shops and there were still people, walking home arm in arm from nights out, a man in the doorway, smoking a cigarette, a woman sporting a large jumper, bare legs and furry boots, shivering by a poodle who refused to pee.

The street lights glowed, their classic black design making them seem like something from a past era, and for a moment she could imagine she was stepping onto the street fifty, even a hundred years ago.

She'd promised Juliette she'd get a cab, and she would. But instead of calling an Uber to meet her outside, she decided to walk to the station and pick up one of the cars that would be waiting there to catch travellers on their exit.

Feeling the colder air start to infiltrate her clothing, she wrapped her coat more tightly around her and was about to descend the steps to the street when a voice called. 'Bella?'

She looked up and gasped. Standing a few metres away, dressed in a shirt and tie, jacket over his arm, was Pete. It took a second to register, to understand that he was here, in Paris. 'Pete? What are you doing here?'

He walked towards her, put his hand on the railing. 'You said you'd think about it. Then you didn't call. I— I suppose I wanted to show you that I was serious about this, about us. I knew you had this big thing on. I was going to— I suppose I was going to come in, surprise you. But then it was too—' He gestured at the hotel. 'Well, it's a bit fancy, isn't it? I felt like a bit of a dick. I mean, I'd probably have been chucked out for not having an invite.'

She smiled, trying to disguise the fact that she felt shaky. 'Probably.'

'So I went and I waited.' His voice, she realised, was slightly slurry.

'Have you been drinking?'

'Not really. A tiny bit maybe.'

'Perhaps we should talk tomorrow.'

He shook his head. 'You said twenty-four hours and it's already been more than that. At least—' He stopped, seemed to be trying to work out the exact number, holding up fingers and counting them off. 'You know,' he said at last.

'Oh, Pete.'

'So?' he said, looking up at her.

'So?'

'Are you prepared to give me – us – a chance?' He stumbled slightly, grabbed the rail again.

She shook her head. 'Oh Pete, I'm so sorry. I just think— I mean, we're so different. I see that now. We want different things. And I'm sorry you came all this way – I should have called. It's just been—'

'But face it, Bella. You don't belong here any more than I do. This isn't you!'

'What do you mean?'

'This... businesswoman thing you're trying to be. I know you, don't forget. You're a school dropout like me. We don't do fancy. We're not like that. Pretentious.'

'I'm not being pretentious. I'm trying to better myself, yes. But—'

'But look at you!' he gestured. 'Not sure who you're trying to fool.'

'This isn't exactly romantic,' she pointed out, trying not to let his words pierce her.

'No, you're right,' he said sadly. 'Look, just come home with me. Or let's make a new home. Start again.'

'I just can't, Pete. I'm sorry.'

He looked for a moment as if he might burst into tears. Then his expression hardened. 'Fine,' he said. 'Fine!' He began to walk off rapidly.

'Pete!' she said. 'Wait! Where are you... Do you have somewhere to stay? I didn't—'

But he had rounded the corner, flapping his hand as if flicking her away.

She sighed for a moment, tried to recapture the feeling of potential she'd had when she'd first exited. But then another voice: 'Bella?'

This time, looking down from the steps, she saw Henri still dressed in his suit, walking, then jogging, towards her. She smiled; he must have decided to meet her, maybe travel back to the house with her. Perhaps he'd be able to tell her what the delegates had decided. Only when he neared, she realised his expression was thunderous.

'How could you do that?' he asked when he was close enough.

'What?'

'Tell my father about me. About the business. How could you do that?'

'Henri! I didn't! I'd never do that!'

'Then how does he know?' Henri folded his arms across his chest. Now that her eyes were adjusting to the dull light of outside, she could see that his were red-rimmed. He'd been crying.

'I don't know. But you have to believe... Henri, that's your secret. Your problem to sort out. I would never— I haven't spoken to him.'

He shook his head. 'Then who?' he asked her. 'Who would do that to me?'

She stepped forward. 'Maybe he worked it out for himself.'

'No. He said he heard it from someone.'

A sudden thought. 'Henri, it was probably us. In the corridor. I mentioned... well, I said to you about lying and...'

'Then it *is* your fault.' Henri's voice didn't sound like his. 'Everything is ruined and it is your fault.'

'Now come on...' she said, taking another step.

Friendship's full of dregs; methinks false hearts
should never have sound legs.

he quoted miserably.

'What the fuck are you talking about?'

Only Henri had already turned, was walking quickly away.

'Wait! Henri!' She made to rush after him, but misjudged the step.

He didn't see her ankle turn, her leg bend underneath her. Didn't notice her tumbling to the bottom of the steps. A pain shot through her lower leg as she hit the pavement, landing first on the edge of her ankle, then on to her knees, managing to put her hands out and prevent her head knocking the ground. The slap of flesh on pavement was both sharp and hard, and the pain of it almost took her breath away. She felt tears spring to her eyes.

A man was at her side almost instantly. 'Madame,' he said. 'Can I help you?'

A woman appeared too, holding out her hand. 'You have fallen, Madame. Are you OK?'

Bella, wincing, moved herself to a sitting position on the bottom step. 'I'm OK,' she said. 'Honestly. I'll be fine.' She forced a smile.

They looked doubtful, but moved on, glancing back once or twice as she sat there wondering what to do next, her ankle screaming in pain.

'You know,' a voice said, 'it's OK to accept a little help sometimes.'

She looked up abruptly. Brad was there, standing in front of her, framed by the soft, yellow lamplight.

She squinted at him for a moment, her head spinning; distracted by pain. Was he really here? Had Pete been? Henri? A strange sense of disorientation came over her.

'Brad?'

'That's my name, don't wear it out!' he said, crouching down.

It really was him. He really was here.

'What are you doing here?'

He looked awkward. Adjusted his stance a little. 'I guess I came to meet you.'

'You guess?'

'No. I did. I came to meet you.'

She noticed then the guitar on his back. He saw her looking. 'I guess... I was going to maybe play something for you,' he admitted.

'You were? What, like a serenade?' She was joking, but he remained serious.

Surely he hadn't been ready to whip out his guitar and sing in the street?

He shrugged. 'I was thinking about it. I mean, I thought about you up there tonight, thought about how brave you've been.'

'Yeah?'

'Yeah.' He sat down next to her on the step, brought her injured ankle onto his lap and began gently massaging it. 'You're pretty impressive, you know.'

'Now I know you're joking.'

He looked at her. 'Don't do that.'

'Do what?'

'That deflection thing. I mean it, you know.'

'Thank you.'

'Better.'

He gently put her foot back on the ground then rose to his feet, sticking out a hand. 'Let's see if you can walk on that thing.'

She stood, tentatively putting weight on the injured ankle, but winced in pain and grabbed onto the stair rail. 'Pretty sure it's sprained or something.'

'Right. Only one thing for it,' he said. Before she could object, he lifted her in his arms, carrying her like a damsel in distress, shoulders against one of his arms, the backs of her knees against the other.

'Brad!' she said. 'I don't need... We can get a—'

'For God's sake, Bella, not everyone is going to let you down. Let me look after you.'

'But—'

'You're still the strongest woman I've met.'

'I am?'

'You are. Now shut up and let me rescue you.' And he leant

towards her and brushed his lips to hers. She closed her eyes
and let him kiss her, relaxing into his arms and feeling, for the
first time in so very long, utterly safe, protected and loved.

53

NOW

It was odd not having anything to do. After visiting the emergency room and having a boot fitted, she'd been advised to rest. Claudine, more than happy with her work and overtime in recent weeks, had told her to take a week off at least. And Brad had made her promise she would.

But after three days of 'rest', she felt edgy. It was strange, moving from full, high-pressure days to ones filled with options and time. Her mind, free from thoughts of delegates and Superior rooms and presentations, decided to fill itself with other thoughts instead – thoughts about her potential future, about her divorce, about the hotel and Brad and the Versailles house share.

Brad had been on hand since her fall to help her around, but had disappeared today on what he'd called a 'secret mission', making a face that had made her collapse with laughter when she'd likened him to James Bond.

Odette was out of the house and Henri, while now a little friendlier towards her, was making himself scarce.

From her position on the sofa, leg raised on a pouffe, she could hear the daily rumble of noise outside – of people and purpose and life. And while her leg still ached, she suddenly felt that she didn't belong in this quiet, restful room, but somewhere else – outside with people and sunlight and colour and noise.

She found the boot a little clunky to walk on, but there was hardly any pain. Heaving herself up, she tentatively stepped forward and, gaining confidence, grabbed her bag and made it out onto the street.

She felt a little stiff-jointed, but otherwise OK. It was pleasant to be out in the sunshine, despite the fact it was a little chilly without her cardigan.

As she walked, she thought about what the preceding months had brought – Pete's bombshell, the house sale, her trip to Versailles, Hôtel Benjamin, Henri and now Brad. The lies she'd told, the fallout, where she was right now.

The truth was, although she'd been relieved not to lose her job, she wasn't certain that working at the hotel was something she wanted to do long term. And she knew she didn't want to live in a shared house for much longer. The sale of the Peyrat property would complete in a couple of weeks and she'd have a little money. The world in so many ways was her oyster. Only she was afraid to open it, in case instead of a pearl, it simply revealed scratchy grains of sand.

She thought about time, about her fear of it running out and how unfounded that had been. And about her mother and how much her unexpected death had coloured everything else in her life. About Dad and his new life and the fact that although he claimed to be there for her, he really hadn't been.

Bella walked for almost an hour before her leg began to

ache and she suddenly realised how tired she'd become. Her mobile pinged – it was Brad asking where she'd got to and she felt a stab of guilt. He'd be worried, of course. It was easy to forget there was now someone who cared where she was, whether she was OK. It would take some getting used to.

'Just gone for a walk,' she typed.

'Whereabouts?'

She looked up at her surroundings and her eye caught sight of a small white feather, resting against a black painted railing. Beyond the railing was a school of some sort, a square, modern structure covered in windows, reflecting the light. As she bent to pick up the feather, it moved slightly, passing through the gates into the grounds of the institution. She stepped through too to retrieve it.

Picking it up, she straightened and noticed a sign. She was on the edge of a college campus.

It was funny how, despite the fact this building was miles – and years – away from her old school, there was still a familiar atmosphere to the place. As if the energy of thousands of pupils' homes, dreams, stresses and achievements had been absorbed into the building and its grounds.

She thought of her own experience at school, and how her stomach had dropped when she'd opened her results. How in that moment she'd known she'd let her mother down, even though she hadn't been there to see it.

She realised that she'd been running away since then. Trying to find happiness, stability. Trying to create a world in which she felt safe.

Only it hadn't worked, not really. Because the feeling wasn't to do with anything external. It was buried inside her.

'Near the college,' she replied.

'Shall I come get you?'

'No. But I'll be back soon.' She paused, feeling something flood through her. An idea. No – more than that. A realisation. 'And I've got something to tell you.'

54

NOW

'We got it!' Claudine was almost alarmingly not like herself. She burst into Bella's office waving a piece of paper. 'We actually got it!'

It had been a month since the presentation and each day they'd waited, hardly daring to hope.

'The accreditation?'

Claudine stopped a moment, deadpan. '*Oui*, what else could it be?' Then a grin spread over her lips. 'We actually made it, but it's thanks to you.'

Bella flushed at the compliment. 'I had a lot of help,' she said.

'So, the job is yours if you want it. Permanently.'

It had been Bella's dream to succeed in this role, and she allowed herself a moment to soak up the news. Qualifications or not, experience or not, she had pulled it off. And that was something to be proud of.

Subconsciously, she reached out and touched the feather she kept in her pen pot. 'Only...' she said. 'Before I can accept... There's something you need to know.'

'Then you'd better tell me.'

To Bella's surprise, Claudine was relatively relaxed when Bella relayed the news about her true CV credentials. In fact, she shrugged. 'Hotel, *chambre d'hôtes*, I do not see much difference,' she said. 'You have experience, and you have that certain *je ne sais quoi* that you don't often see in candidates.'

'A *je ne sais quoi*?'

'*Oui*, I don't know exactly what it is, but you have a resilience. A drive. And you proved it too. Perhaps it was what made you able to pivot after the fire. But it is surely a quality I need in my hotel. So the offer stands.'

'Although I did have a bit of help,' she reminded her boss.

'Yes, of course, your wonderful friends made it all possible. And the art Odette provided!' Claudine gave a chef's kiss. 'And Madame Roux, that was quite a surprise.'

'Yes, she's very talented.'

Claudine nodded. 'Did she tell you I've asked her to stay?'

'At the hotel?'

'*Oui*, if she wants to. For as long as she wants.' Claudine shrugged. 'I felt as if she was a burden, and lonely here. But when I took a little more time to talk to her...'

'She's happy?'

'She likes to be in the centre of things. It suits her. And she told me,' Claudine leant forward, 'she is not ready to be in plastic knickers yet.'

Bella barked out a laugh. 'Oh, she's brilliant.'

'Yes. I think she could actually be quite an asset to the hotel. She has some fabulous ideas for the decor in the restaurant. But this is not what we are here to talk about. The job is yours. Will you take it?'

'Well, yes. I'd like to. It's a great opportunity. But do you mind if I ask you something else?' Bella said, making a face. 'Before I accept?'

Claudine's eyebrow had begun to travel north by this point, arching incredulously as its owner looked at Bella, half-smiling, half-frustrated.

Bella took a breath. 'I just— I wanted to ask whether you'd consider giving me a little time off first. Then perhaps... maybe slightly lighter hours?'

'Oh my goodness! You are pregnant!' Claudine said, clapping her hands together. 'This is wonderful news!'

'No, it's not that.'

'Oh. Well.' Claudine straightened her jacket, self-consciously. 'Then what?'

'I'm going to England.'

'Oh!'

'Not permanently. But for a few weeks. I want to stay with Kitty, really spend some time together, you know?'

'This is the sister you can't stand?'

Bella felt her cheeks get hot. 'Did I say that? Poor Kitty. I think perhaps I've made her out to be a bit of a monster.'

'She is an older sister. Of course she is a monster, it is her job. She cares,' Claudine said. 'Of course you must visit her.'

'And when I'm back...' Bella drummed her fingers on the desk. 'There's something I really want to do.' Taking a breath, she told Claudine her plans. The three-month course at École Ducasse where she'd learn to make all the French delicacies – pastries and chocolate, bread and viennoiseries.

Claudine's eyebrow arched. 'But you know you have a job here, you don't need this.'

'I don't need it. But... I suppose... I want it.'

'And it will become your job?'

Bella lifted a shoulder. 'Maybe, one day. Or maybe just a passion.'

'But to go to school, in your thirties?'

'If not now, then when? I'm not getting any younger.' Bella smiled to herself, thinking of how she had shaved fourteen years off her age recently. 'It's just... after my mum died, I sort of messed up my education. It was something she wanted for me, that I wanted for myself. And I've always felt a little... poorer for it.'

'I understand.'

'And until recently, it felt as if it was too late. You know. I was married, I had a business. I'd left that fork in the road behind. Only I realised something. That life isn't linear. Or it doesn't have to be. When Pete told me he was leaving, it was like sliding down a snake.'

'I am sorry. A snake?'

'Yes, you know. Like in snakes and ladders. The game.'

'Oh yes! Where you slide down!' Claudine clapped her hands again. 'But this is not a good thing.'

'No. Not really. But then I realised that there is no right time to do things. And there isn't such a thing as "too late". Not really. Things happen, and you move forward a few spaces, back, up a ladder, down a snake... Look at Madame Roux – almost in a nursing home, but now she's going to be advising you on the hotel.'

Claudine was nodding. 'I understand. I think.'

Bella smiled. 'I'm glad. Because I have no idea how to explain it more clearly.'

'So, you will be living two lives. One as a student, the other as an executive?' Claudine asked. 'How will you cope?'

'Oh, I think I'll manage just fine.'

'Then it is fine with me,' Claudine smiled and leant in a little closer. 'On one condition.'

'Yes?'

'If you ever need anyone to taste your pastries, you know exactly where I am.'

November and the winter had truly set in. But the lights strung across the streets and blazing in the shop windows brought warmth and a sense of excitement to the dark evenings. The air smelled like ice and smoke and warm winter foods being rustled up in restaurants.

It was Friday. Bella had just arrived back from picking up Kitty who was over for the weekend, this time with Ty. Ty was already tucked up in bed, fast asleep after his journey; the rest of them had all gathered in the kitchen.

It was her last night in the house. Tomorrow, she'd begin the process of moving her things to a new apartment she'd rented in the city – close to the college and closer to the hotel. It was unfurnished, so she'd be able to move in the things from Peyrat she'd kept and put into storage after the sale. Her stomach was a quiver of nervous excitement, but she was ready.

'So you're moving out?' Brad had said when she'd told him a month before.

'Yes – time I moved to somewhere of my own.'

He'd mock pouted. 'What about me?'

'Well, I'm pretty sure you'll be there a lot of the time.'

'Glad to hear it.'

They'd discussed moving in together, but things were going so well between them neither wanted to rock the boat right now. There would be plenty of time for all that in the future.

Tonight was about endings, but new beginnings too. Bella had bought two enormous bottles of champagne and had invited everybody to join her.

They were all there: Odette, who'd finally secured a meeting with the gallery owner for next month; Henri, whose father had apparently come round to the idea that his son was an academic rather than a business mogul; Claudine, who'd just arrived, sporting a long winter coat and furry boots which she'd kept on, complaining that the house was 'too draughty'.

Bella sipped her champagne, feeling slightly queasy. When Brad had invited them all to come together, including Claudine, she'd felt that it had to be more than a simple collective drink he had in mind. Conversation was stilted; they could all feel that something else was going on.

She reached over, squeezed his hand. 'No offense,' she said, 'but what's this all about?'

'Can't a man share a drink with friends without there being a hidden agenda?'

'A man can,' she said, smiling. '*You* can't. I can read you like a book and you're definitely up to something.'

He grinned. 'You got me!'

Then to her surprise, he looked at Claudine, who nodded slightly as if to give him the go-ahead. He stood.

'Well, I was going to announce this later, only Miss Smarty-Pants here figured I was up to something. So I'd better get on with it.'

For one horrible moment she thought he might propose. That was something she might want later down the line. But not now, not yet.

'Claudine here has agreed to let me invest in the hotel. We're going to be partners. I kind of... It feels like a safe investment. Something I can actually be involved in properly. Although it has to be OK with you, of course,' he said to Bella.

'Hey, I'm just a general manager.'

'True.'

'And I'm not even working right now.'

'Also true.' He picked up her hand. 'But you're also pretty important to me, so you kinda get the last say.'

She looked at him, grinned. 'OK.'

'Yeah?'

'Yeah. It sounds... I mean it's a really great step.' She raised her glass.

'Not so fast!'

'There's more?'

Claudine glanced at her watch. 'Shortly.'

As if she'd conjured it, the doorbell rang out at that moment, making them jump.

'She sure is punctual,' said Brad.

'Who? Who is punctual?' Bella asked.

But he was silent as Claudine disappeared to answer the door. There was the muffled sound of talking and then two steps of shoes clipped towards the kitchen. As the door opened, Bella was surprised to see her boss with an arm around a woman in a chequered wool suit, with red shoes, holding a bemused-looking dog on a lead.

Bella rose to her feet. 'Madame Roux!' she said, smiling. Rounding the table, she gave the old woman a hug which surprised them both. 'Call me Élise,' she said. '"Madame Roux" makes me sound old.'

The sharp, discerning eyes looked around the kitchen, taking in the basic decor, the large wooden cupboards, the scattered plates and mugs. 'My God,' she said, turning to Brad. 'You said it was ugly, but this is—'

He grinned widely. 'You'll have to help me decide how to decorate, Élise. Whole place could do with a refresh.'

Bella brought another chair to the table for Madame Roux to sink onto. She had a strange feeling that there was a joke that everyone else was in on but her. 'So, it's lovely to see you,' she told the old lady. 'And you're going to help Brad... decorate?'

'*Oui*. I will not live in squalor. I made that quite clear.'

Bella's mouth dropped open. 'You'll be living here?'

'Yes. Once you move into your new apartment. Just while they repurpose my room at the hotel. Claudine here feels that if I'm to be a permanent resident, I need a little more luxury,' Madame Roux said. Coco barked, as if in acquiescence.

'And perhaps,' Claudine added, 'one or two adaptations...'

'Oh, adaptations!' Madame Roux flapped a hand. 'Anyone would think I was an old woman!'

'Well,' Bella said, nodding. 'I think that's brilliant.'

They raised their glasses again. 'To new starts?' suggested Bella.

'Wait!' A voice at the door took them all by surprise.

'Yves!' Bella exclaimed.

Yves looked very different out of the office. Gone was the smart suit and sharp tailoring. Instead, he was wearing jeans, a black sweater with the picture of a guitarist. 'Sorry I'm late,' he said. And Bella was about to tell him not to worry when she realised he wasn't talking to her.

'It's fine,' Claudine said, giving him her cheek to kiss.

Yves slipped an arm around Claudine's shoulders and they both turned back to the group.

'Oh,' Bella said. 'You're... You two are—'

Claudine gave the slightest incline of her head. 'Someone once told me that younger men can be a lot of fun,' she said with a playful shrug.

'So, we all here now?' Brad said, looking around as if expecting someone else to turn up.

'Yes. Get on with it!' Claudine said.

'Thank you. So, I also wanted to make a toast.' He raised his glass. 'To all of us. To the future. And most of all to overcoming.'

'Overcoming?'

'Yeah, you know. Odette and her paintings. Claudine, well, you know, it was hard for her for a bit with the hotel. You, going to see your sister, and working through that stuff,' he nodded in her direction, and she returned the movement. She didn't want him going into any more details just yet. 'And to Henri,' he said, 'who's finally got his father onside.'

'And you,' she said.

'With the business stuff?'

'Yeah, and the rest,' she said, winking and thinking of the night before when he'd played the guitar softly to her as she lay on his bed. He flushed and she raised her glass, echoing Brad's toast. 'To all of us.'

'To all of us.'

'And to teaching an old dog new tricks!' Brad added.

'Hey!' Bella said.

'Oh damn! No, not you sweetheart. Not your course. You're a young... dog.'

'Thanks... I think.'

'Then you are calling me the dog?' Madame Roux asked disapprovingly.

'No! Of course not. Bad expression. I'm talking about me! Claudine's going to have to get me up to speed on everything hotel-related. I'm the old dog.'

'To old dogs!' Bella said, lifting her glass, much to the bemusement of the rest of them.

'And to Hôtel Benjamin!'

'*Non!*' Claudine said abruptly. They all looked at her. 'There will be no more Hôtel Benjamin.'

'But—?'

'What?'

'*Non.* I have had enough of Benjamins to last me a lifetime.'

Brad's mouth fell open. 'But surely—'

'*Non*, do not worry,' Claudine grinned mischievously. 'It is not the end of the hotel. Merely a new beginning. Time for Chez Claudine?'

'Chez Claudine?' Brad mused then nodded. 'I like it.'

'To Chez Claudine!' cried Bella.

'Yes! Chez Claudine!'

And in that moment, looking around at her friends, at Brad, Bella realised that she was no longer afraid. People would come in and out of her life; some staying, some moving on. There was no such thing as stability, not in any real sense. Things would change, times would change.

But there were different types of change. The change that happened to you, or the change that you drove yourself. Change could be terrifying. But it could also be exciting.

In that moment, she knew without doubt that she was strong enough to step into her future. And that whatever happened, she had what it took to land on her feet.

* * *

MORE FROM GILLIAN HARVEY

Another book from Gillian Harvey is available to order now here:

https://mybook.to/GillianBackAd